SHATTERED FOSSILS

ESSENTIAL PROSE SERIES 179

**Canada Council
for the Arts**

**Conseil des Arts
du Canada**

**ONTARIO ARTS COUNCIL
CONSEIL DES ARTS DE L'ONTARIO**

an Ontario government agency
un organisme du gouvernement de l'Ont

Canadä

Guernica Editions Inc. acknowledges the support of the Canada Council
for the Arts and the Ontario Arts Council. The Ontario Arts Council
is an agency of the Government of Ontario.

We acknowledge the financial support of the Government of Canada.

SHARON LAX

SHATTERED FOSSILS

GUERNICA
EDITIONS

TORONTO—CHICAGO—BUFFALO—LANCASTER (U.K.)

2020

Michael Mirolla, editor
Interior and cover design: Errol F. Richardson
Guernica Editions Inc.
1569 Heritage Way, Oakville, (ON), Canada L6M 2Z7
2250 Military Road, Tonawanda, N.Y. 14150-6000 U.S.A.
www.guernicaeditions.com

Distributors:
Independent Publishers Group (IPG)
600 North Pulaski Road, Chicago IL 60624
University of Toronto Press Distribution,
5201 Dufferin Street, Toronto (ON), Canada M3H 5T8
Gazelle Book Services, White Cross Mills
High Town, Lancaster LA1 4XS U.K.

First edition.
Printed in Canada.

Legal Deposit—First Quarter
Library of Congress Catalog Card Number: 2019947052
Library and Archives Canada Cataloguing in Publication
Title: Shattered fossils / Sharon Lax.
Names: Lax, Sharon, author.
Series: Essential prose series ; 179.
Description: Series statement: Essential prose series ; 179 | Short stories.
Identifiers: Canadiana (print) 20190158166 | Canadiana (ebook) 20190158182 | ISBN
9781771834858
(softcover) | ISBN 9781771834865 (EPUB) | ISBN 9781771834872 (Kindle)
Classification: LCC PS8623.A9425 S53 2020 | DDC C813/.6—dc23

To John, my Virgil.
To Annie and Louis and to my mother,
who have joined me on this journey.

And among such as these am I myself.

For such defects, and not for other guilt,
       Lost are we and are only so far punished,
       That without hope we live on in desire.

Great grief seized on my heart when this I heard,
       Because some people of much worthiness
       I knew, who in that Limbo were suspended.

—**Dante Gabriel Rossetti**, *Inferno: Canto IV*

Contents

Dawn Ascends

DAWN ASCENDS OVER cityscape; the lit buildings call him, name him. With no thought to what might be left behind, he enters the painted sidewalk.

An Ark of Gopherwood

Surely, Thomas, you've overheard Araceli's request. A request that resonated, despite the haunting dripping of the hydration machine. Funny, isn't it, how all the other machines are quiet? Araceli told me you'd requested ending it, stopping the hydration. I suppose that's it, isn't it, B Natural? A note beyond the noise – as in that horrible pun, *be natural*. Dammit, Thomas, I still can't believe you're leaving us.

Consciousness to the last breath, they say. So, perhaps you can hear me. Before you join crazy Virgil and his entourage, I … don't know how to tell you. Damn, Thomas! All this beeping. But the machines *are* advising us on the condition of your heart. Even through this noise and the fog of morphine, you might've heard the remonstrations of that man-nurse with the anaemic frame.

"A friend," he practically screamed. "Your husband needs you! What urgently needs to be said to this *friend?*" Araceli threw him one of her killer stares.

She knows that I need desperately to tell you. Now that you're – I don't know what's crazier, that I'm by your side or that you're here, in this shitty hospice. Crazy that you're on your way – Dammit! I'd throw everything in the garbage for you to come through! Thomas, you CAN'T leave before Labour wins another round. Was that a smile? Can you hear me?

This is what I need to say. I'm sorry, my friend. You know, I've always believed you recognized our indiscretions: the faint touch of a shoulder, a head turned too suddenly. Yes, you know. Still, I have to say it. Finally say it. I slept with Araceli, with your wife. I know what you're thinking, lying on this … frankly, in this casket. All these machines, tubes; your skin, still smooth; your smooth chin, though your face is pale. But isn't that odd: After

the radiation and chemo, there's so much hair, obstinately clinging to your scalp. "Unlike my own head, to take from Eliot: With
a *bald spot in the middle of my hair.* And, yes, our colleagues do
say: *"How his hair is growing thin!"*

Maybe I should open these crusty windows. London's draft
might whisk you away. *The yellow fog that rubs its back upon the
window-panes.* I'm letting Eliot into the room, and here you are,
prone, and somewhere else along a dusty path. As for Eliot, well,
both he and I are American, both with a woman driving our pas-
sions. There's one bit I won't lay claim to: Eliot's virulent anti-
Semitism. Not I, Joshua, grandson of a Jewish grandfather, whose
sense of adventure from England to America saved his sorry ass.
And, come to think of it, my return across the same body of water
… you, Thomas, how right you were when you called me 'Mid-
Atlantic,' straddling two worlds. "Lucky you," you told me. Yeah,
both of us, lucky dickheads. Still, there's one thing to be grateful
for. There's only one bed in this goddamned room.

Wherever you're headed, there'll be no dirt-encrusted windows,
no damp floors. And on this side, where goings-on can be traced in
liveries and stones, in the Thames' brackish waters, we'll go on being
slaves of time. I imagine, Thomas, wherever you're headed, you'll
be winding your timepiece; while down here, I'll be waiting around
for a woman who makes Purgatory look like Paradiso. It's you she
loves, Thomas, despite your poisoned arrows piercing her muddled
speech, whenever her nerves betray her, in her adopted tongue.

"Too romantic," you've called her poetry. "Too much drama."
My editorializing – your words were scathing – lancing Araceli,
as she roamed the rooms of your Chelsea; yes, like the historical
hotel, teeming with guests. But you would remain in the study,
among your books of old heroes, attending to shattered fossils.

Here I am, burying everything in sentiment, when all that's
ever riled you up are the collected records that we call history.

Facts. Actions. Deeds. As for sentiment, I remember your advice after a student challenged a thesis of mine. "Joshua! Get rid of every kernel of sentiment. It'll make you permeable."

We were heading home, the sun in attack mode. It comes to me so clearly. And that headache I was nursing! Despite the hot afternoon, I teased out a cooler version: evening's shrouds over Oxford's colleges. You were rattling on about Pythagoras' purification of the soul, release from the body's prison. Drawing a hand across one sweaty forehead, you cursed. "Fuck this heat. Course Pythagoras was a sentimental fart; life *and* death in his rusty brain carrying some higher meaning. Considered philosophy equal to religion. Considered it a release."

"Release?" I was broadsided by a vision of the ancients masturbating religion.

"Joshua, Joshua, always throwing up doors, locked and barred. I'm talking about matter that becomes numerical essence. And, there, my friend, is where we experience boundless joy. Even blithe Pythagoras was spirited away by this dense stuff ... and then, unfortunately, by the gods."

Thomas, you probably know better than anyone now what the gods have in store for us.

With more luck, you'd have lived three hundred, one and twenty-five. That's what our German Wortham neighbours might have said. Like Karl Auger – you'll be seeing him again soon. Yes, Auger, sneaking up, mocking our equivocation on historical precedence. "'Was glänzt, ist für den Augenblick geboren; das Echte bleibt der Nachwelt unverloren.' Goethe on Heaven, gentlemen. Mephistopheles brought news on the ways of men, who torment themselves. Don't concern yourselves with today's events, gentlemen. Posterity will do the choosing."

At the time, Karl was trying to resuscitate interest in the leader of the peasants, Thomas Müntzer. Posterity chose Müntzer, indelibly imprinting the end of his life onto the historical canon, with his sorry head on a stake. Death chose Auger, soon after that research. I suppose posterity was Auger's destiny. Mine? Who knows? Clearly, Thomas, yours is the odyssey.

Sorry, but it's a relief to get this off my chest, to tell you, to finally tell you. I doubt you're wondering, but I'll put it to you this way: Was it *love?* I'm not a fan of that word. For Araceli? I'll never know. Did I ... did *we* do anything wrong? I'm sorry, I still can't bring myself to say we did.

Almost seven years ago, your wife and I were on your tweed Chesterfield, sipping Merlot, trying not to spill. You were off 'conferencing,' your manuscript open on our laps to a discussion of the infeasibility of locating stray planks of Noah's Ark on Mount Ararat. You'd referenced the Babylonian flood told in *Gilgamesh*. So much ink you spent on the landing of a vessel by someone who heard voices. Aerial photographs hint at remains. Feverish disbeliever in the very field you fiendishly defend, disdain for the *process* of history: your arguments threaded along the idea that intractable narratives threaten our reconstitution of events. As I read your words, I recalled Coastal Salish and Cowichan legends I'd heard back in Seattle, about the Raven, Creator of Light, and a flood that swallows the earth. Araceli was reading your theory on the inevitability of legend after a natural disaster. I burst out in laughter, startling her; she sighed loudly. 'There are clues in legends,' you'd written. 'Perseverance is not enough, however, in rewriting the past. There are complications. In examining multiple narratives, archivists of course must resist the tangential. In this rewrite, we might well ask whether it is the story told of an event or an adherence to some material authenticity that dissolves in our hands as soon as it is shaped. We must also resist the tendency to become caught up in the operatic aria written by subsequent generations of cataclysmic events. At the very least, we have clues. Why not consider these clues, however fantastical?' More to myself than to Araceli, I murmured something about the *we* and *our*, a pronoun inured in our psyche, as historians who fancy ourselves the scribes.

What was most noticeable is that in the search for an ark in the Caucasus mountains, you'd let down the drawbridge. Caught up in what to keep, what to destroy, you'd given myth a syllogistic whirl, promoting stories as 'evidence' even as you dismissed this form of extraction later on. Araceli and I moved closer. I pointed out your economy with words, sewn within seamless phrases. She jumped in. "He's referencing Uruguay!" She was utterly convinced, while reading a passage describing certain elements familiar to her, that you'd included her beloved country. I could have set her straight, not reassured her, as I did, that, yes, it is a possibility. I might have parroted your inflection and dismissiveness. If anything, you've always discredited her homesickness.

All I did was suggest deleting a paragraph. She'd fallen into an idea of yours. I was alone, in the absence of her presence. She was with you, admiring your modelling from the remains.

Just laying it bare here, Thomas. Along her neck was a distracting, spicy fragrance like patchouli, but more refined than the kind we get a whiff of in those cramped lecture halls and corridors. Her oils: arranged like a night choir in her … in *your* bedroom.

"Look, *Gjoshua*," she said, riding my name over Uruguayan syllables, tucking loose curls behind an ear; the rest falling over her shoulders. She laughed. "I see the world as a poem. Thomas imagines it is an argument, but we are similar, with our epitaphs for fossils."

That's when all colour drained from that capricious landscape, everything drowned but those eyes. "Fossils. Yes. So many species are gone, just within the last while. The West African black rhinoceros; the dolphin Baiji, from the River Yangtze – species we know are disappeared. But there are millions too small to detect.

That is what Thomas does not understand. He does not understand this Earth." Her eyes, dark gashes in cedar. What could I do, my friend? When the world's pouring in, what would you do? I kissed her. That evening she became … my paramour, I suppose.

Later, I gathered my jacket, ripped and a bit ragged, worthy of an adjunct lecturer waiting for tenure. I'd left my scarf, no longer caring if I littered. As I pressed my arms through ripped lining, Araceli set down your work, the Tiffany's light trained on the sofa where we'd just been. "Here." She wrapped the scarf around my neck. "Promise me *gjwill recuerda* this" – 'you will remember this' is what she meant.

Remember the story, the very same story the world over. The one that begins with a kiss and ends with a promise.

So much for modern myth making; what you perhaps missed is that myths are the guillotine, set up by the fearful, hoping to avoid detection. On one occasion, when you and I were passing Oxford's gables and cupolas, we came upon no actual dead, until rounding a bend, in the distance, in the window of one stone tower – there! Blue lights floating about, like ghosts, admonishing us. I stood a moment to watch. Coughing, you pressed forward. "I wonder. Do ghosts have a smell?" Suddenly, as if inhabited, you cried out. "That's it, Joshua! Launching into Auden: *The glacier knocks in the cupboard / The desert sighs in the bed / And the crack in the teacup opens / A lane to the land of the dead.*"

Damn this infernal heater! And these monitors … but they're our only way to know, Thomas, that you're still with us.

And this sunlight reminding me of the blinding reflection off of moats. We were passing Oxfordshire's gables. You were recounting a winter's tale of one empress, Maude, escaping the armies of her cousin, Stephen Blois. Lowered over the walls into the stillness of snow, she manages to elude his feverish clutches.

"Glorious anarchy!" – the usual Thomas catty dismissal of life and stories laced with intrigue and intent, if not bravery.

"More of a utilitarian sense of urgency, with the help of snow."

"I'll give you this one, Joshua."

The both of us, two buffoons in London, entering All-Hallows by-the-Tower or standing beneath St. Mary Woolnoth's clock, wound to the Queen's Time. In the middle of a patch of American tourists, you turned to look skywards, then towards the stone façade, reciting: "Where Saint Mary Woolnoth kept the hours …" The tourists actually burst into applause. I looked away, mortified, imagining you in a previous iteration, pulling the tenor bell for Pastor Newton. Pointing to Starbucks, you shouted: "Saint Mary survives air raids, only to be sucked dry by *that* barnacle!"

"Sure, Thomas, but over in that direction is the Chamber of Commerce. No big reveal: sucking people dry is part of human history. Occupiers and the commercial thread, way before Alfred and the Norse occupation."

"True, true, my friend. Churches, cathedrals, citadels of our capital pride. And we, poor minions, beholden to the almighty pound. Great bathrooms, though, in our commercial chambers."

While I sulked, with manufactured guilt, you enjoyed a getting-away from "this wall of victims," you called it. Other times, you labelled your grief, *The Burden of History*, "A once and constant presence. Look at us, Joshua. We still haven't prosecuted the killers in the massacres in Derry, the ones who gave the orders."

How often did I have to hear about Ireland? As it turned out, many times. So many dead, still to be claimed, still to be placed in their yet undug graves. How wrong you were about trials that "had to happen in order to put this whole thing to rest." How much I never grew tired of telling you how wrong you were. On the other side of the heavens, would Noah's drowning neighbours have been content with a trial? At times, you agreed about leaving the past in rubbish bins. It'd be better "for my health," you actually told me, to heed the angels of the future. "Never dote on the ravages of the past!"

Dammit. I'm slipping words into your mouth, Thomas. And you're – Exeunt, Death! *Angelus Novus!* Only you don't believe in winged creatures, do you, Thomas, outside of birds, bats or bugs.

Speaking of wings, remember our discussions on Walter Benjamin, his reference to Klee's painting *Angelus Novus,* and his argument against eulogizing the past? We were in the courtyard, your voice carrying over spring's blooms, had managed to vacate one bench occupied by beleaguered students. Behind us, engraved on Oxford's wall, the poetic musings on our revered rowing boys. I was anxious, flushed.

Courage was the foci of this discussion. You'd decided Benjamin had shown none.

"If it weren't for his monstrous imagination, that crazy European would've survived. The Nazis weren't anywhere near the Spanish border. Benjamin was impulsive, taking his life. For nothing!"

"Easy to judge, Thomas. Courage looks like cowardice from the vantage point of safety. Anyways, no need to make things up here. Hannah Arendt revealed everything in her letters. He had a visa. No passport. *And* he was Jewish, for God's sakes!"

We spoke of Benjamin's creative (but maybe flawed) image of the winds of time carrying us into the future, ruminated about the senseless hope for this future, when in all likelihood there will be none to worry about. Benjamin wanted to save history from the idea of continuum. In disputing the modern idea of progress, he was prescient. As usual, you craved an argument. There'd been an issue at the university. I know you recall this. A student accusing Collins of stealing his work, delivering the ideas at a conference. The student had reason. But there goes Thomas, defending our "right to mimeograph immaterial ideas."

"Joshua, Benjamin's take on the painter Klee's *Angelus Novus* – it's not … he's not opposing progression. His project was to rescue the past, to leave us with a sense of rescue. But there lies his problem: with memory and how little it can assist. Still … the single catastrophe's compelling. Leads back to the sentimentalist's preoccupation: historical materialism. As Gramsci reiterated, 'idealism, upside-down.' So, my answer –"

"Your answer?" I said, interposing.

"Too close to God-searching, seating the mission of history in some philosophical exercise."

But I was busy, redirecting your attention away from my flushed cheeks. Araceli and I had argued – because of you, Thomas. She was begging me to forgive your support for Collins. I was trying to steady my racing thoughts: "Forget Benjamin's architecture of historical materialism. What about the Marxist project? He poked holes in the whole thing."

"Worthy attempt. Completely wrong. Benjamin's point is that history's a remembered sequence of events, leading to catastrophe; and, of course, we can't take his 'continuum of progression' any further than he allows. Anyhow, 'the project,' as you call it, wasn't Marx's."

At some point in our conversation, I left. While I can't remember what ticked me off, I remember the anger, remember standing and leaving you on the bench. Maybe I was trying to drive you away. With too much sun or drink, there it is – our dissolute souls! And that party Araceli arranged for you, after the publication of your Noah's Ark book? God, I remember that. In the décor, rather than two-by-two's, three-by-three's was the theme. She'd arranged everything. Three tables, with salads, sandwiches and desserts. Along the bar, grains, hops and grapes. Araceli, you,

I, the Kabbalah's mystical three, entering the beloved garden of Eden. In that story, only one emerges unscathed. I'll lean closer. We both know, Thomas, who that unscathed one would be. And I think you can hear me. At the party, you were shouting. "In Euclid, we have a *true* poet! A TRUE POET!" Anyone who's ever read Araceli's words found you especially brutal.

That, Thomas, is where I enter: my love for her words, for her writing, her portrayal of the lie behind the truth. Poetry that is a bouquet of lies. There's beauty and strength there. Maybe you'd agree. Poets are our sages. Pity our sobriquet for them isn't 'cipher.'

And the Tiffany you'd procured for her twenty-eighth – at the time, you were what, late forties? And newly divorced. The expensive lamp came on the heals of your marriage proposal, but this is one thing you got right. Araceli's gift to the world is the cast of light through coloured glass. Her words catch flame. Once, Thomas, she showed me *her* gift to you: a stained-glass panel with a cerulean blue constellation. Scales of justice in Inca gold. *Libra*: misfit of the zodiac (funny, you and I, born under the same sign).

Opening the closet, pushing aside your pleated trousers. "He keeps it hidden here," she said, smiling. That's the effect you have. She smiles at your insults.

"What a sham!" At that party of threes, you strode among the ebullient houseguests, past inebriated philosophy grads, up to their necks in Hannah Arendt's human condition, boating along to Kant's revelation on judgement, on envy versus jealousy. (How I appreciated that one!) Maybe this too was about drowning because your reaction was to drown out everyone else. I imagine there was some rancour there too: the Tories had won; you were pissed to hell.

"These days, we've broadsheets on boredom! As teachers, we're just helping the internet along. No adjudicating on matters regarding societal rage or apprehension. And there's the terror, the source of our night sweats. Despite everything, technology, science's advancement, despite our preoccupation with social media, we've never stopped living in the Age of Psychoanalytical Victimhood. It's the '50s and '60s all over again!"

I glanced over at Araceli, ducking behind three gigantic flowering cacti.

You were riding the tide. "Manufacturing bills of magnanimity instead of stuffing the nouveau riche inside history's dresser drawers. Talking, drinking tea and espressos, distinctly not SUPPORTING the adventurous spirit, when WONDER is what students are saying in every paper. And between the lines? BOREDOM!"

With aplomb, you continued sacking educators, criticizing obstructions we place like chess pieces before students, many of whom were in attendance.

"We've GUTTED ourselves!"

Gliding among the illustrious guests with the ease of a two-bit dancer.

"I'm speaking of hazarding. RISK-TAKING!"

Ranting.

I stepped in. "What about the critical souls, the ones in classes I've taught who've spoken up about Churchill's sharpening his sword on a 'savage' Pashtun warrior – yes, 'savage,' Churchill's name for their solicitous colonized crew, in India, his rice famines? Risk-taking right there. Certainly, *they* haven't lost anything by attending classes with craven souls like us!"

A scattered few in the room laughed.

Later, I caught you in your study, ploughing verdant fields with Nietzsche.

"This is what the conclusive aesthetes argued," you said, leaning back against Araceli's knees, as she rested on the summit of the couch. "'We're drowning in our conversions,' conviction dictating beauty or rigid abstinence, biased by faith, even compassion. Still, Nietzsche had something. We take hot bubble-baths in our own suffering."

Araceli offered the famous Turin story of Nietzsche, passing a driver flogging a horse, throwing his arms around the poor beast. "My dear, this is your Nietzsche? Critical of compassion? One thing he *was*, was authentic, a compassionate philosopher." Her liquid-browns were doing what they do best: piercing through the mottled skin of arguments. "Read what he wrote about love. Several sides. Several sides to a story."

You inhaled. "Authenticity? When he passed the asshole beating up the horse, he was an old fuck. Like me! His landlord spied him dancing, butt-naked, playing piano. Clearly, he was confronting his mortality when he met that horse."

Later, in the kitchen, I found Araceli alone, framed by the infinite night. Chrysanthemums, planted in a colourful pot, were blooming, in fits of violet, fuchsia and yellow. Closer, and "Here we are," she whispered. "Taking up the kitchen with my bad manners." She brought a sushi-roll to her tongue.

"Just so," I whispered, moving closer. "You don't have to talk."

The crease in her lips, a comma between two clauses. "Ah, the mystery!" She lifted her face. Through the window, the moon lit up the night, glancing off the stone façade.

"Mystery? Of the raw fish you're consuming?"

She chewed, swallowed. "Cucumber, my dear. I don't eat animals."

"Fish, you mean."

"I mean fish and everyone else."

"You must be the only Uruguayan who dislikes seafood."

"My dear, of course I like. That is why I don't eat them."

Even this idiocy was precious.

Damn! It's cold in this room … I want … I want to say that despite that blasted heater and unlike history, boiling over with vanity and conceit, it's fucking cold here! As for your Noah, waiting to for rare gopherwood trees to mature, I know you'd be howling, "For God's sakes, he wasn't sitting around!"

His wife? This I'll never forget: "Women, Joshua, are our Corinthian Sirens, waiting to break us silly sailors. We eviscerate them, excoriate their attempts to mirror our egotistical selves. We stand, catcalling. Men pincushion, while women kindly unravel."

You know your dear wife once asked me, "Why do we always become what you men want?"

And, Thomas, you never spoke about any indiscretions, but of course there were many. Yes, of course I knew. That's what you do: forget the ones who surround you, the ones who get close. You admitted as much, that day on the bridge.

Remember that beautiful Shakespearian professor, the one who left for Madrid?

As for my excuse for knocking around with our colleague, without Araceli's – let's call it, commitment – well, you understand, yes, Thomas?

"Shakespeare," our colleague told me one evening, her lips forming delicious words. "Tickled by Pythagoras, brought out pathos in *Twelfth Night's* Malvolio. Offering supplication to class and its finery for Olivia's love, Malvolio would perch on an ass's head to move above his station. The Fool, disguised as priest, asks the silly dandy, drooling over Olivia, whether a bird's soul can inhabit his grandmother's body."

Well suited, isn't it, Thomas, to Araceli's universal-soul ideology? And how appropriate for this moment! *Twelfth Night* and a confession.

When this colleague, now in Madrid, petitioned yours truly, I took full responsibility and gave her what she wanted. It was one blessed night. In bed, pillow against cheek, of all things, she recounted Ginzburg's *The Cheese and the Worms*, about Menocchio. You know, Thomas, the peasant who believed life originated from rotting fruit or flesh. "History is meant to be tasted," I remember her whispering. "So, what happened? Called before the Inquisition, that unknown miller Menocchio spoke of the divine as earthbound … only not in those exact words, and he did get a few things wrong, like spontaneous generation, worms from cheese. For all of it, even for his less ridiculous claims, like portraying Jesus as human, he was called a fool. Like Malvolio, who is quizzed by the Fool. That's the game."

"What game?"

Propping herself up on her elbows, so close I could smell our sex, warm along her breath. "The game of imagination and logic. Having a stake in the way it's framed, imagination's free to frame logic as it pleases."

"And sometimes," I said, "it comes up as we hope: heads instead of tails."

How I wish, Thomas, you'd OPEN your eyes! But I'll say it again; it's the infernal heart monitor that gives us hope that your heart's still beating. That's what hearts do – a good sign, yes. I've heard there's a surge of life before death. This, I'm afraid, you won't have. The machines will perhaps.

I'm thinking, Thomas, of when we first met. Long ago and far away, yet close. I squeeze in the bellows, while you have no say. We were at a conference, in Exeter. In a clamorous café near the university, you strode in, wearing a herring-bone tweed (who wears that now?), throwing back frothy hair. Sitting down, you asked whether I was "appreciating" the lectures. Without waiting for an answer, "Ah, you're eating here. Don't recommend it. Go for the tea … Joshua, is it? I tell you, avoid, at all cost, what passes as edibles. "

I was off to a panel on revolutionary transcendentalist Americans. Leave the Loyalist ranks and look what happens! When we met again that evening, let's just say I knew it wouldn't be the last. Then, I met your wife … what I think drew me in is her laugh; it's like raw silk. I fell into its depths. I was falling the first night you had me over for dinner. Such paradisiac odours from the stove. At dinner, the both of you were composing a duet along your house crystal. Caught up in the sonorous ringing, you offered: "This reminds me of a story my ex-wife told of a suspension bridge in northern California that collapsed." Yep, bring in the ex, Thomas. "Mirror of London's bridge," you added. "I suppose we have many collapsed bridges."

I was being literal. "Most bridges are unstable. Look at Olaf's Norsemen taking down the first incarnation of London's."

Araceli laughed, then noticeably blushed.

You referenced your ex-wife's research on faulty engineering. "The architects weren't versed in music. They miscalculated. Tonal chords, all that wind and clanging-about is what brought down the bridge."

Through the echoing sound chamber inside my head, sound waves collided, wind whistled through iron. Music, the culprit; resonance, its co-conspirator. "Almost a perfect fifth," you added. "The 'Pythagorean chord,' the cosmic chord that Saint Augustine speculated we hear at death's door. Not the tritone, the Devil's chord. Blasted inferno." You smiled and swayed to some melody only you could hear. "No, no. The fifth we accept; that's what moves us. The music of the spheres. Earth's rotation. This … polyphony, really, this music of the universe: I've always believed it's in B. A B5 Chord, whose fifth is F#. Some call it the power chord. To my ears, in imagination, it's the music of the spheres."

Above her own woven tablecloth, with her hands, always expressive with her hands, Araceli threw gravitas to merriment, Uruguayan palatal over plosive consonants: "But, Thomas, dear, how can we possibly make this … this guess about what we hear when we die?"

I can't remember your answer. What is it now, Thomas? What universal chord do you hear?

It was only after reading your manuscript on Noah that I passed by the Bodleian Library particularly to open a book, a book which in my uneducated, pre-Thomas mind hadn't existed. Along the gilded pages of the Book of Hours was our ark builder, his wife and sons watching churning waters swallow their cousins and neighbours. God, haloed above, bends a rainbow. Like an archer, his bow.

I'm not apologizing. What I … what we did was shameful. Yet, in those kisses was an indentation in the fabric of possibility. Once (although it was hundreds of times over the course of our affair), Araceli, who must've been determined to break the spell, mentioned your name. "Dovish Thomas, duelling with unseen enemies."

"Maybe I'm in constant battle," you admitted. "But it's infuriating, following threads of meaning, much like some of us approach religion: believing in the divinity of the device. A wry trust in deceitful things."

As historians, we're like scientists watching cells divide, ruling on mitosis, "when it could be anything," I hear you say. "Arbitrary should be our rule of thumb."

Very soon, I'll be leaving. I'm sure you'll be happier. But I have to ask: What were you thinking with Noah? You were never religious, "ever-rarely an Anglican" (your words). You're an historian, in mind and body, caught in dismantling legends, irreverently quoting. "All sorts of holdings become our answer to the imagined bogey-man, the treachery of anarchy."

Pointing skywards, you blamed smog for the death of blue. We were nowhere near London. I was imploring you to help secure my tenure. Diversion was your tactic. Appropriately, we were passing Oxford Castle's slimy stones, William's hand-over to Robert D'Oyly, the stench of rot in the air. No promises that spring. Just rot and damp grass. And you, nonchalant.

"'Life's an act of faith,' said Babbitt. 'We don't know in order that we may believe; we believe in order that we may know.' Eliot asks, how do we throw away Christianity or faith in Babbitt's humanism, without throwing away humanism?

"Course, we can!"

I was frustrated over your refusal to not play a larger role in the faculty's upcoming decision in my fate.

"You already know what I think, my dear Joshua. Never mind humanism; never mind religion. Civilizations are birthed in times of faithlessness. We commit atrocities because we can, ever faithful to our perverse ability to wreak havoc. Chaos enters, the truest state (so say quantum physicians), until everything re-arranges itself. We call this rearrangement civilization."

Your hand on my shoulder had the strength of ten. "Eliot opened his critique of Babbitt with a caveat: easier to destroy than to construct. Anyways, he was speaking of Babbitt's construction of humanism."

With flourish, you gestured toward the ancient castle whose walls later held a prison. Currently, a hotel. "Pretty savvy, converting a prison into a hotel, don't you think, Joshua?"

My mind was flitting about. If debtor's prison, why not one for adulterers?

"Joshua, I see you're angry."

"I'm … frustrated."

"You know I'm doing all I can. Now, who's doubting Thomas?"

"But you understand that Americans are still underrated here."

"Don't worry. I'm involved in a most auspicious way."

I suspect but will never know how much you assisted in their final decision.

While our paths crossed, our subjects rarely did; your nose buried in almost anything European. Meine Nase immersed in migration, while my mind was desperately seeking 'release' from deciphering artefacts.

One strange evening, Crimea was on your mind. Recovering from the flu, I somehow had no resistance to your call to hit the pubs, where I'd forget everything: my students, how things were going with Araceli, forget … yes, Thomas, forget what I was doing to you.

We were walking, chomping on crisps, discussing civilization's malcontents. How strange, memory. I lurched forward, spit out one bad chip, caught on a passing student's cellphone. You pulled me close. "Good draft'll ward off diseases! Worked wonders for my last bout of gastro!"

"Gastro and beer?" But my mind was on whether Araceli would catch my flu.

"What's that, Joshua?"

For a moment, just for a brief moment, it'd felt as if you'd wound a finger around my thoughts.

"This is sinus, Thomas." Whispering, "I failed that little fart with the cellphone."

You drew me even closer. "Don't worry, my friend. 'Rate Your Professor' will bear his retribution."

We were off to the Turf, where, chins wagging, students commiserated, dunking youthful epiphanies into iterations of foam.

I've always found that wooden interiors add mystery. Trap doors, treasure-chest lids, all from wood. Course that happens only in legends. Not in real stories.

Indoor smoking had been banned. I desperately wanted a cigarette.

"Try hashish," you advised. Reaching for your hopping hops, clearing a dram of whisky, "I know," you said.

I choked.

"I know what you think, Joshua. A symbol of religious strife. That's Crimea's embattled history. Eternally involved in proxy wars. Quiescent little Crimea …"

You'd missed my great sigh of relief. Quickly, I pointed out that the sorry case with Crimea was a linguistic one. "Like all good empires, Russia (could be Putin, could be anyone) is convinced they have to annex any country where the good mother language Russian is spoken."

Bang! Smacking the table, you spoke your mind. "Doesn't matter that it's Russia. Don't doubt *for a second* there's a patina of religion in the brokerage of Crimea. Started in Jerusalem. Eventually, we Anglican Brits enter, gouging out a geostrategic base between the Balkans and the Caucasus. Centuries, battling over an island, surrounded by the Bosporus Sea. That island is really a pulpit to defend paltry beliefs."

"Trade interests and power brokerage. You forget: My mother was a lapsed Catholic."

You took a swig. "And your father was Jewish." But you were already on to something else. And, Thomas, what was that: *Your father was Jewish?*

"So, now, Joshua," you continued. "What I'm doing to wile away the hours is reading a novel about an early-nineteenth-century husband who believes with all his soul that 'suffragette' is a bandaging technique invented during the Crimean War."

"I wonder –" But you cut me off.

"Imagine. A man who can't do a damn thing when it comes to women, not even give them a moment's thought, not one ounce of muscle to figure out the meaning of that word, a fucking word, for Christ's sakes! That's it, Joshua: we hominids are no different than monkeys, than bonobos. Only with us, religion drives our war lust. But just like bonobos, sex drives it out."

I was picturing chimps heading off to battle, returning for the sex. Uninterested in monkeys, some of our biped cousins way back when had invented charioted Ares and the more level-headed Aphrodite; Eros, product of their union. Faith to offset lust. You reconsidered your statement. "Sex is dictated by too many physi-ological functions to give it any more thought, whereas violence is dictated by a slew of forces, villainous and heroic."

"Still." I was recalling a BBC interview. "No one can radicalize without a context. The passion is there, but what we do with it –"

Why was I referencing passion? Well, you can guess, Thomas. The conversation went on a bit, moving from one subject to another, losing all sense as the hopping hops kept on coming, until you brought up your sister's visit. "The crux of our relation-ship, Joshua, is her vision's Hegelian. Storytelling, with some con-voluted Spirit guiding events. I agree with her, though, on 'Bricks of London.'"

"Bricks of London?"

You ricocheted a few strident phrases off of the pub's walls: "Blake's mortar for our nightmarish visions: a corporeal mani-festo. Reflecting or *deflecting* civilization's power. 'The stones, Pity; the bricks, well-wrought Affections.' Blake's mythical Gol-gonooza. London's primeval past. We worship buildings and stat-ues. What is that but base mythologizing?"

It became my mission to shut you up. "You're letting senti-ment in through the gates of historical materialism."

"Blake's referencing architecture." As you swept the table of crumbs with one unrepentant hand, you cried, "Odes to dust, Joshua! We have to remain resolute against poetic whimsy. Like we see in Araceli's –"

No way in hell would I let you shit on her work. "So, you're saying beauty and legends authenticate experience, turning us into war-lusting chimps?"

"Don't bury your head, Joshua. Not authenticate. Dangerous times when stories author our world."

Days later, I was in the campus bookstore, admiring your book. On its cover was a talented rendition of Noah's ark, in tawny brushstrokes, splashes of purple-blue and white. The illustrator was definitely referencing Turner's *Retiring of a Navy Ship*.

"Sir, can I help you?"

I'd been standing, bleary-eyed. Nights spent researching the writings of those stealing aboard galleons and armadas, staring out portholes at the drowning. Editing, correcting, skivvying on 20-year-old scotch, deliberating what should stay and what should be deleted from my lectures. Yet, there I stood, before your book, wondering why the raven in the Noah story doesn't return. For the dove, return's essential. Maybe the raven had found grains of truth.

That's it, isn't it, Thomas? Let me lean closer. Last spring, on the bridge, that's what you meant. I was to dole out the grains. That's why Destiny's my friend, carrying around her handbag of irony. Just a month prior, I'd been on that very same bridge with Araceli.

April, the more earnest trees flowering. Everyone was so busy I don't know how we found the time to breathe. Araceli's book had been awarded a university prize. My congratulations sent over social media inspired her to call. You were away. I chose the city, late afternoon. Along the bridge, our embrace was sudden, her kiss full of intention. She took my hand. "Tonight, *Gjoshua?*"

How, after all these years, would I respond? How, after all these years, would I *not?*

We'd arrived separately in the city, joked about leaving separately. When I showed up at your door, she seemed genuinely surprised ... your home, your bed. On the nightstand, a book with a cover photograph of two lovers. Had you set this up?

She's off to Argentina, Thomas. Araceli's in perpetual motion, while you and I are mired in the muddy waters of stasis.

A month later, there you and I were, Thomas, on that very bridge, surrounded by the eavesdropping fog. You were leaning over, staring at some untenable point, murmuring. "I'm leaving."

To Argentina? Shit – I'd almost spoken aloud, hadn't meant to cite your wife's dreams. You were staring at the water below; the air, cool.

"Listen, Joshua. I mean, listen to that." There were muffled human voices; then a birds' choir.

"B?" I offered. "B Natural?"

You smiled, then coughed, covered your mouth, pretended laughter. "But now, I must tell you. There's something more critical. Soon, I ... I won't be here –."

"What is it, Thomas?"

"I have a favour to ask. Think of it as ... well, a gift."

Redirecting your chloric greys: "I've been horrible. I ... I destroy, Joshua." You stared down at your hands on the rail, returned your gaze to the blue obscure. "So many women ... and I've never told her." You, sighed turned to me. "Well, Joshua, I suppose every one of us is guilty, every one of us off to Dante's hellish underworld. But I need you to ... I won't send out any reminders. It's just that I've never been able to tell her, to show her, not in any way she'll ever understand. When I'm gone, someone will have to make absolutely certain –"

"Gone?"

"Yes."

"Understand?"

"That I love her."

You're silent, but your voice resounds. I recall an interview with a woman from the Pyrenees. "I'm not afraid of dying," she told a reporter. "I'm afraid of the tunnel."

On that bridge, you brushed a hand over your face. "I'm so … so knackered these days."

Finally, I noticed.

"Christ, what is it?"

"They've diagnosed a pancreatic enemy, Joshua. How's that for turgid?"

Shock took its throne. Your mouth was moving, but suddenly I was deaf.

"This earth, Joshua, carries such beautiful music. How is it that the infernal dog comes nipping at our feet when we *finally* realize this? The 'perverse charm of violent undertakings.'" You were quoting John Banville. "That's what it feels like. And what am I leaving? What am I leaving any of you?" You turned away. "Nothing."

You're wrong, Thomas. And I've seen Araceli's answer in her poems, the way her words – the way they … like the Tiffany's light through gold filaments. That is her response, not to me or to anyone else, but to you.

And now – do you hear that, Thomas? Across the River Acheron, songs of the dead are entering like insect wings. Where virtuous heathens go, Doubting Thomas and Aristotle, drinking champagne. In limbo. Imagine! With Virgil as guide, you'll never be rid of poetry!

Here's sentiment: Araceli asked me to record her reading her own poems, so you'd have her voice. And I or she would play the recording for you. In a flash, I realized, all I've ever needed is there: her words, life-rafts.

I sense you're speaking, Thomas. "An ending should be brief," you're saying. Along Acheron's shores, you'll be forever debating the dilemma of endings. Endings and return, Malvolio-style. Somewhere inside the dreaming of philosophers: *L'ombra sua torna, ch'era dipartite.*

Here. I've brought along that poem by Blake, the one you recited at our favourite pub. And here's the rest: *Labour of merciful hands; the beams and rafters are Forgiveness.* Forgive me, Thomas. Forgive me for loving her; and yes, forgive me, Thomas, for loving you.

The Earl of Beaconsfield

WE WERE SITTING in the parlour, curtains drawn.

"Wouldn't you prefer the library?"

As the portrait artist considered my question, it was his moustache that drew me in. The delicate hair above his lips moved of its own accord. However, as our country's greatest poet has written, appearances are deceiving.

It has been rumoured that I would benefit from a moustache, that it would add distinction to my face. What a shame that would be! I firmly believe attributes should be carved by bold experiences, not by facial hair. Besides, I once had a bit of beard. Was I more distinguished then? Doubtful.

More interesting to my tale is how a Jew, baptized, has become Prime Minister. My public sees me as a man from the Hebrew tribe, but primarily they view me simply enough, as a man, erring but ever astute when it comes to sacrifice. I am a man (of sorts). I say of sorts, as this relates to where I reside: on the blank page between.

The portrait artist disagreed with my choice of the library. "No, Sir, Mr. Disraeli, Sir," he admonished, brushing his hand across that waxed moustache. "I'd rather paint you in the parlour, a more suitable climate for your complexion."

He is an artist, after all. I conceded, laughing and quickly changing countenance. Although I am practiced, the threat that I would reveal all … that I will reveal everything is a regular occurrence, especially indoors. My fear is similar to the man's who is afraid of heights: not that he would fall but that some compunction might animate him to jump. I was worried I might easily let down my guard, as Shakespeare's Viola eventually does.

Ah, sentimentality. It is a modified equation of reason. We have reason, so we shall keep sentimentality. In this enlightened age of lionized texts, its stalwart queens and perplexed parliamentarians who ask, how I, a man of the Hebrew tribe, took the stage. They are correct in asking. I have been a pariah my entire life. I call myself a parvenu; although there is this: Shakespeare's inked pariahs are clowns, fools who see, with the exception, perhaps of Lear or the Venice merchant, mirrored in my own brows. Like the merchant, I have Venetian roots. Unlike him, I have no revenge to take, no pound of flesh.

"Ah, that is better, Sir. Yes, that is good." He was smiling.

These portraits call for remarkable feats by their subjects, and I do not have the mortal strength to avoid the call of the spirit to move about. Were it not for my careful watch of his practiced hand, I might have changed course. I might have wavered. Yet, I was entranced by this artist's craft, his symphonic wash over the canvas. "Tell me, Sir." His lips turned up slightly. Was he indeed amusing himself, at my expense?

"Yes."

"As you pose for this portrait … I often ask my subjects a question. Unfortunately, I now cannot find one that will suffice."

"You are asking me to find a question with a suitable answer?"

"Sir, my brush will better suit the tone of your skin –"

Had I heard correctly? Had he found me too dark? So fused was this man's focus with practice, he could barely distinguish between his own version of actuality and what actually was.

I obliged, as he dipped into paints, rendering my face a shade paler.

"Perhaps a story?"

"It would indeed help."

Should I reveal? Should I finally breathe? He was glancing at the portrait, the yet incipient draft of me. "I will tell you my story, then, but you must swear."

Surprised, the artist turned to me. "I swear."

"Swear …" I suspended the rest of my thoughts.

"Swear, Sir? On what?"

He had stopped painting, then offered his father. "On my father's life, I swear. I would have no reason, Sir, to tell anyone. Not a soul."

"Yes, this is an important story that most importantly must be confidential."

He turned and continued his work. Not once throughout my narration, did this evidently fine interpreter of character interrupt. He did not stop his brushstrokes nor artificially cover for discomfiture.

I know what will be asked. What was it that overcame me? Why would I finally tell my story to a stranger? A stranger, I repeat. And, yet, I knew. I knew it was time and that it should be he. I am not regretful that I shared my story with this man.

"Well, then, you have heard Ovid's story, of Hermaphroditus and Salmacis?"

This sparked a change. The artist lifted his attention from the canvas. "Yes, Salmacis, a nymph who fell in love with Hermaphroditus. I have read *The Metamorphoses*. What kind of artist would I be, if I hadn't? Salmacis is a jealous creature, clinging to Hermaphroditus, as he swims … as he tries to escape her salacious grasp."

"Have you ever wondered about that tale?"

"In what way, Sir?"

"The unfortunate Hermaphroditus is punished. The source of his punishment is a woman, a naiad, a nymph."

"Yes, a nymph who wants from the gods."

"Pardon?"

"Who wants from the gods, Sir, who wants too much, as all goodly and godly women do."

"Yes. She obtains it, in this case."

"She does, Sir."

"They become one, and I quote, 'Being one, they seemed neither and yet both.'"

"One creature; that is what Ovid wrote. May I ask you, please, to turn slightly to the left?"

"Like this?"

"With your chin, please. Yes, much better. Thank you."

It is like this …

I brace.

Brokering, I brace against what I cannot tell anyone but of course my wife, although there have been a few lapses.

While brokering, I am creating from investments a future for this country. As I do this for my country, I, Benjamin Disraeli, First Earl of Beaconsfield, Prime Minister, a Jew of origin, progeny of Isaac, have almost managed to fool myself. What amuses me, often more than I care to admit, is that there are so few who know.

The man you are representing with your brush is …

I am not a son but a daughter *and* son. I am both, Hermaphroditus and Salmacis.

[The artist did not blink. Had he heard comparable stories from other sitters?]

I wear my clothing against the inclement weather, to conceal what I am: three silken vests, which rid me of what may have already died. Indeed, I wish that it had. An individual may never be truly certain, but at this time, I would allow for such certainty. Let all doubt be put to rest. If, however, another element of equal denomination should be revealed, then such it will be. What is life, if not synonymous with change? What is life, if there is to be no brokering? Ultimately, we broker with death herself. I enjoy prosperity, although a fickler friend than death but interesting in this regard.

There are others who share my secret, other trustworthy guardians. I have made compromises, leaving some, I am afraid, in the shadows. The trick is knowing where the ignorance lies and who those trust-keepers might be; to know that in trusting, they are content to remain ignorant of the entirety. The substance, the *who* I truly am, is a constant threat, ready to charge through everything I have built, with the grit of those Parliamentary devils, who go on about my purchases and actions, both of which they cannot truly vouchsafe and thereby resolve to abhor.

I brace against what they know or believe they know. I brace against what they cannot believe. It is the same with these vestments, thus represented with the portrait artist's slick brush and palette. Words clothe the nakedness. For as I tell this, I nevertheless have purchased the oratory and addition of dirt to my grave. Yet, I am always fearful of the wafer-thin parchment that lies between the *who* I truly am and the *what* I reveal. Will everything disintegrate when exposed?

It is a constant worry. Will they find reason for insurrection? I keep the lions at bay with negotiation. I oversee the building of canals. I oversee conduct and legislation. In this, I give my admirers *and* detractors meaning, and a taste. If they ask for more, G-d forbid.

They did want more of me, regarding the Corn Laws; although any man worthy of his bread would be proud of that legislation. Look what it did for our domestic vitality!

I am more than I appear. What lies between, I am.

I am the in-between.

In this, I take heart. Beneath, there is another, more permanent wearing-away. Nevertheless, what would I, could I ask of influence, of passion, of flamboyancy? What, of disguise? Modesty pulls no weight with me. I had to dispense with it, as one would with any cloak when the collar's crispness has faded. Holding the cloth against my chest, I engage language as further disguise. In truth, I have wrapped my chest in yellowing bandages. Not much of a chest, not one whose revelation would be admired; although *ma spectacle* may serve as a momentary respite. Herein is the rub: my chest has become manly, even while it has maintained a womanly form.

[The artist began to speak. I dissuaded him.]

What breathes beneath this clothing is the truth, and what it is people imagine they see. However, all of it is a lie. You may ask, why a lie? Had I reason to tell, to tell the full story, perhaps the greatest curiosity would be my lovemaking. Here it is. I love women. I have never loved men as I love the delicate – but ah! Not so delicate sex. It is only at night when the contra-alto sings from this womanly chest, almost plaintive, that I know as a woman. As the Baroque artists understood, as musicians understand. Politicians do not, which is why they argue and why many forfeit the finer arts.

Distinguishing passion from reality and dreams from substance are most difficult allocations for the mind to uphold. Even I, an Earl, a first for the borough of Beaconsfield, would say that politicians cannot distinguish. We leave that for artists.

I, a Jew, baptized Christian, which Saint John might laud, Salome condemn –

["I am sorry, Sir," the painter interrupted. "Could you move, this way? The afternoon light has shifted. It is more … shall we say, soothing, from that angle."]

Now, how *did* he detect the frown that had begun to form?

I moved toward the sunlight's thread through diaphanous curtains. All other curtains in the dim room were drawn, as they sometimes are at this time of day. I then revealed my story.

I am woman.

I am man.

I am the in-between.

Some women I have been with know; some do not. My siblings have always known. In deference to the Word of the L-rd, I am baptized. Yet, I am neither Jew nor Christian, man or woman.

[At this point, the artist was so engaged, he barely glanced my way. I wondered about the accuracy of his portrait. I believe his rather perplexing disinterest encouraged me to tell him if not the entire story, the salacious parts.]

A woman-man in my position cannot leave anything to chance. Someone for whom fragility does not begin to explain its quality must plan every minute. Thus, I ask, how might they ever see that this rogue, this purveyor of ill course and disastrous discourse am not and never will be whom they believe me to be?

I am Benjamin, Son of Yamin. My father, Isaac, Laughing Isaac. My father, having suffered a falling out with his synagogue, became Christian; yet I trained myself to decipher the ancient texts. Thus, I know that Isaac was his mother's laughter. My own mother was stoic. I have inherited my grandmother's laugh. When I am dreaming or in my quarters, I laugh, as there is the possibility that I am fooling no one.

History will chronicle the Earl of Beaconsfield as a politician who did not offer broken promises. Along with my brokering and lionized texts, they will eye the portraits and indeed this portrait, the sombre background within the frame and the persona within. Is this not what circumscribes all our lives: the art of creating who we are to become? Each of us has our calling. A contra-alto bellows. A swallow swallows, her cry a lament. A nightingale ... ah, yes. How is it that a nightingale's song touches us so? Her dulcet voice bears a necklace of mellifluous harmonies. Yet, even I, cloaked figure, cannot figure out how it is that a nightingale's voice reaches so deep within us, the strangest of animals.

My parents disowned me, although they claimed otherwise. They disowned the *what* and certainly the *who*. The midwife delivered me and then the news with the suggestion that they raise me a daughter. This was inconceivable to my parents, more terrible than their having birthed, as my mother would sometimes whisper to my father, an abomination. My country woman Mary Shelley, daughter of Stateswoman Wollstonecraft, a mother who died soon after she was born, this Mary Shelley, author of a monster who read Plutarch, Goethe and Milton and abandoned all hope of acceptance or pity, knew well what lay within their hearts.

I would be raised a son.

How might I forgive my parents? How would I not? And is not this the horror I witness along my countrymen's faces for my having been born a Jew? Some envisage me as a Hebrew whose roots are tangled in the tubular arms of the epitomized tribe. This is the page onto which they have placed me. I may well leave my identity to their prose. Knowing of my baptism, they are yet overcome with anguish over my roots.

Yet we must keep in mind the insignificance of all their attempts to categorize. "My good man, Disraeli," her Lovely Queen Victoria once had the audacity to publicly express. "What is your religion? You were born a Jew, and you forsook your great people." Her lips curled in a question; and I could have kissed those lips, however straight and firm they remained.

Our Royal Regina crooned: "Dear man, no one believes you are a Christian at heart." There was something there, ground into the mortar of her inquiry. O, dear, Lovely Laurel Builder, Charmer, Our Queen, if only you were aware of how close you came. Regarding the others: I have acclimated, but the aggrieved are pursuing the clues they have accumulated along their journeys.

"Yes," I answered her. "I am a Jew. When the ancestors of the right honourable gentlemen in this room were brutal savages in an unknown island, mine were priests in the temple of Solomon."

She laughed. I believe her admiration grew.

Not satisfied with being only a broker, I became a writer, as well. Such is the duality of my nature. Certainly, there is truth between the tasteful lies. Yet, I am no longer interested.

"Paltry writing," my detractors have claimed, their noses turning at the mere whiff of parody of their genius. Granted, these critics might perceive the lancet poised above their corpses, and I, ready to rid them of that superfluous tendency to breach all odds and exist: Whigs, Tories, all in this reputed party, along with Gladstone, stand as armies against my radical proposals.

I exist.

What I am not is a medical student, to my parents' grief. As the pages of legal elocution dry, the sight of certain bodily juices, blood of a Whig, for example, disturb me. Blood runs from a wound, drawing life. I cannot bear the sight, however.

I am.

I chalk.

Onto this dry slate, I ask, why would anyone destroy? Why make this the aim of writing?

I care not about their paltry lives. They do not move my pen. Certainly, they are quite capable of wielding the pen against anyone they abhor. They criticize my having penned them into my writings. Perhaps they desire a duel, but enough with the pen!

I confess I am not without my faults. My critics who are not in politics have an insatiable desire to see some politicians brought into the light, in my writing. My wife would never allow me that pleasure. On my father's grave, I have made light of no one. Yet, I am dismissed, shunned; my writing and character considered 'flamboyant.' This writing, they say, is not worth the paper on which it is printed. I, my wife, as well as the Queen, one of my most endearing advocates, would disagree.

My subject matter, it is known, has been liaisons, unbridled human passion: no humbleness in this 'flamboyancy.' Through the pinholes, I have seen this odd criticism published: My narratives are too fetching. These critics, the very same who, in my company, feign interest in my prose or in my (wife's) gift for storytelling and romance, go to remarkable lengths to prove that I have, in my publications, eviscerated citizens whose title or name bear no mention here. Suffice to say, these are the same men who wish me ill-fortune, who believe themselves perfect parliamentarians: grave and unerring, critical of most ventures … stoical, as well, and they protect this stoicism as if this is equivalent to bravery.

We might well blame their error on my physical nature, on what lies between my legs, which of course they do not realize they have discerned. Hiding, I have managed to disclose. These bandages have become an allegory. What is buried, *oh cruelty!* is revealed on occasion, that which cannot be abided by myself but intuited by my enemies and friends. Yet, despite the admonishments, despite the bad reviews, I must confess I enjoy this equation: The more I conceal, the more I reveal – an equation bearing more of a resemblance to the holding of a secret than to a burial.

[The moustache-winged artist, hair curling over protruding ears, asked that I freeze: momentarily, he promised.]

And so, the weaker sex, the sex victorious in its reticence – it is here, inside, as well.

The Parliamentary world in which the two of I inhabit is fitting for both. If, in this world, these bandages were to unravel, would the headquarters of the highest office or indeed of the lowest still ill-suit me? Man, woman, we are both suited to govern. G-d has given me the capacity to take up matters that might be unsettling to good citizens, to take up the grim tasks of so-called 'men' and make of them soldiers.

What every figure of this country cannot see is that in this country's charter, there is a certain eulogy. Empires remain, as long as they rise. A country can rise only as far as it recognizes the depths to which it will eventually sink. Beneath the layers of earth, there is a shaft, a mine. My country, great England, needs this canal, this water beneath the crust.

I know.

They think I am crazy.

They are always thinking.

"They think you are a fine man," professed the painter.

Perhaps. They have helped train my indubitable patience. I am the indubitable patient, claims my own doctor.

[With a swing of his brush, the artist asked then if my doctor were informed. I still find it interesting that this should perplex him.]

Yes.

Anna is my doctor's daughter. I will return to her.

This you know. Mary Anne Disraeli is my companion. Our feelings of endearment are unrivalled. There are rumours that I have married for money. These are rumours, befitting small minds. I may be a profiteer, but I am no thief, especially of a woman's heart – the basest thieving.

Perhaps philandering is base and yet another form of thievery. Let me add, this is not my usual comportment. My wife and I are happy, her wit akin to mine; her wry sport with words, a match which I often lose. Her mind, greater than any woman's, any man's. 'Reasonable' and 'passionate' become savage misnomers when we use the former to mark men and the latter, women.

[The artist sympathetically shook his head.]

However, never tarry in rancour, I say, the rancour I have for the treatment of women by our pitiful society. This is not about my wife … take any woman, Emilie du Châtelet, mathematical genius of our last century, from Versailles, who died after childbirth, it was rumoured, with Voltaire's child. It is said she had a mind for Newton's equations and a passage to her chambers for many lovers.

My wife's passion is astonishing. In politics, we are compatriots. She is fascinated by any discourse about lands she has not visited. She is the ink to my pen, the pen to my ink, offering the greatest assistance in the editing of my writing. She is my co-author and remains untroubled by my kinship with both the Hebrews and the nymphs. A most enthusiastic woman, Mary Anne reveals pleasures, I must confess, of which even I have heretofore been unaware.

[The artist seemed to be readying to ask a question.]

Ah, yes, Dearest Anna, the doctor's daughter.

[He nodded.]

I let my heart become an entity, a wastrel. I will craft a verb: I was *wastrelled*.

My dear Anna …

The nightingale, whose way through cannot be calculated: She is of this and the time before. Anna, my doctor's daughter, the evening I sent her a letter was my downfall.

The nightingale's song does not end happily.

When I was with her, night's veil was thrown down upon our nakedness. She saw and smiled, this songstress who was silent in our bed. No words escaped her lips. Nothing but a womanly sigh, when I stiffened inside her. She pulled away the bandages. Bosom in bosom. And now I make mockery, but this is how it transpired, and, here, I have added more detail than is necessary.

Everyone knows. Nevertheless, my wife lay with others. Who, cuckolded? Who, beguiled? Anna told me she was leaving for

France, but this was not the end. As our affair continued, she grew angry. This opera star, diva extraordinaire. *She*, angry with *me!* There were threats.

[The artist lifted an eyebrow, a gesture of compassion?]

I cannot begrudge her this reaction. She attacked me, claimed I was 'another monster.' Who was the first? I did not ask. A disdainful evil, she said and would tell everyone. What was that requisite event, pushing her to reveal all and almost ruin my life? My leaving her. I refrained from speaking. Better leave her with the possibility to tear my flesh; a far more dangerous threat would have been her fury. I would not be able to suck out such venom. I therefore let her go but with no farewell. I have imagined her sonorous voice. Nothing further than that. When Anna returns to our shores, I will leave on business: something fractious in my ranks, something I will have to fix. Perhaps I will voyage to Bismarck's unified Prussian states.

She and my wife are the only two I have truly loved. They, and my parents, my dearest sister, Sarah and my brothers with their ridicule, their taunting. Dear Sir, I was not left unscathed by the midwife's briny hands. My brothers wondered how it was possible that I was filled with resentment over their illustrious student careers at Winchester, when I had none of the riches handed to my siblings. Rather than Winchester, my parents sent me to Hingham. What no one knows is why. It was not due to my appearance that, upon closer examination, would have been discerned, the Hebrew etched into my cheeks, my chin. It was the womanhood I carry alongside the masculine.

My student days were uneventful. I guarded the truth, having no need to shower with my fellows. Nor was I required to undress beneath their surveillance. There was delicious gossip about the ladies. Of course, I honoured my violet peacock feathers and indulged. I remember a young woman's Anglican graces, her eyes!

She was not my first, but I was hers. Darkness, of course, was my foil. Eventually, there came Henrietta, but you may have read of her and will read more when I am gone.

[The portrait artist objected. "Oh, Dear Sir, I –" and appearing to reconsider his 'Sir,' he continued. "I cannot foresee that my life will be longer than yours." I objected. G-d will decide our fates. The man is younger in spirit as well as in physical forbearance.]

I took peace in the neighbouring Epping woodland, escaping the school property and its sputtering inmates. There, I entertained my *wanderlust* in the pages of books, beneath the solicitous trees; and there I indulged in the forest's wealth of smells, the precious elm, a solitary oak, under which I might station my ineffable heritage. Who else but the trees would be so accepting?

During school breaks, I stretched out alongside the Lea and Roding, their grassy banks conducive to my contemplations.

My passion for the Epping trees, for their magisterial stature, has been shared with our Queen. She agreed to visit, with the intention of naming the forest for the people. Indeed, she shares my interests in narrowing the girth between the working class and the landed gentry. No doubt she believes that the former need their land, as well.

Ah, yes, our Queen's sardonic wit. In this, she resembles my dear wife, who, once, out of my earshot, responded to her majesty's comment about my wife's wonderful alabaster skin: "Ah, yes, but you should see my Dizzy in the bath."

Learning of this, I feared she had spoken of my effeminate qualities. How near she drew those in the royal court!

[I paused here, told the painter that I felt such comfort in speaking with him.]

Anna, whose silence I bought with smoothed, polished stones, set in silver and gold, gave me death: such death that I thought, if this is death, how delicious. Ah, the taste of a woman. I have admitted of my knowledge of their prolific ways in keeping secrets between their thighs.

[Of note, this was not spoken in precisely the language stated here.]

As for my wife, she knows how to press her lips into mine, my lips upon my face perhaps less interesting than those below. She pulls so gently. "Ah, dear Dizzy," as I lie on my back, soothingly, lifting my masculinity aside. She whispers, her voice, a moistened indentation, dips in her fingers. My lovers are fed, as am I, on legions of love. At the moment, there is no other knowledge than the fragrant.

[Most of the artist's response was contained in a sigh, as he walked over to draw the curtains. "The sun," he said. "It is a volatile beast."]

"For history, Sir," he asserted. "Stay still for history. The office will wither your countenance."

"Wither my countenance?"

"An idiom. I will offer another. There is no cover. I always ask my sitters to wear no cover."

"Ah, I like your riddles, but what do they mean?"

"I think you know," and there! He had his portrait! Upon my face, bewilderment, eternally etched. There, for the world to see, but I do like that portrait. I do.

When the artist gracefully took his leave, he turned, once. "Your secret will remain sealed within." He pressed a fist to his heart.

Not seven days hence, penning his and my name to paper, white and fragrant, he wrote: "Dear Sir: I thank you for sending me a copy of your book, which I shall waste no time in reading."

And I, forever wondering if I should have remained silent. I did not tell him that my wife, my lover and alibi, gave me the strength to broker this new deal for our country. It is due to her unearthly yet solid temperament, her marvellous mind, that we will have the Suez Canal. She took me in her arms, called me by my name. This is how changes are made, in the arms of dreamers.

Four Characters

The Writer

"Sweeter than wine ... softer than a summer's night." Lou Reed's yowling lyrics were on her mind last Friday, inside Montréal's Gare Centrale. It was 9:02, in red, on the black screen; the swan-like 2 and rounded 9 too gracious to accept anything as foolish or regrettable as his transgression, which had been made bold and plain as day by a silk scarf – yes, the scarf, far more than the woman wearing it: a scarf dyed the colour of trains, rain and ashes. *Springtime* was what the writer remembered thinking when she first spied the translucent material, though it was October, the drizzle washing out morning in the way only a devious autumn hand could devise.

It was then, over the course of one insomniac night and the shedding of so many tears, that the writer experienced the revelation like a reverberating gong: four years of her life entirely wasted. The image of the damn scarf flitted across her very own screen, its arrogant fluidity brushing aside any attempts at distraction. Silver reflections haunted her midnight black. She'd forever remember the figures swirling, twirling along the material, decorated with turquoise swirls, not unlike the swirls cartoonists like George Schultz use to indicate dancing.

And what guts, meeting him at the station.

Sure, the woman was beautiful. If one were to go with first impressions, in the woman's brown, expressive face, arched brows, protrusion of chin, there was an even quantifying of life. She was holding a book, with a vaguely familiar front cover. In the writer's memory, the illustration vaguely resembled the cover of one of those *Lonely Planet* guides.

The Scarf

Fashioned from the finest silk, the scarf attracted the attention of anyone who drew near. Its exquisite strokes of artistry had been applied by a methodical hand in the Hunan province, during the early part of the imperial war-torn century. Among the dancing, operatic figures, in lavish gowns and elaborately beaded head-dresses, was a musician, cradling a long-necked pipa, her fingers dipping, as a poet's pen, into river strings.

Suffering was both the scarf's birthright and character, lending the painted dancers and musician a tacit aloofness. Recently, the scarf had made its way overseas and even more recently had been excavated from an accessory-bin at a Montréal estate sale by an artist who gave it as a gift to a doctoral student. Now, extolling in its own brash beauty, the scarf bore witness to the joyful council of tired eyes, long habituated to the drab and washed-out colours of forgetting.

The Scholar

The smile on the scholar's face, later noticed by the writer, emerged over years and years of pointed discussions the scholar had had with herself. It was as if having been seated at a conference table with all her worries, she'd finally conceded to their presence – a smile seasoned with a beguiling wit that often rescued even her own self from whatever deep misgivings plagued her soul. A few years back, she'd moved from Chicago to attend McGill, only to throw herself into the thick of things: a PhD in Post-Colonial Literature. And now, here she was, Friday morning, a half-hour before her lover's arrival, tensing her grip on the métro pole. Across the car and mirrored in the magnet-black window, her smile beamed exuberantly above the scarf, her face melting into the never-ending night of the endless subway tunnel. "Obsidian," someone had once said of her complexion, and she'd responded by giving the neoliberal idiot a piece of her mind. "Black. I'm black beautiful." *Black girl magic,* she thought. To the idiot: "Don't need to play tricks with that word, my friend."

She glanced again at the reflection. Her stylistic winter coat seemed more distinguished against the scarf's deep turquoise, festive dancers celebrating along the silk. She released the métro pole and pulled on the scarf, to loosen it, elongating the painted pipa player. The métro, packed to the gills, unexpectedly jolted, and she fell against a suit alongside, who cast a lowered-lid stare. She scowled and turned to her book, to Lodovico Castelvetro, discussing Aristotle's *Poetics*, and at this point in the text exploring the three unities: time, place and action.

Like some of the other riders, the scholar's heart was raw, with an equal amount of worry and morning's promise. She was headed towards Bonaventure, *aka* Central Station, where her new*ish* lover, the artist, was arriving from Halifax. She laughed, remembering his first portrait: Her face in so many shades of black, she literally couldn't stop laughing all way home and into the next morning.

"Alright. Maybe it's unintentional, but your …" – waving a hand over his drawing – "this is comical. Authentic representation?"

She'd asked if he'd ever heard of OBAC movement and the Wall of Respect – South Side, Chicago.

He hadn't. Crumpling into a gigantic beanbag chair, he'd sighed. "I'm being an idiot."

But it had bothered her. Was this a racialized moment? How much of his mistake was simple, conceited blindness? Was he so oblivious? He *had* gone and read up on OBAC, on artists like Charles White (from her neck of the woods), on Daniel LaRue

Johnson, Alma Thomas and Suzanne Jackson ... true, his research on the women came a bit later.

The scholar's arm fell to one side. Castelvetro's book seemed to have put on weight. She caught her reflection again in the métro window, the train hurdling towards ... was this destiny? So many sleepless nights, the end of her dissertation nowhere in sight. But her question to that face in the reflection was why him? Surely, there were many. So many.

Returning to the book, she tried reading, but the words on the page ran together: letters transmuting to gyroscopes.

Sister, sister. You speak of my peril. Your ink, my skin, my life. When you call my name, white sister, you know nothing of my language, and I, every crevice of yours. Your words have never been mine, words we've never shared. Tools of our master's house I do not own, until in claiming, I regain. Dismantling of the mantle's rich meaning: This is mine – she'd coined up this little piece during a bleary-eyed night, writing her dissertation, after an umpteenth reading of Audre Lorde's call to bring down the master's house. Maybe that was a good recipe for liberation. Still, how had she been rising to the challenge?

The scholar exhaled. What was critical was keeping her immediate objectives in mind: to finish the fourth chapter of her dissertation, the culmination, really, of her investigation of postcolonial literature and the geopolitical relationship of Haïti to North America, illustrated in the literature of both countries. She breathed in sweat, stale perfume and something so vile she pinched her nose; then thought better of holding this pose and relaxed. All around her, shoulders and elbows, faces asleep and half-awake, pleated trousers, faded jeans, briefcases and backpacks.

As one prof had poured forth to a full lecture hall, humans live in the world of the relative, building on what relates to their own experiences. In this car, there had to be three-hundred relative experiences. Relatively speaking, she could've fallen for anyone … any man, woman, someone who is non-binary. So, why *this* guy: his sallow, pasta-coloured face, his charcoal and 'obsidian' palettes of paints, none of which expressed her physically, spiritually or intellectually?

Prima facie. In her narrative, stupidity was at the wheel; and she, smack in the middle of a dilemma. *Dasein, Being? Acting, Doing?* As in, what the fuck was she doing? Mostly wondering why above it all, what she fully wanted to do was gather him in, in that Hollywood impresario imitation that he loved so much. Maybe acting was her calling, like it always had been for her mother.

The Artist

He didn't believe in destiny *per se,* except … well, in the trickster involved in this chapter of his life. Currently, he was living the aesthetic, not ascetic life, and like some famous Greek hero, facing a momentous decision. Número Uno: to take off with the McGill scholar, who he'd follow to the bowels of the earth, if it weren't for the other, Número Due: the writer, who, as luck would have it (his mistake), was now his fiancée! From the moment he'd met her, with her ridiculous Mata Hari bob … granted, he'd found it attractive … there had been issues, hadn't there been? A writer, who once upon a time was, to him, and to him alone, a movie star, minus the jewelled crown. But things had changed. And what had that been? Enter, the Chicago-born scholar with the *Wow!* smile and her inimitable expressions that, with one brushstroke, changed the ever-known to something surprising and beautiful. Actually, it was a friend's party where he'd met her, and it *had* been just like in one of those movies.

He regarded his hands. On the one, the scholar. On the other, the writer. He thought of their recent trip to the Laurentians, the way her breath inside the cramped tent literally stank. Sure, he'd fallen for her unique expressions and the music she plucked out on her guitar, the amazing range to her voice and, last but not least, her fascinating collection of paper clips: red for quirky stories with crazy plots, blue for the more straightforward ones. And, sure, their biking trips had been pretty amazing, riding through his home province, Nova Scotia. After all that weed, they'd fallen into incredible laughter that had pulled his insides out, before both had been sprayed by a skunk and kept laughing. He'd have to give some credit to her applaud-able (or was that *laudable?*) way of never budging from the margins. Or that thing she'd done, penning-in his family's birthdays on her surrealistic calendar that had great prints by Yves Tanguy, Dali and Magritte. Kind of cute. Kind of hilarious.

But toss in her annoying habit of forgetting to do the dishes, forgetting to swirl the peanut oil into the peanut butter. Her habit of leaving crumbs everywhere. And now all her pestering about moving in together – to his cramped apartment, where there was ZERO space. Sure, her place had far more, but it was out in the boonies, in the West Island. Was that really where things were headed? He turned to the window. They were speeding past flat, boring panoramas. Like the rest of his life with the writer. Her wall full of those insufferable Klimt prints. Nope, he'd never been a fan of, in a word, kitsch, or, better, the Québec term, quétaine prints of gold upon gold lovers hibernating in gilded robes. And her awful grey filing cabinets. Creepy, in fact. All those years ahead …

Impossible to believe, but it'd been four years since they'd met in front of the corner store, the dépanneur near his place (dilapidated but nevertheless selling a superb collection of micro-brewed beer).

She'd been falling, slipping on ice. He'd caught her. "Good thing," he'd muttered, realizing he'd said it aloud. Sheepishly, he added: "In a parallel universe, you'd have been lying on the pavement."

"In that universe," she offered, her voice surprisingly quiet and alto-low. "I may have met with similar compassion."

Her grey eyes bore Scarlett O'Hara holes in him. Like O'Hara landed in Rhett Butler's arms *before* his celebrated: "Frankly, my darling (or was it dear?), I don't give a damn."

Now, *that* was an interesting story, minus, of course, the atrocious racism.

In front of the dépanneur, he cradled her, as his eco-friendly bag fishtailed before the squealing wheels of a beige Corolla.

Sure, he remembered it all.

And things had been pretty good. It was just ... well, with her refusal over the past year or so to give two shits about what he was thinking. Sure, things hadn't been constantly straining. They hadn't been constantly draining, but he was straining. And he was drained, like a caged hamster, running on a treadmill: there was some exercise but no cardiac arrest. Until now.

The Scholar

She absolutely wouldn't address the question, although it had been asked: What was beneath all that theory of relativity in her laugh? The scholar was indeed conscious of her ability to demolish inhibitions that fell like walls of Jericho whenever someone bewitching entered her life. Sure, she'd been warned. Her mother had thought to tell her that her head was a little too turned towards sanctity, towards inviolability. Still, no one would call her sanctimonious ... well, maybe, but only on occasion. And who wouldn't be, just a little, after all her experiences? Take that time out on a boat with the dreamer from Greece: the sway of his baritone voice under pitch-black skies. In the waters of Antalya, he'd recited the writings of a medieval Turkish poet.

The fact was, for her, life was diffuse, spread out neatly and cleanly, with no need to be taken seriously. She was very much like her mother in this regard. Her mother, a Chicago actress and director of a theatre company, was always being hit up for what she called 'the black tax,' lambasting society for its blind spot when it came to anyone who didn't have a "a pale, honky ass." Completely, utterly blind. Her daughter, stronger still for having to "always handle this shit and keep her humour," told her: "It's the same with you – where do you think I get my steady self-assurance?" Her mother reminded her that one X chromosome was from her "brilliantly hilarious" father.

Born with her back straight, head high, this scholar had damned well made up her mind to never stretch too far to the skies in search of answers. Such imperviousness expressed itself as a gift: an unerring ability to create a lasting impression. And how might she begrudge her wiles, as she steered a rational course over super-irrational dreaming?

OR ... Wait. One. Goddamn minute. If she didn't care, why was she here, in the pit of the beast: Montréal's Gare Centrale? He'd purposefully expressed the desire to see her not today but tomorrow. And wasn't that strange?

She looked up to take in the bas relief, a strange inlay Constructivist relief of Pink Floyd's Just Another Brick in the Wall's pasty-faced, churned-out-meat kids. An incredibly ugly showcase, against '70s suburban blue: a frieze pretending to be for the workers who built this country. Yeah, sure. As for her own labour and that rather tentative possibility, tenure, good luck. Just get through the year, she told herself. Finish the dissertation. Go on the circuit. Find a job at some ... well, hopefully not at a middling university.

High above on the inlay, where no one could lay a hand on the so-called 'art,' the archetypes of Law and Surgery, Broadcasting and the Arts looked down at those waiting for a train or to meet someone arriving by train. The male-like and female-like pasty figures – the women representative of grape harvesters, the other's arm extended to a wine barrel – bore their Canadian-proud métiers with austerity. Then there was that Haida mask and a totem pole. And beneath the generic Indigenous caped chief, the words: O Canada … True North Strong and Free, O Canada, We Stand on Guard for Thee. South and West, above Bureau en Gros, its familiar *red* band – Red, thought the scholar. *Patriotism, chauvinism, Canada*. She stared at the flag, with its maple leaf, then scanned to Québec's fleur-de-lys. Of these two, which did she now consider home? Québec, probably. At the opposite end of the station, alongside the golden arches were the words, Nord et Est, and along the frieze, O Canada, terre de nos aïeux, ton front est ceint de fleurons glorieux, car ton bras sait porter l'épée, il sait porter la croix ton histoire est une épopée, des plus brillants exploits. If this ridiculous cast of characters grabbed her attention at the moment, that's all it was: a momentary lapse, before the next shit-exploder of a thought came barrelling through. The artist's caginess.

High above, through the station's windows, nascent sunlight filtered through giant-sized raindrops. No, not raindrops. Looming dragons. She lowered her head, bringing the Castel-vetro book close. Off to the right, she caught some Second Cup idlers. Remodelling had obliterated the café's cachet. Blinding lighting and tacky tiles had replaced the Roman-triclinium floor plan: three sofas beyond the proscenium arch, with a few actually decent wood chairs. The bureaucrat capitalists had also emptied the place of anything retro and unusual, including a table, reconstructed from an antique spinning-wheel. Once, sitting at that very table, with the artist from Halifax and while sipping a chai latté, she'd cranked the wheel and laughed. He'd murmured: "Dizzying."

"Dizzying?"

A word, he revealed, not strong enough for the way he was feeling, as his eyes pierced her chest like an arrow through feathers.

The Artist

K-chunk, k-chunk. The vibrations wracked his body. He shifted. Bathroom break. But he couldn't move, couldn't do much of anything, as he remembered that telephone call he'd made back at his parents' house in Halifax, and the near cardiac arrest, soon after his father's "When ya' marryin', kid?" Remembering the sense of WOW! when she answered, his elbows propped on the lump of his captain-boy pillow. This incredible woman his parents and friends had no idea existed, spoke, as he spoke, but more like moving air through vocal chords, as the rest spiralled out of control, his fingers absently tracing the illustrated wheels of trains, cars and bicycles along his bedsheets. If only she were there with him: the Chicago-born scholar, his muse, the one who gave him all the reason in the world to 'rainbow-sheet his apartment in cotton and rayon peace cranes' – *her* words for his billowing sail-like creations.

He absolutely needed to tell someone. Anyone!

There, on his twin mattress, he'd ended the conversation with "Drinks? Saturday?"

She'd asked what time he'd be arriving. He bristled. Hadn't his girlfriend insisted on meeting him at the station?

"Sure, I'm coming in Friday morning. No need to come meet me, though. I prefer arriving alone, love those edgy first steps."

Her answer had been laughter: an $e=mc^2$ that started in his head and made its way down.

Now, sitting in these seats (seats because, small miracles, he had had two to himself), he wondered about the lies, then sighed a sigh that ballooned into his surroundings. Apprehensively, he turned around, hoping no one had heard. Having had this extra seat on this *k-chunk* train ride west had done nothing to calm his nerves. Abruptly, he stood up. Off to that stinky toilet ...

The Writer

9:02 will forever be tattooed on that immutable screen in her head and framed by the intense clarity of the city beneath a haze of precipitation. Forever imprinted on those grey cigarette ashes, landing with immunity on her weathered loafers. Fucking Christ-all, she should've covered the whole damned pavement with those ashes, along with an outdated version of herself, should have left everything behind at Montréal's Gare Centrale, for others to sweep away.

Take him, she'd felt like hissing into the scarf, into the ears of the *woman w*ho strode over for the penultimate embrace.

The Scarf

One-hundred years into sunset, a silk painter had curried favour with a trader and purchased the material for the price of a meal, which the trader enjoyed before giving himself over to the painter. Under night's canopy, the artist had curled her brush into figures rising, mythical, from her swollen imagination – dancers and one musician. She gifted the scarf to her daughter on her wedding day. Sadly, a year later, the mother fell ill, present in spirit to comfort her daughter, at the grave of her daughter's newborn. The mourning mother reached about her shoulders, pulling the scarf close, as the earth swallowed her pain.

Time passed a smooth hand over memory, settling on the last hour of day, when the scarf's next proprietor uncovered love letters in her husband's secret cabinet. Flowery script substantiated her suspicions regarding his love for the girl. Stepping into action, she purchased and applied a fatal dose of poisons along the onion-skin paper which her husband was to use as wrapping for the silk scarf. She was no more than sixteen, a mere girl whose fate was now cast into the most pernicious hands. Happily, destiny had more auspicious gifts, and the intended victim hastened to a neighbouring village.

The Writer

9:02. Pretty easy to put a finger on the exact minute when he'd shown his nakedness, in an umpteenth rerun of the *Emperor's New Clothes*. Then again, maybe it was her nudity that had been revealed. One minute before his arrival, she'd been checking the time. The numbers spun about in her head like the sharp LED on her clock radio. Numbers and their equations had always been spinning about in her head like dizzying insects. Math, once, had been her joy. Now, manipulating language was what fed her. Maybe this had been her problem all along. While she'd been concentrating on language, he'd been pursuing other arts, the librettos of which had been offered by that damned scarf.

The Scarf

In December 1933, a relation of the vengeful wife removed the onion-skin paper, saving the dancers and musician from certain asphyxiation. As recompense, she decided to keep the scarf, breathing nothing of the deed or her self-approved reward. When the sounds of artillery fused with the miracles of modern cures, there came another owner, who, while guns raged, sought refuge in a cave bordering her village. Somehow, the scarf's owner survived. She'd later swear that in its whisper-thin demeanour, the silk had protected her. Ferocious winds assailed. Yet, its beauty became a respite. With an indelible spirit and valiant youthfulness, she danced as much and as well as anyone hiding out could or might dance, and with this, defeated the terror besieging her country.

Years later, when death held her close, she requested that the piece accompany her in the coffin. Nonetheless, her son placed her hand on her heart and the scarf in a box, with his mother's other possessions.

The Writer

With the *clink* of a loonie, several toonies and a puff of her first cigarette in many years, the writer took in one catastrophic gulp of air. What a crime scene she'd left! Only paces away from where she was waiting for his train, that strange woman was embracing him! Over the woman's shoulders, the King Idiot stared. Someone should've offered him a crown.

The Scholar

9:00 was probably when the scholar noticed the 'other' woman, who, admittedly, was striking: a '20s ink-hair bob, intense irises excavated from anaemic skin. And she was texting. Shouldn't the scholar be doing the same, giving 'her guy' a head's-up? For one, in so many words, he'd told her not to come.

Crazy comes as crazy be. Ever since that party, when he'd ambushed her – followed by a night of comic moves – she'd been falling. At the party, as she exited the washroom, this 'dude,' hazel green eyes, mulish mess of hair, had requested that she wait for him while he used the facilities. Stupidly, she honoured his request. Really stupid. Maybe it was a *sui generis* thing with him. The guy was one of a kind … and charming. He claimed he'd been carrying something around all night for her. So, uncharacteristically and foolishly, she waited. As he exited the toilet, he revealed that he'd been admiring her "cool tunic."

"It's European," she said.

He nodded, adding something silly on his "great luck" at finding someone with some material (he pointed to her scarf), and "hell, even a necktie would've been meaningful," that so resembled what he'd been trying to achieve with his art.

The Scarf

After heading south to the province of eternal spring, the scarf attuned itself to a life of leisure. Those who learned of its existence felt blessed. This was the case with the next proprietor and with everyone this proprietor met. Along the scarf's spine, the dancers shared in her innumerable lovers: men and more secretly women, who inhabited her in that indeterminate way rain gathers in bamboo – softly, momentarily, their faces tunnelling into silken crevices.

After some time, the weightless fabric was folded over, displaced with enviable ease by its revolutionary counterpart, a swathe of red. The dancers, with their bourgeois inclinations, found their world consigned to a closet, where they endured the accumulation of dust and hushed liquid voices. One fine day, the scarf was lifted, cleaned and lain out in a valise bound for North America, where it was found by the artist from Nova Scotia, who gave it to the scholar, now waiting inside Montréal's Gare Centrale.

The Artist

As the train slowed, entering the city, he held his head in his hands. Still battling a shit of a headache, like the one after the clashing Swedish punk group concert last August: a concert with … well, with who else but that woman everyone expected he'd be spending the rest of his fucking life with. To be frank, the pounding had begun literally hours ago, when he'd spied Lake Ontario. There was that vacay he'd taken to Port Hope, with … who else? The scholar with the American accent and mystifying scent along her neck. *And oh!* What a neck. One of Modigliani's beauties: dark waters to face; eyes squinting under a Mediterranean sun, her serpentine throat even more insanely gorgeous with that silken swathe he'd given her. When she wore it, the colours lent her face the impression of a beacon surrounded by a Turner sea. Rich brown irises, mesmerizing and full of more wit and art – yes, art – than the eyes of any woman he'd ever known.

The Scholar

Maybe she was insane. Her lover certainly was *dream-crazy*, living in his cozy apartment, built at the turn of the century, in the Montréal neighbourhood known as the Plateau. "Not much of a plateau," she'd said during their 25-minute walk, during which they passed her own residence in that nod to bohemian 'poverty,' the McGill ghetto.

That entire walk was spent talking. Nothing polemic. Just … well, about things. When they'd entered his place, HOLY SHIT! Warm air escaped her lungs, as Sam Gilliam's *Carousel Change* came to mind. *This* self-proclaimed artist's walls and ceilings ballooning with fabric, masts of fuchsia, mandarin-blue, the corners of soft cotton and rayon knotted. "Reasonably-priced and decent apartments like this are pots of gold," he'd informed her.

"That's not what I – this!" She danced around the room.

He reached out to kiss her … not really, not yet. First, he needed to provide a lecture on his billowing, knotted fabric work. The ensuing lesson was brief: on reef knots and round-turns, clove-hitch and bowlines. Sailors, he told her, signalled their speed with their number of rope knots, which also represented nautical miles. Before everything grew heated, he had more information on ancient galleon captains, how they were responsible for exacting latitudinal and longitudinal measurements and even to exact measurements of time. He was whispering into her neck.

She turned. Sweet smell of man. Grabbing his body, something she'd never done in this exact way, as that place between her thighs (what the …?) began flooding the lands. He laughed, his lips brushing her skin. She let him remove the tunic he admired, then her bra, as she pulled at his muslin shirt, lifted it over his brown-flecked nipples, dug her teeth into his flesh. *Vampire!* He pulled her closer, murmuring something about knots, scarves and infidels. Then – nothing. The memory eluded her. Had he fallen backwards? Had she thrown herself against him? Had she pulled at his belt, unzipped his pants? Well, this she knows: nakedness and fury – a frenetic, incredible fuck session! Succinct. Simple. Delicious.

The Writer

Maybe she should've listened to intuition, should've stuck to the old narrative: Boy meets girl. Since she hadn't paid attention, the narrative had wheeled on ahead without her: Boy goes about his business, meets another. As for her own stories about friendship (the best ship, she heard punned once) and love, what those narratives needed was more realism about assholes, something the literary magazines had obviously been requesting with their comments about too much backstory, too much poetry and motion in her prose.

Well, she'd damn well keep her prose, along with lonesome characters, wandering through salons that were managed by singing bartenders, emptying love songs into highball glasses. She'd keep her manuscripts, pinned together with Pez-coloured paper clips and all her boxed guitar picks, some of them still plucking out the riffs she'd played a thousand times too often to be of any use to her now.

The Artist

The two extra-strength Tylenols he'd taken had had little effect. He covered his mouth against rising acid. She'd be meeting him at the station, his girlfriend, the one his parents adored. Down on his lap was his iPad screen, pulling him in. There, the front cover of the Chronicle Herald: a mugshot of the el-sicko engineer who'd tried to murder his wife and son. Psycho-brains, who happened to have lived in the old section of Halifax, where the WWI ammunition explosion had levelled the houses. Who in all terrible hells would be so obsessed with such darkness that the only way out was destroying the light? It was like everyone was freaking out these days. What was needed was a grand overhaul, something huge – maybe mass extinction? Something beyond yoga's cat stretches and half-lord-of-the flies (or was it fishes?) poses. An emptying out of all that bad karma. He brushed a hand over his screen. Alongside the photo, a byline declared, 'Home Renovations Not Up to Code.'

What the fuck?! Someone's trope was all screwed up. More to come with that shithole for president. That's why he hadn't been reading any papers or much of anything recently.

Too soon, he'd be seeing the writer. She'd probably texted him, but his phone, thankfully, was turned off.

The Writer

This was how she'd tell things and continue to tell things, again and again, as if re-telling would reverse the narrative, something that John Cusack's character does in *High Fidelity*, after he's located all his old flames. Conclusion? There's no cause for regret. As in Aristophanes' prose or Shakespeare's plays, what's set up to happen usually does. Even in the real world of the arbitrary, it's entirely plausible there's such a thing as destiny. *All those scoured lives for the gods' good laughter.*

Whatever it was, is, has been, she's had it with posturing artistes who wax opaque about Rothko's bloody squares. Fucking enough of idiots who chase women around, including those wearing elaborate silk scarves, pretentiously curled about, like cats' tails.

The Scholar

While waiting for his train, it occurred to the scholar that laughter was generally the preferred reaction. If she were to be asked how she viewed the world – her response? "With brevity, like a straight line through glass." Which is how she responded to the artist's question one evening: "What would you really love to do? Something you've dreamt of?"

"Let's sail, six knots!" Or, more to point: "I'd like to walk, holding your hand, along a shore I've never visited." Totally cliché, but this was something an Alice Munro character might have said – Munro being an interesting Canadian author. Still, lest we forget, the best of the best: Dionne Brand and Esi Edugyan and their extraordinary writing.

What transpired was one unforgettable weekend. After a train ride to Port Hope and check-in at an inn, rented along

Lake Ontario, the full moon had complied, the wind whisking the water treacherously onto land. This brief sense of danger had given her cause to embrace him, a gesture he'd passionately returned (whispering how Turner would have appreciated the furious waters – he apparently reveres Turner).

One delicious weekend. But since then, they hadn't been hanging out together so much. Sure, he was occupied with his paintings and nautical bed sheets, and she, with her dissertation. Both of them were dropping promises like pennies into a pond, admitting things would have to change.

"It'll have to," she said. The chemistry between them was burning. It was, in a word, sublime, beneath those sheets, tightly bound, crying out. Not since her post-teen years with a sullen Swiss architect (on a yacht, off the coast of Malta) had she been able to express herself with such reckless abandon. Limiting such nights together hadn't been so terrible. With all that was on her proverbial plate, she hardly needed the mess. Theirs had been so far a light but passionate engagement.

The Writer

Gare Centrale. That's where she was, having been offered the morning off, thank you very much. Nothing was ever certain with that shit-of-a-boss, whose my-way-or-the-highway was going to anyhow be a distant memory come January. Standing, she texted the artist. Maybe he'd lost his phone? He hadn't answered her last three texts. Above, near the ceiling, the weird bas relief, with small-p propaganda art: in relief, grape pickers and a lab techie, who looked like the Dr. Bunsen Muppet, with thick-rimmed glasses over a faceless mush of a face. Above, the timetable announced departures to and arrivals from various Québec towns up the Fleuve Saint-Laurent, to and from Toronto and Ottawa, the nation's capital. All aboard! Soon, the rare train from the Maritimes.

Soon enough, after his train came in, they'd be winding their way up the iron-wrought staircase to his one-bedroom, where those crazy art projects uglified his ceilings – 'art,' he called it. 'Sails.'

More like cotton and rayon sheets imitating dead fish flopping about.

Gare Centrale. The central crossroads for all Montréal trains, the 9:02 in savage red. So many, too many trains along the rail ties. He'd be riding the escalator up to this floor very soon, beaming at her, with that smile.

Several days later, looking back, she realized she should've recognized the cheerleader-cherry flags, waving on the one black-and-yellow bumble-bee race car, hers, the one vehicle that just didn't get it. Maybe he wasn't meant for monogamy. So? Was she? Nope. No. Wait. Surer than that: Definitely not! Still, she'd never be found searching for answers in someone else's crotch. She'd never turn her head, as he always did, telling her what a treat it was to imagine this or that beauty in bed. And what had she been doing? Wondering why she couldn't be as blasé as Joni Mitchell advertised to the world she'd been: 'He picks up my scent on his fingers, while he's watching the waitresses' legs.'

To the artist's confidential joking about other women, she'd tried, sometimes answering with laughter! She'd been laughing, for Christ's sakes!

There they were, on that October morning, 9 a.m., 9h. Two women, waiting.

A cool female contralto, in French, then in English, announced the train's arrival. Anyone waiting might have imagined curtains rising, as the first passengers ascended, their faces flushed, as they glanced about.

At 9:01, wisps of his hair were visible. At 9:02, there were his pouty lips, his head tilted.

The Artist

Rubbing an eye, he regarded his girlfriend. *What the – ?!* Behind her, the Chicago-born queen, smiling like the bright side of the moon. He felt a constriction in his throat, his chest.

The Writer

The writer wouldn't rush to greet him, not right away. He was standing, strangely wide-eyed, while she glanced momentarily at the 9:02 on the timetable. That's when the air filled with perfume and a scarf; and there the woman who'd been holding that strange book, walking towards him, her lips set in a wide smile. The rest wasn't easy to recall, except maybe there was a loud gasp – hers – as the woman threw out her arms. Maybe, despite her better judgment, the writer screamed. And maybe that scream was answered with woeful stares. Not maybe. She did scream. And it was answered with stares.

Later the writer would try to justify the pack of du Maurier Lights she spent a pretty penny on at the newsstand. Stepping out of the station and holding back to light her first since quitting years ago, she noticed the city, beneath the drizzle, giving way to a startling brightness, like Technicolor seeping through the filter of a very old camera. Metallic office buildings seemed washed in nuclear blue, the whole downtown core bathed in hyper-real acrylics, unfamiliar shadows flicking their eager tails. Everything appeared obtuse, except, weirdly, for one address she will probably always remember: 1008. The 1, 0's and 8, chained and bound, with the Clash's break-out-of-jail song playing in her head. Inhaling tar and tobacco, the writer wondered how she'd locate that somewhere far-from-here place.

The Artist

Inside the station, the scholar and artist formed an arabesque, the scholar's arms over the artist's quaking shoulders. That scream – from the writer, only a half-metre away, staring, as she watched this embrace.

Over the loudspeaker, there came an announcement the artist couldn't make out, as he tried to stay afloat, drowning in the shock of this incredible situation.

"Sorry," he was murmuring, pinning words onto the now tangible screen between. He began pleading. "To hell with everything." The beautiful Chicago-born woman was the one he needed, wanted. But she was stepping back, glancing at the screaming writer, then back at the artist. Unfortunately, he was suddenly voiceless ... watching the sway of his lover's shoulders and *oh!* that wild perfume.

The Scholar

Now, so much wiser and certainly more in control of her faculties of reason, the scholar stepped to the side, then up to home base to slap him. Only she didn't. Damn that face! Ridicule, personified!

So, that's who the pasty-faced woman was. She turned, leaving the sonofabitch to his tearful display. Later she'd erase the whole thing from memory. With a gesture worthy of *Instagram*, she tore off her scarf – his gift – and walked away, with the deliberation of one who would never again deal with such trivialities. Ahead were only tomorrows. She'd grab a coffee. But later tonight or tomorrow, she'd grab that well-deserved drink, at a bar near this station: a place she knew well, where the stale, burnt-orange walls breathed out maudlin stories, blown into Kleenexes.

The Writer

Outside the station, the jilted fiancée, who, from now on, would tune into all red flags, took one more drag of her cigarette, then ground out her remaining self-pity into the wet pavement. She handed over her pack and a loonie to a man asking for change. "Et les cigarettes? Merci, Mademoiselle!" She remained vaguely worried about the ethics of her action. He puckered, inhaled, thanked her again. She contemplated returning to the station, instead opting for the rain-drenched road, curving up into morning mist.

The next evening, Saturday, at Gate 13, she thought about her cellphone, ringing nonstop until she'd blocked his number. Sniffling, she made her way to a little hole-in-the-wall she hadn't visited in years. Under the phantom glow of the streetlights, she imagined a fiddler offering lullabies, with all the identifiable marks of lost love or something more valuable when found.

The Writer and The Scholar

Saturday evening, at the bar, the two women found one another. In low lighting and smooth music, they decided to sit and 'talk things out' at a wine-coloured booth, yellow bulbs illuminating their foreheads. On stage, a talented musician was pulling bass lines from steel strings, his velvet voice combing out Leonard Cohen's lyrics: "Suzanne takes you down to a place by the river …"

Two women, two characters holding back on the inevitable discussion of a third. Drinking and clinking glasses. "To new friendships."

"To possibilities … and," added the scholar, "to unity."

"Unity?"

"Of time, place and action."

The writer laughed, although she had no idea what her new friend meant.

The Artist and The Scarf

Lodovico Castelvetro's idea of unity wasn't lost on the artist, that Friday morning, inside Montréal's Gare Centrale, where the scholar had given him her scarf. With this gift now back in his care, he grasped the material with the futility of a desperado, hunkering down for a lifetime of despair. Fuck Life, Incorporated. He was bearing the weight of the entire world just like a modern-day Atlas but with something far heavier than any Titan could bear.

Unable to keep his composure, he started to cry. Rising above, along the train station's wall, Charles Comfort's frieze sang out, *Oh Canada!* Eyeless Muppet scientists mixed chemicals; eyeless women gathered grapes. All were demonstrating their Canadian spirit. There were other faceless members of society: a man tying reef knots; another was dancing some strange version of manifest destiny. But it was the one right above the artist, the violist, who performed the last treble-clef notes of this drama, with her sweet, languishing solo – although to virtually everyone she was silent. Directly below, backpack against stomach, her audience of one had collapsed into a plastic chair, burying his aching head in the scarf's spiced perfume.

.

Life is but a Dream

BEAUTY AND CALAMITY in equal parts, that's what she remembered: a headline on grey newsprint. An equation for infinity. Atomic love – the phrase, the equation, across slate-blue …

In the great cavity between waking and sleeping, she rode the GM's '74 Chevy Impala, its rear-end curved into a flame and bordered by a chrome fender. As the world of consciousness receded, the slick asphalt rose to meet her, folding into a burning wave of petroleum. Below, the land was an inviolate green … and desolate. No little Lego houses nestled in the valleys.

She knew where she was headed. Gripping the vinyl cover, she glanced into the rear-view mirror. She was twenty again, cheeks lean, unmarked, though those so-called 'crow's feet' had never bothered her. Eyes bright, lids no longer heavy. Smiling, she pushed back phantom frames, rolled open the window and shouted. Every detail of the car was visible: the side panels, two dents along the back fender. It was like she was driving along a Mobius strip, or more like she'd been folded over, opening into this world. She recalled the turned-over coloured squares on those paper origami games her students used to make, a fortune under each flap.

Outside, summer's crisp greens and browns bled into a union of landscape and motion, a joyful absorption of symmetry. Wide sections of fields dropped to lush grassland, with several shades of green vegetation along the hillsides. She scanned these hills, as burnt-sugar vocals floated up from the FM. The song … what was it? Everything about this road, this place was familiar, even the sound of pebbles ricocheting off the car. The asphalt changed to gravel; the guardrail to her right, laced with bowties. She had arrived, in this fabled language of dreams: a country known intimately, like the taste of one's own blood. There was a name for this place. Beyond the guardrail was the grave, with its clumps of upturned soil. Alongside a diminutive knoll was the cross they'd firmly driven into the soil, its wood planks uneven.

She turned off the ignition; the engine's percussion dissipated into the chattering of birds. Rounding the fender, she ran her palm over a scratch in the paint that spooled out to blue ribbons, baby dolls and sleek stallions, highways that stretched into lonely roads, beneath a reclusive bass and melodious treble. Straightening, she took in the Johnson grass, the teal sky. With two tenuous steps, she found herself in front of the freshly dug grave. There was a pungent odour of soil, then a stale, cloistered smell, like hidden libraries. Inhaling deeply, she knelt before the cross, concentrating on the streaks of time through white paint, the uneasiness of the nails, the whole marker of the grave leaning against the warm breeze that swept past, carrying the tangy odour of chlorophyll. They'd buried their brother here – she and Quinn had buried Michael.

Early September 1951: That's when the baby's breathing changed and something unnamed began its journey, a slow, methodical ambling towards their house. Cowering in a corner, she closed her eyes, as the house grew smaller, became a teardrop on a blank face. Still, the monster proceeded.

With a sudden fury, she shook her head, breathed in hard.

Michael was born in the early part of the day. Golden light strayed in, shattering along the floorboards. She and Quinn were playing cards, their grandfather leaning in to watch the plays, his stale breath mingling with the musty odour of the room.

"No, not that one! This! The club!" Directing their moves, while their grandmother chastised. "Stop encouraging them! It's the Devil's game."

From within her parents' bedroom came a great wailing – their mother. There came a ferocious scream; then a lengthy cry.

"Well." Her grandfather leaned back, turned to the window whose glass panes were oblivious to the merciless sun. Scooping up the cards, she turned to her brother Quinn. "Don't worry." He was older, but sometimes she found herself comforting him. His eyes filling with fear. Not long after the last haunting wail from their mother, followed by a definite baby's wail, the bedroom door opened, and their father stepped out, cradling the newest member to their family. "You two, come see your new brother. Michael." The baby's name danced over chipped teeth. She touched her new brother, his baby-wet skin; tiny fingers.

Now, kneeling before the grave, she felt it in her throat – a deliberate descent, slow suctioning of sky. If only she could let go, let all that ever mattered run out like the frayed threads of a sweater no longer adhering to form, sewn by a diligent mother, a stitch every year, until all was lost in the thicket of memory. Squeezing her lids tight against the image of her mother on that bed. She opened to an almost blinding brightness, but the birds had stopped singing. Silence. Such is a dream. Such was her baby brother, although he was no dream.

Rising, she saw that the gravel road had narrowed. In the place of the Chevy were two children's bikes, the larger hitched to a cart, hewn from solid oak and painted cherry red. Both bike and cart fell to one side.

"We've both come."

She spun round. "Quinn!" Her brother was a kid, and he was holding a music box, a miniature ballerina pirouetting to the *Waltz of the Flowers*.

She was eleven again, the rising violet light drawing her from summer bedsheets. There wafted in the aroma of griddle cakes heaped with syrup. Through her sleep, she heard Quinn's padding. He'd entered her room. "Get up!" It was summer '51, the fields so wide they engulfed everything; summer days exciting the compelling, the unbelievable but true. Fresh grass promises embraced even the saddest nights. That's when their baby brother was born, early June.

July's melting-wax heat refused to dissipate; indecisive August's hot days were relieved in evening's cool star-blanket skies. At month's end, shooting stars. Excitedly, she made a wish. In September, the dogwoods were taken over with the wine-red of weeping, the fawn-coloured grass drying in the sun. In the hidden grottos of corn, she directed theatre of the absurd: worlds of animals with vast knowledge of things. Evening entered through open windows; the bone-dry howling of coyotes. Inside, greedy mouths closed over succulent molasses ham. The slaughter.

Baby Michael's crying at first was cat-like, a mewing between heavy, uneven breaths. The doctor came and propped up his leather satchel outside the nursery. She leaned against the doorframe, the leather smelling of horse saddles. From inside the room came a bass lament, as the doctor gave his prognosis: Michael's heart was defective. A deflated organ, soiled pink like a barnyard sow's sick baby: a heart beating, spluttering into grey. Only a trip to the city would save their baby brother, to the city hospital. The city, where dizzying concrete buildings sprouted cellophane eyes, and you were caught in tunnels of sound. But at least doctors would take care of Michael. Despite both grandmothers' plea to leave the children at home, she and Quinn were to go as well. Sure, "some school would be missed," said their mother, but no missing of hard-blade rulers smacking knuckles or straight-back rows of pine. There'd be a reprieve from dividing wholes into parts.

The wind blew heavy over tin-dry fields.

On their beds, inside suitcases, their clothes lay neatly folded. That night, it rose from inside the Earth and, in a deep whisper, entered the house, then the crib, releasing its secret.

All those days and nights that followed: hot salt pouring over raw faces, onto flannel sheets. Their mother lay on the bed, wouldn't move, her strands of hair bunched up on the pillow. The whole house was balanced on whispers. Despite the burning inside, she, as the eldest, had to open the front door for the minister, who placed a hand on her head, his ancient body steadying itself. Under the weight of his marbled fingers, the bedroom door gave way, tempting anyone lingering around its frame. She waited, while Quinn left the room and then the house. When the minister finally came out, he was carrying a small linen blanket, which he took to the window, where he began praying, as the fiercest light of day left its imprint in rose and orange along the horizon.

Minister, reverent reverend.

Out here with the singing birds and even shifts of land, the words were changing to a filigree of wildflowers running through tall grasses. So much pitiless green, the absurdity of spring. Soon, she'd find the madness of autumn through a worn aperture.

Little Quinn, still here, pushed aside his bangs. Somehow reminiscent of the minister's shiny forehead, as he stood with Michael's body before the window. It was supposed to be to the Lord the minister was calling. "Give … to take," but no one was taking Michael. Ever since she was very young, she'd been reckoning with the sinless notion of the spirit. There was no spirit, no edification of the soul, and no sins had been requested by any horned devil. Nothing during the church services about the electricity of long-blade grass over bruised knees, the bitter crispness of uncooked corn. And now Michael was gone. No one was taking him. Clearly, they'd have to bury him.

"Don't worry," she assured Quinn, whose spirit was absent after Michael's death. He seemed to have travelled through this life and gone on over to the other side. "We'll do it ourselves." In the full moon, they lifted the small body from the bassinette, surprised at its lightness.

Quinn frowned. "He's light. Aren't the dead supposed to be heavier than the living?"

Maybe, but this act would call their mother from her cave. She'd be theirs again. Everyone would have more space for breathing. Plus, the Lord, our Father, and Jesus, his Son, needed to finally take the body of Michael, since they had his soul.

Twelve-year-old Quinn, lips uneven, repeated: "We did it." The children, united, as they stood before the grave. She hesitated. How could that deep, wide pit hold something so small without losing it? Above, glacial clouds rolled out.

Her brother's focus was on the resident hillsides, now filtered in lonely blue. She realized they must have come a long way from the open meadow to this place of endless rises. The kid Quinn who was standing before her called out: "Where's Michael? Do they go up or down when they die?" Chin diving into chest. "I think," she heard him say. "Everyone who's dead must go down."

"It doesn't matter. He's gone." Sighing, she moved towards the road.

"Don't! Don't leave! Please."

"I have to." Along the road, the perplexity of gravel, indented with fresh tire marks. Their bikes were overturned; the crate's lid, open, like a broken neck. She reached to the back of her own neck. It was damp, her hair too. Her brother's face was eclipsed by sun; his eyes, grieving; his lips, pursed in that familiar mournful expression. She knew what was next.

"They're going to find him! Then he won't be ours!"

"He was never ours."

Her brother's "Nooo" lengthened, as his body unravelled.

There was a rattling confusion of narrative. Breathing easily, she found herself in the driver's seat, the land passing rapidly, the car's gauge indicator swinging from Theta to Omega. It stopped at the figures $2\pi \sin(\phi)$, then swung around, settling on the pagoda-house pi, veering sharply to square root. She tasted the chalk dust and musty erasers, beneath rows of equations and solutions filling blackboards.

The motor was slowing. Glancing up, she saw she was entering a parking lot, her hands on the wheel, edging the car into a narrow space between two Peugeots. Nearby was a gargantuan chain-link fence – the sheer breadth of it! Like chains to hold the giants at bay. Barely visible over the top were fairground rides. A great metal-clanging hurt her ears. But she had no time to worry. There was a sudden rush, a swirling of scenery and shifting shades of violet. She had landed in a sky-blue rollercoaster. Peering at the small people below, she experienced vertigo, sat up straight. Alongside was a young man, his face, angular, pitch-black hair framing eyes, painted grey. His head lifted, as she moved closer. Those people far, far below were cheering. The car jumped, the tracks reared and split into two steel roads.

Only relief and freedom met her deep, oxygenated breaths, as she slid out of the rollercoaster onto one of the silver ties. The crowd below had grown, and she knew somehow that she had to entertain them. She knelt over and embraced the great steel tie, as the crowd below cheered. Turning, she saw the beautiful man waving, his hair lifted by the wind. As the rollercoaster moved, his expression was lost, but she detected a great jubilance. The rollercoaster dipped, followed by a volley of screams, and the cars moved like the ringed casing of an *Alice in Wonderland* caterpillar.

Whoosh … closing her eyes, opening to the crowd below. Holding onto the steel tie; even from this distance, she could make out a young man beyond the crowd, his shoulder blades rising as he turned a carousel's copper crank. In her throat, the sweetness of caramel, the pain of possibility, a childhood and freshly popped corn. The boy's sixteenth summer, a kitchen door swung open. "Got that job, Mom! Working on the carousel!"

Below, felicity swept over his face, as he ushered children onto the coloured horses. Entering from far, far away was the burlesque minor chord of an accordion. Inside the melody was a dream within a dream. A film, perhaps: 1940's film noir. Spirited horses and jousting knights, riding candy-cane poles. In smeared daylight, the rollercoaster reappeared, cars swerving, the whole thing swallowed inside a seam of air.

Below, the carousel had changed course, moving counterclockwise now. And she, contemplating the life that might have been. A grand carriage, not for a horse but for a baby; a boy, an aviator piloting through boiling mass of sky. In that circular inferno, Icarus falls and brushes off cinders from seared wings.

Squinting, she made out other rides: a Ferris wheel with bright red and white seats; a whirligig whose swings were flying straight out, the children caught in centrifugal force. On her left, one bright cable car moved along a rope strung between two stations, like a spider along her thread. A girl leaned out of one, waved; and she returned the greeting. Fairground music climbed wildly up the scale and down. There was that feeling again. She was being thrown about, trying to right herself inside some world where a red-hot iron moved along a wrinkled surface. Back in the Chevy, she found herself pulling out of the parking lot. As she drove, evening overtook the land; the air cool, licking her shoulders. When she stepped out, Quinn was there, eyes wide. "See! I told you, you shouldn't leave."

Legs growing heavy, as she watched him press his hands together. He turned to face the grave, his upper body falling forward, staying at a 45-degree angle over the open pit. And her spade – propped up by a shank of earth it had cleaved. "You're too close to Michael's grave."

"I'll move. But you shouldn't leave."

Behind came the faint whisper of forest. Brushing a hand over her forehead, "We should finish the job."

But when she reached the spade, she found she was alone, longing for the rollercoaster and carousel. Releasing her shoulders, crescendo into setting sun, cathedral sky.

Breaking the solace of quiet, a familiar baritone called out. "Marry me. We have to take care of this; we …" Hesitation in the voice gave her purpose. She turned to the man she probably still loved, hair falling over shoulders, familiar grey irises – a wildly handsome face but inside (she remembered now) an awful gloom she'd been compelled to explore. Power of attraction. The mysterious divide between absence and the substantial humours that fed his blood. With that guitar slung over his shoulders, he was playing far too softly for such strong, steel strings. No! This was her song, her story. Behind him, the horizon bled ruby.

"I can't marry you." She waited. "And that's my song."

"Yours?" His lips rounded, formed words, inaudible. His eyes softened. *Strum, strum.* With a watery stare, he implored her; then closed his eyes. It looked like he was praying.

"Nothing to understand," she said. "I can't marry you." His lids flew open.

"Anyhow," she added. "If we were meant to stay together … this baby."

"*Baby?*"

The land below tumbled; desolate fields stirred. They'd never found Michael's body, wrapped in a blanket. Her parents had never found the child. And, here, before her, the man who came much later, the one who imagined he was the father – but not of Michael, of another baby who died, the one she never named. Before he spoke, she had to warn him. "You're in front of his grave," the force of her voice singeing the air. But the pain! Grabbing her belly, her waist. Her insides were exploding. Her muscles, clenching.

What was happening? Her thoughts, fireworks, burning her eyes, but it was the man she'd loved who was crying them out. The volume of his plea was diminishing, his voice siphoned off by an invisible hand.

"Stop!"

She felt the insistence of pressure and pain. Stooped over, she clamped her head with her elbows, concentrated on the green long blades, doing back flips inside the weird opaque colours cast by the setting sun. The pain in her gut, in her womb – the fore-telling of nightmares, shadows through caves. Wracking her body. Something was tunnelling through.

"I'm not ready!"

Between her thighs, drenched in furious sweat and blood, tissue-damp, there was a great suctioning. Weakness overcame her. She felt an emptying and then a dull thud. The baby's legs were kicking, its mouth gasping for air.

The body seized; then was still.

Slowly, moving her hands towards those tiny arms, legs, as the child grew transparent, filling in with the cast of the dying sun and the surrounding hills. She searched the face, gem-sized eyes, lips parted.

Above, came a sharp, piercing cry. A crow. A creature she once found elegant was now a menace.

"Take him!"

The crow dived, clamped a beak firmly in soft flesh. She thought she saw the baby stir. No. Her arms fell to her sides, weightless. "Well, then." She let herself roll onto the ground. The physical cramping was gone. There was supposed to be another birth, the birth of the baby's placenta, but this birth never came. "That's it." Dry air tickled her throat.

Quinn, far older now, along with the other man who had become her lover, stood above. Her brother, a man with fiery eyes, wild hair framing his jaw.

Threateningly, he moved forward. "What the hell? You knew!"

She felt sick, swallowing her own stinking saliva. Turning over, kneeling, she vomited. Thick acidic sourness scalded her throat. Bent over, she concentrated on the grass. If only she could be this bile, threading into the ground, with no mind, no care. Somewhere far from this madness, maybe she'd shed it all, like a snake its skin. Then again, she was the one who'd given the baby consciousness, given life. Then, the child had been taken.

Quinn was yelling, anger pulsing beneath the thin skin of forehead. "You screwed up! You screwed up my life, you sick –"

She cut him off. "You came to me! Sick shit!"

"You were the one! It was you. Don't you remember? You leaned against me, with your stockings … your underwear."

And, here, now eighteen, maybe twenty, with that horrible wet tongue between salivating lips, was her boyfriend, strumming his Fender strings. His chords, louder, angrier. His voice, a whispering spirit in a tail wind, surprisingly beautiful. From somewhere back in the days of remembering, came an image of the two of them singing in unison.

As for her brother, his lips were moving, though he was thankfully silent. She threw her palms over her ears, then dropped her hands. His voice ripped through: "Why did you make me want you like that?"

Someone's voice – hers! Screaming: "You sick fuck! Call it by name, Quinn! Rape! Now you know why I've refused to see you all these years! You could die for all I –"

There was the *twang* of steel: her boyfriend. "People used to be locked up for this!"

Her head aching, her breath, heavy, lungs filling with mountain air, she sighed, as she spoke to these men who knew nothing. "People lose everything when this happens. Anyhow," her legs buckling. "It's over." She scanned the evening sky, now doubling in on itself: a pageantry of deepest navy. Irony, she realized, as she pulled up her knees along the cool grass. In a rush, all associative thrill with archetypes left her. Here, beneath the barest ghost moon, everything became literal.

Relaxing her shoulders, "It's a book, a novel." Sweeping her lips with the back of her hand. "Although in the novel, this never happens, Quinn. Your counterpart just imagines it happens." She looked at both men. "*He,* by the way. It was a boy. Died before he was born." She patted her belly, now content with the space it displaced. Slowly, she stood, shook off the grass and mud and flexed her fingers. "Now, you both know. He wasn't ours. Not yours, Quinn. And not yours." She motioned to the singer. She was done here. She turned to the road, to the bicycles and cart, to the parked car, addressing the men but refusing to turn around. "This baby was mine. The other one, our brother Michael, was never ours."

With Herculean strength, she heaved the bicycles and the cart onto the roof. No need to secure them. They'd balance just fine up there. She grabbed the chrome handle. Its coolness felt like a salve beneath her palm. She stepped into the car.

Finally, the name of the place had found her. Here, Quinn had wrestled her to the ground. She could taste the incense of autumn leaves after the rains, heavy against the back of her thighs, the pain inside, as she bled. "This is the song," she half-whispered: an atomic love song, with sopping wet atoms and nuclei.

How she could do this, she didn't know, but she wished them well, the men who wanted to suck out her bones, pluck out her heart. Grabbing her belly – they'd have swirled the warm liquid inside, if she'd let them – she slammed the car door. A look out the window revealed the grave. The men were gone. With the finality of endings and the belligerence of memory, she called out to the rounded hill: "It's over!" Against her back, the crush vinyl seat, with its vertical strips in shades of brown, provided comfort. Out amongst the shadows was the cross; now illuminated, arms budding leaves out of thick, velvet veins.

"This is the tale," she said, putting the motor in gear, hitting the gas. The mountain was lit by the bequest of moon. "I wonder who's doing the telling."

Realizing that answers rarely puncture the fabric of dreams, she loosened her grip. Along the pebbled road, she kept one eye on that trickster moon, which first was a grey wisp, then a brilliant celestial disc, backlit by the hot gases of the sun. She cranked open the window all the way and serenaded the night. Thinking of the men she'd left back at the grave, the men who had meant nothing in the end, she added to her song: "Such sound and fury. Signifying anything but nothing."

Freedom

With a rumble, the walls and floor heave, clench, loosen. A long time before now, when the whole place was moving, the frozen ground beneath entered hooves, travelled up legs. Her entire body has been numb for as long as they've felt the motion beneath, after they were prodded, burned, pushed into this suffocating darkness. Now, there is no longer movement below, but there is another kind of motion. She counts the frequency of the surges through unyielding. An acerbic uric sharpness tears through sensitive tissue. Blood trickles from the skin of those alongside – children. There are two older ones like her. She can't see them but feels, hears them, above. She speaks to them with thought-words. One of them repeats, *Resist.* Desperately, she opens frozen lips. *Yes, but how?*

These children, with their eyes folded shut; others wide and wet with tears. Some, on their sides, their breath falling, rising, battling the frost. Rows of skin burst with pustules, beneath sprouting hair, as the cold enters bone. She's been shivering forever, a deep uncontrollable shaking; her body aching to push blood through frigid veins.

But, now, there is something else. Not the awful, not the breathing. A shimmering pale that smells … could it be? Like the spine of life.

Some of the children are closer to the large slat windows, where ferocious winds enter. Yellow is the odour, tired and sweet. Towards the great metal openings, she manoeuvres her aching limbs. Along her legs, on the backs of others, lacerated skin. Rot and blood and bruising. The taste is different, now deeper. She takes in a long breath, settles her face inside the slats, chin on frigid metal, lifts her snout into this place of blue. Something unfathomable is moving out there: many of those steel rods and painful kicking objects she's only ever known as fear, hate. Horror pounds at her jaw, steely and cold.

But there are many colours outside, so much movement, odours she never detected back at the Place. Violets and reds, the bluest white, the blackest green. And, yes, somewhere out there is splendid or some other land which she feels blessed to have discovered.

From beneath, there is a great tremor. The back-lift opens. Into the blinding, one of those awful furies lifts itself into a frame of light, screaming: "Okay, off now. Get."

Sweat pours from its face and body, a smell of milky dampness worse than anything here. Her hooves, this square of shit beneath. She breaths into the fear.

And something new. A sensation, like a wave, riding through her stiff legs, releases into her heart. She wants to tell the children, slunk over, some staring at the *it* by the door, wide-eyed. She wants to tell the ones who are moaning hot sounds. She wants to say the word.

For so long, in the darkness, she never spoke. Silence, when they'd taken her infants and swung them into mud puddles, bleeding red, her children's voices calling. Then, stilled; her breasts aching with mother's milk. Silence when they'd come at her with their rods, stabbing electrical currents through her skin.

But it's music, which comes to her as a seed, slips into this calloused sight. She realizes what she must do. With every muscle, she breathes, funnels the stale, acrid air into rhythm: 1, 2, beautiful measurements. 3, 4, 5, the colour of thirst, quenched. Sweet oxygen. Briefly, her song. Her music. She tries sharing this voice of light.

She tries, as her mates push their heads into soft, aching flesh, as they cry out. She's singing once more and, yes, she knows, one last time. Taking in the out there, the pale aromatic, she holds herself above the cold rush of ending. She calls out word-thoughts to the two elders above and to the children alongside. Music bursts forth. Sensational Joy, warming her hooves, sliding from her knees to her throat. A sweeping bliss rising above the stench. She feels it bring her forward. Freedom. They are getting out, going into the light.

The Left Eye

TALKING ABOUT LOST TIMES is never taxing, and I believe kids should hear everything, as long as you got someone around to remember. For my own children, this 'everything' is a story; it's a gift. Same with the grandkids, though my daughter Cecilia tells me I'm long-winded and tend to "give into speaking thoughts they shouldn't hear. They're just kids. Let them be." But this way, by repeating, my grandkids are going to know the inside and out.

My particular favourite is my own grandma's story about Great Aunt Cecilia, who gave my own sweet Cecilia her name.

It was 1964, Kentucky. I was nine or so, nine and a half actually. The spirit of change was evident, some experiencing the spirit more than the change. And in my life, there'd been way too much change.

One particular day, I was taking the country road to Grandma's house, bending over to pull clumps of mud from my loafers. Even with all the worries I had storming inside, my lungs were ballooning with April's sweet promise, the fresh scent of new buds lending me the kind of high you only get in childhood. The cathedral sky was crayon-blue, and those Kentucky's orange-breasted robins, red cardinals and the yellow-plumaged birds were throwing their plump chests into song.

Course, I desperately wanted to join them, but my thoughts were elsewhere – first and foremost, on the state of my younger brother, James, who was having his tonsils removed in Lexington. Mom and Dad had both gone down. I was sore they'd left without me. But there was something else. My grandfather had just died, and it was still an open wound.

That morning, leaving for school without James had been stranger than one of those crystal blue winter storms – what my dad called that storm of winter, when the skies and land against the first chapter of evening were so white, they seemed blue. But there was no storm. It was April, damp April, and just like Little Red Riding Hood, surrounded by deep woods, I was making my way to Grandma's. True, it was better to be leaving school rather than going to it. Triple true, "Tonsils aren't something we need anymore," and in all likelihood, James was going to be just fine.

Before they had left, my mother had been whipping out assurances, in that strange tone you'd use for babies. As if, to be perfectly honest, she wasn't so sure herself. But what I felt was the sourness of a whole lot of lemons. Why was everyone pretending? Nothing was ever 100% certain; nothing ever 100% in-the-bag. My brother might perish beneath the surgeon's blade, and I had had the oddest thought: What in Sam Hill was going on when people were born with parts they didn't need? Not like my feet in those muddied shoes or ears tuned to the crazy chattering above. Made me think of a girl in the second grade … can't remember her name, but I remember her story. "My daddy axed his thumb right off." She drew in a long breath. "He never needed it anyhow. Found a way to use his other fingers." Imagination's a monstrous thing; I saw a thumb in a blood-red lake, corkscrewing down a drain.

As I walked to Grandma's house, the image of blood left me, while Little Red Riding Hood's grandma's red flesh between a great wolf's canines took over.

All around, though, was nothing but spring woods, and beneath and before me, gravel and asphalt. I had my school satchel slung over my shoulders and knew it was pure silliness to fear someone or something behind the poplars, especially in daylight and especially with cars on the road. I stopped, thought of Mom's "Janice, my dear, don't worry. James'll be much better. The doctors know what to do. We'll see you soon, honey."

What I did suddenly realize is that James had probably had the surgery already and was stretched out on a gurney, in a bleached-white room. Maybe, just maybe, there was some blood pooling next to his head. Into imagination's gruesome scene came Grandpa, his fingers "riddling" over his banjo strings, as he liked to call it. Along the fingerboard, his other hand bounced around like bullfrogs.

The banjo, he'd once told me, hailed from Africa, where they'd hollowed out a tough-skinned gourd fruit and scythed through bamboo for a fingerboard. Just a year before he died, we were out on my grandparents' porch, on his porch swing, taking in the orange-sweet summer. Demonstrating the technique of scything through a gourd, Grandpa made such an impressive display, I swore I caught sight of a blade.

"The long-reed bamboo's strong but flexible. Strong as bamboo means you bend in the wind, never go down," he said.

"Not even when elephants come?"

"Elephants?"

"In Africa."

Laughter spouted out, looped with spittle. I was angry but wouldn't show I gave a rat's ass what he thought ('rat's ass' expressed in mind only – I'd never utter it out loud). Like every kid and certainly every adult, I hated being made fun of. I jumped up.

"What's the matter?"

Fuming, I stood, silent. Nonchalantly, he turned away, whistled some tune – no one else could ever whistle so fine. When the fire left me, I sat back down.

He caught his breath. "So, as I was saying, not even a stampede of African elephants can break that bamboo. But here's the thing: Bamboo's nowhere's as strong as ... well, as that big ole tree over there, but its power is in bending when it needs to. Bamboo has the strength of, well, of a herd of elephants."

"Not strong enough to stop being cut down, though."

This time, Grandpa's laughing came out fiercer. I had no time to react, as he was immediately seized by coughing that wrenched his insides out. Mom used to say that it was like pulling teeth to get him to quit smoking. Have to admit that I loved watching him stitch the small dried tobacco leaves into swatches of paper and watch his yellowed fingers roll the paper.

"Grandpa, you okay?"

He nodded. "Yep. I sure would've liked a gourd banjo. That bamboo makes a lasting keyboard."

GOURD – a round word. I pictured the blue and green drawing I'd seen of Africa in a world atlas at school, but what those slick pages had to do with the real place, I had no idea. Things don't have to be read in books, I knew. I sure learned a whole hell of a lot from Grandpa.

Just that winter, snow cracking over split leaves, they'd lowered him into the ground. Throughout the funeral and with all the talk about God, our Father, Jesus and Heaven, two thoughts were looming like giant road signs in my head:

1. How on earth could they dig through that frozen crust?

2. Why did Grandma keep murmuring the same line over and over again: "He lived as well and as long as can be expected," along with her "Amen"?

Right up to his death, he'd been riddling away. Grandma swore that "without all that playing, he'd never have made it this far."

Sometimes my brother and I would join in, our voices cutting spirals through the cotton-stiff summer. During the snowed-in winters, our tunes surrounded snow-laced windows.

Making my way along that road, I turned to look at spring's budding poplars, coffee trees and cottonwoods, all those blooms having risen from nothing. The lemon trout lilies were popping out; others still folded-in, with their sad, puny smiles. Every so often there were spots of purple, mostly from the prairie crocuses. Soon there'd be hide-and-seek summers, tall-grass afternoons, evenings blown in cool and rippling, ripened fruit falling, worms snaking through their bruised corpses.

As I walked on, the birds were going on like they had something to say. I finally felt fit enough to give it a try.

There's an old stream, that I long to cross.
And Ol' Man River.
He'll just keep rollin' along!

Grandpa was always naming things. He especially liked naming the birds. "There's that sparrow. Crazier than an outhouse rat, determined we don't forget its infuriating trill." There, on the porch swing, we had tweezers for ears, capturing the bird calls. One song seemed higher than the rest: a whip-poor-will, with its four-notes.

"Singing the way of things," Grandpa said. "Knows a mighty more than we do. Knows that Mighty Mississippi, carrying freedom. Yep, Paul Robeson sung it best."

"Paul?"

"Robeson, singing *Old Man River*. That voice of his – what a voice, belting out all the stuff people have been through."

"What've they been through?"

"For hundreds of years, horrible, horrible things. Slavery for one. And that's enough to push the light out forever, but then you have the Jim Crow –" His voice fell. "Those laws that push folks around, tell 'em they aren't human."

I was confused. Most times, meaning arrived long after what was spoken, but then I was hanging around a lot of adults. Grandpa nodded sympathetically, took his reading glasses out of a shirt pocket, along with a wiping cloth, wiped the lenses and placed the glasses back inside. "Course you don't know what I'm talkin' about. Some people are treated differently, just because of who they are, just cause of skin colour." He sighed. "It's been like that for as long as I've been around. Inside some men's heads there's just too much whistling of crosswinds. They act like they own the world." He put his hand to his mouth like he had a cigarette there, but there wasn't one. He wasn't allowed to smoke when he was sitting alongside. "That's how it's been since God made us, I suppose," he said. "Some men think they're better, and they won't let anyone else be in their kingdom of one."

I remember those words, although at the time I didn't understand them.

Above us, in the afternoon sky, the gibbous ghost was already up, waiting its turn. Evening would bring with it the crickets' choir and the orchestration of other night critters. And, since it was August, there'd also be a shower of shooting-stars. I had my wish ready – for next summer. Dad had insisted I wasn't old enough yet to set off July 4th firecrackers, like the flaming *Salutes*, pistol shooters. But a wish could extend to next year. And with all the stars, shooting across the dark sky, I ran a pretty good chance. I swung out my legs, watching my bare toes wiggle. Over by the door, limp socks stuck out of a pair of brown-toed shoes of champions, my birthday present from Thom McAn's, out in Lexington. That was one crazy shop, with a fancy wooden flora-scope, or X-ray machine, in the back. Just to put on a show, once, Mom, who was later pissed to hell with herself for doing this, stuck a foot underneath (not advisable for adults and certainly not permitted for kids). I remember seeing her glowing toe bones. There, on the porch and beneath our feet, the wood planks were holding the porch together. How odd. A thousand bones to hold a person together and just some wood and hammering nails to hold down a floor. As we both swung ourselves out over the porch, a breeze swept in, whispering.

"Y'know," Grandpa said, taking out his tobacco and rolling papers. "All's we got are those two notes the warblers sing, until the third that reads the world."

Birds, singing the world.

On my walk to Grandma's, I felt the sun's warmth graze my shoulders. I stretched out my neck to the insistent sparrows, who were belting out their songs. I could smell it, taste it: the orange-lick flames dancing in the fireplace and Grandma and I sucking on candied caramel, melting in a sea of hot cocoa. I bit back on a sudden *can't wait*, generally reserved for days like this day: a Friday, with one Monday already gone and the other one far ahead.

Just like tonsils and left thumbs, Mondays weren't needed. Nor was the whole of this year, spent in fifth grade, with Miss Pettigrew – *Miss Petty P-U*, we called her (I'm pretty sure she knew). She was awful. Not at all like Miss Allison, who'd taught us in the fourth grade. Miss Allison would flip her bright orange curls, throw hands into the air, sketching vibrant impossible worlds; being in her class felt like we were on a journey. She was up from New Mexico. New was her style. She told us to use her first name, but then we weren't allowed to. (I think the principal had had a word with her.) Her always-new stories came out all fluttering and real. I remember she had us choose an animal who would stay by our side for the entire year. I used bright chalk over creased black paper, crayons and watercolours: a howling-to-the-moon coyote, lavender eyes framed in licorice rims.

That was fourth grade, but the year I'm talking about, in the fifth grade, I was enduring a lifetime of sorrows. That afternoon we'd been reading a silly book about a boy named Stanley Lamb-chop, a boy crushed by a bulletin board (certainly those boards can be dangerous). He's flattened like an envelope and, in this particular story, sent in the mail. For our first discussion about this careless creature known as Flat Stanley, Miss Petty P-U called on Mattie, the new kid whom she loved pestering. Mattie was from Chicago. She'd arrived just after Christmas vacation.

"Why don't you tell us, Mattie? What can Flat Stanley do, now that he's flat?"

Long brown hair, freckled nose, Mattie pushed herself up. Her eyes bulged behind thick, Coke-bottle lenses. In a sense (and in my older, non-discretionary judgement here), those eyes resembled a bug's underneath a magnifying glass.

Whenever she was called on by Miss Petty P-U (which was most of the time), Mattie would jump a little, then push her chin into her shirt. Right then, a rash was spreading across her face.

Miss Petty P-U brought her hand, *Thump!* down on Mattie's desk.

"I'm speaking to you!"

Mattie swallowed. "He – he – he can – he's flat."

"*Ye-e-es.*" Miss Pettigrew twirled a finger in the air. "What can he do?"

"Sent through the mail? He can be sent through the mail?"

But Miss Pettigrew wouldn't let up. She wanted a full literary critique. "Yes, and what does this tell us, about Stanley, about being flat in this world?"

"Uh … maybe … maybe it shows us … shows us how things … how much easier everything is when you're flat and other things you never thought about become more difficult to do."

Then Miss Petty-P-U didn't seem to know what to do. "That's fine, Mattie."

Another time, snaking through the desks, *Smack!* Her hand flattened Mattie's Kleenex box. "I asked whether you knew 'bout the problems in *Chicago*, with *tho-ose* people."

Mattie's neck extending from her shirt was like a turtle's extending from his shell. In our school, it just so happened there were no Colored – I mean, African American – kids. I know it's crazy, but that's how it was.

"Uh, Ma'am, I … I don't know about those problems you're talking about."

"Well." Miss Pettigrew sniffed. "I've heard otherwise."

"I don't –" Mattie's voice slipped beneath the desk. I remember thinking of a mouse we'd found in the classroom. I'd shushed two other girls. We'd put the creature in a box and placed it outside. Course it probably came back in, and the janitor probably got to it before we could try out our paramedic training again.

But this day, in class, below Miss Petty-P-U's trained bullying, something happened. Despite the creeping blush in her cheeks, Mattie sat up, and, in her clearest voice ever, said: "Ma'am, I know what you're saying, but I think I might know about what's going on in Chicago."

During recess, I left a super-duper kick-ball game to talk to this Mattie, so different from the other yellow-bellied cowards.

On my walk from school, I was finally, finally turning the corner to familiar big trees, holding onto their fragrant bouquets. And … Grandma's house! Blue sidings and windows that stared out from cream shutters. I leapt over those three front stairs, thinking of Grandpa, who used to cry out: "Pumpkin, you're as crazy as the Four Horsemen of the Apocalypse!"

"GRANDMA!"

My satchel slid down, as I grabbed the brass knob, yelling as the door swung open.

"What, in blessed God, Janice! Let me take your bag. Good Lord, what's the spirit in you?"

I collapsed on the 'Welcome Home' welcome mat, the greeting so boring and predictable in its robin-egg blue frame.

"What's got into you? Take off your shoes. Come into the kitchen. I've made some sandwiches."

"Not hungry."

"Course you are. You come whirlin' in – you must be starvin'."

I said something about James.

"He'll be fine, hon. The doctors said it was routine. Don't you worry. He'll be up soon, eating rooms full of ice cream."

Settling on the lacquered bench, I unlaced my shoes. Grandma, already in the kitchen, called down the hallway. "Cut some carrots for you!"

Ugh! Vegetables. Those shoes went down with a smack.

(Always in a hurry when we're young. Maybe we become slower later because the older we get, we're spending too much time trying to remember.)

"I heard that! Shoes under the bench."

Like many grandparents' houses, there were photographs on every inch of wall, and the stale, familiar odour of Grandpa's smoking was still present. Some of the old black and white photos were at eye-level; other portraits of family, higher up. Ancient turn-of-the-century family portraits, I had learned, were taken with huge cameras, photographers lifting up sheets to let in the light. From what seemed like a long ways off, Grandma's voice coasted along. "Hon, are you coming?"

Then, like some sign from Heaven, the afternoon sun broadened along one wall, lit up a photo of two sisters, sitting at a kitchen table: Grandma with my great aunt Cecilia, who was turned at the waist to have a look at the cameraman, her broad face painted with laughter. A much younger Grandma was reaching across the table, smiling.

"Janice, hon."

"Comin'."

Alongside was a photograph of me and Grandpa on that porch swing. Sun was in his glasses, so you could barely see his eyes. Both of us were smiling, but not, it seemed, at the photographer, my father. Rather at the person standing right here, right now, before the picture. How odd, that all of life could be captured in a frame. I drew closer to the photograph of my great aunt. She'd died before I was born. Strange, I'd always passed this part of the wall before, but –

Her eye! Great Aunt Cecilia's eye!

"Grandma!" I shot down the hallway, skidding into the kitchen, where she happened to be on her knees, half inside the cabinet beneath the sink, both doors swung open.

"Whadd'ya hollerin' about? Darn, can't for the life seem to get this bugger free of dripping." She straightened, and I saw a pale bucket under metal piping. "You're so fired up, Janice. Settle your good self down and have a sandwich."

I bounded into a kitchen chair, then reached past the lemonade pitcher to a plate piled high with sandwiches and carrots. Oh, that sweet black-currant jelly, slick peanut-butter lathered over soft bread – paradise. When that bit of sandwich made its way down, all my sorrows melted away.

Grandma sighed. "Trying to fix this crazy pipe." She sighed again. "Wish your grandfather were here." Reaching behind her waist, she unthreaded her apron string and, seating herself at the table, let both arms settle on her lap. "I don't know." Those used to be Grandpa's exact words.

A spidery feeling was making its way up, inside.

"Sweetie, would you like some juice?"

"Naw'm okay."

"There's lemonade."

"Uh-huh." Why was she always pointing out the obvious? Plus, there was one large omission on her part, and it was making me feverish, so I asked: "Did they tell you what was going on with James? Did they call?"

"Yes, and I promise they'll call again. As soon as he's awake."
Grandma stood up. Over at the sink, she turned on the faucet.
"OW! Forgot how hot that water is! I've been trying to get this
whole apparatus working ... leaking pipe, hot water coming out
instead of cold, spraying faucet." Sighing, she turned off the tap.
Through heavenly bites, I wondered why she was going on about
plumbing, when James' life was in jeopardy. I too was off in peanut-butter heaven.

"Since your grandpa's left us, nothing seems to be working."
With a few short steps, she reached the table.

"Grandma?"

"Hmm?"

"In that picture in the hallway, what's wrong with her eye,
Great Aunt Cecilia's eye?"

"Her eye? The left one? Good God, thought you knew. She
was fit for a glass eye."

"Whadd'ya mean? Eye's still there!"

"Seems so, but no. Long story."

"Can't you tell it?"

"The story?"

"It's a story, ain't it?"

Grandma shook her head.

"Isn't it, Grandma?"

"Sure, of course it's a story, about my sister, the rebel, long
before the war."

The War. I'd seen photographs. At the library with Grandpa,
I'd borrowed only Grandpa-recommended material. For a good
long time, the both of us leafed through pages of war shots. He'd
been just a kid at the time. During the Second World War, he
wasn't drafted because although he could have made officer, as he
was a bit older than the soldiers, he had a limp: one you couldn't
really tell he had. Only when he brought attention to it did you

notice this minor imperfection that had saved his life. I had no idea how lucky he was to have survived or how unlucky he was to have lost so much – friends who never returned.

"Whadd'ya mean, rebel?"

"Like you. Mud fighting, running around on dirt roads, soft cushions for horses' hooves."

I imagined the horses' heavy hooves imprinting the dirt. "Not so soft now, huh?"

"And not so many horses, just to get from one point to the other. These cars … I was never enamoured, like your grandfather, of those smelly, loud machines. Still, I'm telling you. The horses' odour, their you-know-what, could be smelled for miles.

"Yick!"

She smiled. "Well, cars sure stink."

"But her reb –"

"Rebellin'?"

"Yeah, and the eye?"

Grandma settled herself in her seat.

"It was the middle of summer; I was about your age. Ten."

"I'm nine and a half!"

"Like I said, about your age, and I was out with little … little at the time, Great Uncle Harold. He was about five."

I couldn't imagine Great Uncle Harold that small.

"Even though she was already a young lady, Cecilia was running, climbing that ole sycamore. She and Nathan used to –"

She stopped, lifted herself to her feet. "Do you … would you like some tea, Hon?"

"Thanks. With honey, now that you mention it. But what they … what did Cecilia and Nathan do?"

"My Dear Janice, show a little patience. As your grandfather used to say: 'Hold your horses!'"

Passing the refrigerator, she ran a palm along the door, held it over a dent which Grandpa had made, moving the kitchen table around. From the cupboard, she pulled out tea she used only for special occasions.

"Are you sure James'll be okay?"

"Most definitely."

Grandma set the kettle on the stove. "Didn't think it would be so powerful, missing Nathan."

Reflections of the afternoon sun were settling on her grey-whipped hair. I turned to the pitcher of lemonade. The condensation droplets resembled rain falling on painted yellow daffodils. I poured out some of the most amazing lemonade in the world.

I knew about Grandma's older brother. Nathan had died before I was born, fighting in that same war that Grandpa had avoided. Great Uncle Harold, far too young to join, had never married, had two really great male friends whom he'd bring over from time to time. I remember my mother speaking in hushed tones to my dad about this. Course now it's evident what was going on – he liked men. We carry so many secrets.

On that chair in my grandmother's kitchen, I felt something dark and seeded moving up through mud-soaked roots. The bittersweet lemonade made me pucker.

"Is the story about Aunt Cecilia a bad one?"

Grandma lifted one of those little transparent honey bears, with a yellow tip. She constantly complained about the lids coming loose. "It's true what they say," she murmured. "Long time ago but could've been yesterday. I remember Mother fixing tea on those old gas stoves. At the time, gas was new *and* a luxury. Not like coal, and my mother was so proud."

This story I knew by heart: the set-up in her house, the kids sharing bedrooms, the favourite apple trees, a cherry tree and Nathan's love of animals. One day he brought home a pig. Imagine! A piglet, purchased at the fair. Pink bellied, that piglet grew into a sow, larger almost than a pony! Estie, they called her. She'd fall on her side for a belly rub, I heard.

"Course, after that, no one could eat that delicious Christmas ham. My heart sank, I'll tell you." Grandma always said this. I nodded absently and finished my sandwich.

But that story probably started me wondering. I was afraid to ask about the cows and sheep, the chickens, about how odd it was to be putting something on your fork that once had been attached to a whole some*one*. Maybe my heart was made of the same stuff as Great Uncle Nathan's. Once I'd brought home a kitten; another time, a scraggy dog. We couldn't keep either. Mom didn't like cats. "Unless we had a barn and little mice critters, which we, thank goodness, do not." And James was allergic to dogs.

Grandma emptied the steaming water into the teapot. She placed this, along with two saucers and two cups, on a tray that I'd painted for Mother's Day. It seemed like an awful lot for her to hold. I got up.

"That's fine. I can do it. Let the tea steep. Course you want the honey!"

She turned around for the little bear.

"What about Cecilia's left eye?"

"Patience, Janice. My sister was a strange one. When she should've been doing girl things, she was up in that ole sycamore, which unfortunately for the lot of us had one bad branch that was readying to fall. But no one had given it a second's thought, especially Cecilia, who never thought about anything anyhow. Course, while she's up there, the branch decides to break off. On the way down, her eye must've caught on something, maybe a twig."

"OUCH! GRANDMA!"

"Luckily, she didn't leave us there and then, depart from this natural world."

"Was she screaming?"

"One shrill scream. Then she lost consciousness. My heart –" Grandma's hand hit her chest. "I could feel it, pounding. My mama came out. Nathan too. Little Harold was with me; he started running. I was just standing there. My sister lay on her side. What a scene!"

I leaned into the table. Even knowing all the goings-on in the strange merry-go-round world of adults, even knowing about wars, I had thought their world was different. I realized it could be just as scary.

"As usual, it was Nathan to the rescue. Fell to his knees, ear to her chest. There, in a pool … in my own sister's blood, was Cecilia. Nathan turned her over, though my mother was screaming for him not to. Cecilia was still breathing. Then, I honestly don't recall what happened. Eventually the local doctor came out. Thank Jesus, he lived nearby. Course we took her to the hospital, but it was that doctor who saved her. I s'pose Lady Luck was hitching a ride that day. The good Lord was certainly present."

"And the glass eye?"

Grandma lifted the teapot. I noticed her hands were shaking. "Grandma, I can pour."

"I'm fine, hon. Really. My sister lost her left eye. Much later, she was fitted for the glass. For years, she had a patch, like a pirate."

"A pirate!" With the hot tea steaming, I emptied the honey, braiding a layer on the surface. I didn't stir but set my lips along the rim, sipping the syrupy liquid, blowing miniature waves. Bare-bottom tea: my invented word for stuff I could finish in a flash.

Grandma added her own thick teaspoon and sipped. "Thing is, Cecilia died when you were little, soon after marryin'."

"On account of the marryin'?"

Laughter bubbled up. "No, hon. From pneumonia, though maybe you have something there, with the marryin'."

"What 'bout medicines?"

"Before the war, they didn't have any good medicine for pneumonia."

I didn't want to think of little James. "So, she changed the patch to glass?"

Grandma leaned back. "Cecilia was grateful for the glass; though she didn't have it until a couple years after the accident, when she met her husband. S'pose she was so taken with the sweet nothings he was saying to her. Sweet Jesus, they were nothing! But there was my sister, prettying up her face. Because of him, she went and got fitted for the glass. He paid, of course. But she paid too – not with money. That woman was far from rich. She paid a different way, and that … my dear Janice, is a whole other kettle of fish."

"How did she pay?"

"She paid."

"How?"

"Being married. That was payment enough."

"But she was okay with the nice things he was tellin' her?"

"Maybe. Beautiful wedding. Beautiful bride. And he – if I think back, he had handsome-enough parts, handsome-enough face. Still, he was ugly to me. Always bossin' her around."

She walked over to the sink.

"What is it, Grandma?"

"Nothing."

"Can't you say?"

"I'd rather not." She sighed, turning. "Cecilia's husband was always criticizing her *and* your grandfather."

Now, *that* was sure blowing the top off a haystack. Only the Devil Himself would've had a bone to pick with Grandpa.

Grandma stared out the kitchen window, just standing, as if there were a whole different world out there that no one else could see. "Yep. Grandpa saw right through that bast—. Turns out he'd been married before."

"Before?" I was surprised, couldn't imagine why anyone'd marry again, unless, of course, their wife had died.

"Cecilia would sooner run into the street than listen to us – such a stubborn soul. Grandpa, you know, played at their wedding. Main thing is he was always raising hell, talking about how … how the Colored folks don't … well, he used to lament the way they were treated." She stared at her hands. "How those folks *still* have to eat at separate places. Dear Jesus." She turned to me. "How they have to go through the back door of public establishments or drink at separate water fountains, pee in separate bathrooms. Even die on the road! And Cecilia's husband couldn't stand listening to that. Called it 'horseshit nonsense.'" Grandma inhaled. "He said your grandfather must've *loved* Colored folks.'"

"What's wrong with that?"

"Exactly. Cecilia's husband believed there was something wrong with lovin' people."

The sun was entering the kitchen, creating wee mustard-painted butterflies in the flying dust. I fastened my mind on an image of Grandpa, playing at my great aunt's wedding, remembered his songs about wide countries and travelling, about fires and, sometimes when Grandma wasn't around, about terrifying things he sang in his low, quiet baritone. Surely, my grandmother had heard them.

At that moment, I was clouds away, same as Grandma. Except I was at a cousin's outdoor wedding, at what Dad might've called a "very memorable event." There'd been a great deal of dancing, until everything felt heavy and dreaming had carried me away. That fragrant summer night, I kept an eye on the stars, a whole other kind of sky than the one in Grandpa's quiet songs. I realize now, of course, that those songs had something to do with war, the way anger boils up, blood-red.

Grandma lifted the teacup. "S'pose that's how it goes. Cecilia's husband was a real winner. You know, they moved to Louisville. After my sister died, we never heard from him. Anyone could've seen that coming."

"Maybe his heart ... maybe it was shattered."

"Shattered?"

"Like that window when I threw the ball, when Mom grounded me."

"Maybe."

I sensed a low note of sadness in her voice, what my fourth-grade teacher Miss Allison might've called "a pit of tears." Cecilia had married a man she loved, probably someone battling something deep inside, hateful on the outside. Probably I'd never know. "Grandma?"

"Yes, Janice?"

"What about the sycamore?"

"Well, Nathan and my father went out to chop it down. Cecilia's bedroom faced the tree, and her bed was just below the window. She was recuperating, just happened to be peering outside, when they went out to chop it down, screamed out to let it be. I guess the sycamore was resilient enough. Just one branch, gone. No need to chop down the whole tree. And ... well, as it turns out, she climbed up again."

"After the accident?"

"Yes, Ma'am. And I joined her."

"What?!"

Grandma was tracing laced blue flowers along her cup. "Have to tell you, I loved it up there. You know, Janice, Hon, the house is still around."

I nodded. "Yah, I know."

"But the sycamore's gone. I passed by once and decided to knock. Nice woman came to the door. Apparently, the family's been there for years. The woman knew about the sycamore. Said it had fallen sick. She knew the exact date the tree came down; turned out to be around when Cecilia left us. I guess it's like one life taking another."

I turned. That sun was so strong, I felt like I was outside. It kept shining on the sink and tiled counter. Not a dying light. A birthing light. I squinted into its promise. A thought leapt in. "Grandma, Miss Allison used to say that even when it's telling you things you don't wanna hear, a story can be a kinda protection."

"Hmm, Miss Allison. I remember. You really liked her, didn't you? A shame really that James will never have her as a teacher."

Her sadness caught me off-guard. I swallowed hard.

"Yeah, so Miss Allison talked about how animals can protect us: wolves and bears and howlin'-to-the-moon coyotes!"

Grandma leaned forward, smiling. "Animals, like wolves, protecting?"

"A story can be like that, can't it?"

She sat back. "Janice, you just might have something there. Always with a sharp point."

"And maybe Cecilia would be a kind of bird, up in that tree?"

Grandma scrunched up her face, like she used to do, when she was deep in thought.

"Maybe, Janice."

Through the window above the sink, I could see the branches of Grandma's apple trees: trees that would keep on blooming, just as they had last year. Not even anyone as determined as Miss Petty-P-U could stop what was coming through the forest like a wild beast. I recalled Grandpa saying: "Everything moving miles faster than when I was young." Right then, I missed his voice's scratchiness, the way he wiped his lenses and even – I know this is strange – the tobacco-stench of his breath. It was no one's fault he was gone; just the world changing things.

Grandma's voice interrupted my thoughts. "Funny thinking of my sister as a bird. Most certainly she'd be a blackbird, streak of red on those shiny wings."

My own mind was flying about and settled on birds; then on an image of James, eating buckets-full of ice cream. Maybe he *would* be alright. There'd be no running around, no climbing (apparently, a family trait). Not for a while at least.

Staring down at the teacup's bottom, I noticed an odd stain. Afterwards, I realized this couldn't be. The kind of tea they sold back then did not leave behind any largely visible stain. It was as if someone were down there, invisible, painting with tea: first, a tree, its branches spread over a wide trunk. Where one branch jerked up with meanness was Great Aunt Cecilia, singing her lungs out. Beneath, Grandpa was riddling along his banjo strings, while a flock of red-winged blackbirds (clear as day!) moved like mischief across tea-coloured skies.

Les monstres affectueux –
Affectionate Monsters

Be in this place • Être ici on le peut.

It's ALREADY BEEN more than a few years since the New Brunswick government scrapped those license plates. And Marie-Thérèse was probably not the only one wondering, *Be where?* Removing the plate from her car, she decided to remount it in her bedroom, above the bed – maybe to tempt the fates. If it ever fell …

Blazing sun shoots through bay windows – *her* bay windows, *her* house. Marie-Thérèse's father's words move about the room, inside dust whorls: "Sweating off that blazin' sun. Just the taste of it – murderous." Musky sweat of a good run, sweet pine in her shirt, she pulls, pushes and plucks with the bristled brush at the knots in the dog's thick fur.. So much for that walk among trees dating back a good hundred years and stretching beyond her colonial-style house. There are deer ticks now, who've migrated from the south because of warmer, longer summers.

In front of her house, the street had been christened long ago. 'Indian Road.' Despite the obvious insult, it's retained its name, but recently she's gotten herself a ladder and some paint, crossed off the 'Indian' and written 'Erasure' above. So far no one's bothered with her addition to the sign.

Holding her breath, Marie-Thérèse tries for a clear path through the dog's fur. Thoughts of her twin sister, the dog's human companion, Nicole, who's off with her son for her birthday. *Their* birthday, the sisters' BIG FOUR-O. It was yesterday, Friday, July 16th. Next weekend, they'll celebrate with a trip to the Meduxnekeag River Valley's rare Appalachian forest. "Country amnesia. Opening the windows, letting the goddamned IT out." That's what Nicole reported she'd be doing.

"What's IT?"

"Everything and nothing. I'll be screaming my bloody face off. Getting ready for the big five-o."

"Not for another decade, Nicole."

"Sure, but I gotta lay down the specs."

Nicole and her son have set out for the red cottage not far from the Miramichi River – the cottage, an inheritance from their mother. Towards the end of their father's life, he threw out a reminder they'd be inheriting the cottage, and: "Let's sweeten the deal. I want the two of you to take on the farm."

Nicole's thoughts? "Prodigal daughters, taking on what our never-brothers would've inherited." And what were the patriarch's orders? With a good deal of remonstration: "One or both of you will have to look after the canola and corn." He'd already closed down his hog and poultry farming. "When they go smashing through with their bulldozers and pipelines," he said, taking up his curious inflections when, as Nicole called it, he did his mans-plaining. "Building shit condos and taking prime real estate to resell, sending their earnings offshore, you won't budge."

Just so there'd be no mistaking his intentions, he 'advised' them to "each find a husband to help manage the place."

Remembering her father's words, Marie-Thérèse shakes her head. The dog rides his rough tongue over her arm. Too much breeding and human design ends up in slavish obeisance. This is what happened to a litter of foxes she read about. They'd been bred into affectionate little monsters. *Les monstres affectueux.* After a few generations, their ears flopped down, and, amazingly, each generation of foxes was more affectionate ... slavish even, sickeningly obedient.

"Jeez, doesn't anyone brush you?" Usually, he's not such a mess, his fur unbelievably knotted. In her crazy-ass brain, Marie-Thérèse's ploughing through a whole field of knots.

Back when miles measured distances and fog curled in miles from the shore, Nicole, the older, by a good twenty minutes, and her sister Marie-Thérèse were headed toward that vanishing point, as they took the roadside west. Beyond, the stretch of country road gathered speed, rising rapidly into the horizon, past the barns and crowns of dairy farms and the long, thick necks of granaries and grain elevators. Here, along the spine of country, Marie-Thérèse carries thoughts of her uncles and cousins, who, along the coast, are pulling in lobster traps, yanking in nets of snow crabs, herring and cod. As usual, thoughts of her mother enter.

Dreams extend further back than days can tell, but the memories are as real as this road, Nicole's straw-coloured braid, straight over the back of her yellow tank top. Marie-Thérèse's own scraggly-straw hair sticks up all over the place, no matter how much she brushes or braids the loose ends.

Of their mother, all they've ever had are photographs. No floral fragrance, the kind that you can smell in other kids' hair. From their aunt, they have stories. "Over those strings," their aunt said, speaking of their mother's violin playing. "It's a cliché, I know. But it was magic. Weekends, you'd throw off that coat of armour you'd built up. Your mother, girls, was a musician's magician."

Nicole has always wanted to play. Their father has wanted nothing to do with music.

Leave it to Nicole, who later told Marie-Thérèse that violin bows are made from the tails of dead horses and the strings … weren't they cat gut? "I'll play brass," Marie-Thérèse replied, having no intention of taking up anything. Nicole sought out a different course. Despite having taken up the violin in her twenties, she's become a decent fiddler.

A tired Atlantic breeze carries the sisters, their shoes in hand, naked toes snaking through wide fields of flowers, snow-white, blue and violet. The edible goldenrods, having escaped the farmers' blades, are shooting up like miniature fountains. In one fist, each girl carries bright blooms with a cloying perfume. The ocean's breath streams inland. Brackish waters and plant life stream in, quiet undercurrents. It's the tongue of summer, precocious and incorrigible, days of melting spumoni ice cream.

Back then, Marie-Thérèse thought of things as they could be. Or … did she? Easy to create memories from dreaming, and dreaming from memories. So, how did that vanilla, chocolate and strawberry make their way into her mouth, so she bled sweet cream?

"Y'sure about those June bugs? Didn't see any yet." Nicole shuts one eye: something she does whenever she's up to no good.

"Not June bugs, Nicole. It's past June."

"I know. That's why, stupid. That's why I said it, Marie-Thérèse. Your hair's stuck in your ears. They were s'posed to be around back at the beginning of summer, but there weren't any."

"Anyways, you know they're called Shadflies. Fish flies. Stop fibbing your arse."

"Ha. Well, didn't see the Mayflies either. Betcha can't find no two that're exactly alike."

"Betcha, but you'll have to wait for next year."

"Ah, Marie-Thérèse, that's stupid. Betcha for next year then!"

Up close, on the other side of the fence are four Jersey steers who've come up for a closer look. They have little budding horns that will probably remain as is, as the farmer has probably burned them down. Marie-Thérèse does the math. That's 4 steers x 2 horns each. A perfect 8. The grass on the other side isn't so green. Muddy. She eyes her sister's right-hand pocket. Inside is a candy melt that

Nicole's promised she'll hand over. She doesn't like sweets that much – strangest sister.

Other side of the fence, the young steers are feeding on the muddied grass: a meagre diet. Some grass, corn mash and bone meal. "No need to have them eating smorgasbords." Her father's words.

Smack! Nicole has hurled a mud-slap at her face. Marie-Thérèse peels off the caked dirt. "Goddamn it, to hell."

Nicole isn't caving. "C'mon! What're you staring at?"

The Jerseys call, their voices, haunting. Through the caked dirt, Marie-Thérèse catches one whose large, wet eyes meet hers. He's asking something. What? She grabs a pack of wet mud, hurls it at Nicole.

The dog yelps. "Désolé, Tigre."

Tigre. Marie-Thérèse's nephew was five when he named the dog, the French handed down from their Acadian ancestry. But how strange. Marie-Thérèse pauses. How strange naming dogs and cars after predatory animals. There was that recent documentary on the poaching of a Siberian tiger and one of her cubs, the Siberians so endangered, they might as well be extinct. Maybe Tigre isn't a completely ridiculous choice. Still, the name doesn't suit this dog, doesn't suit any dog. And what about her name?

Marie-Thérèse. Acadian, not the Scottish side: their father's. It's Nicole who's always felt most Acadian: from their mother's side, family from Bay of Chaleur or La Baie des Chaleurs – there, with Deschamps et Louis Mailloux, et tous qui ont fait les batailles, les révolutions, who nobly fought to disengage from Britain's rule. When they were kids, during every Tintamarre Festival, Nicole proudly held up the Acadian tricot-coloured and yellow-starred flag, singing her lungs out.

And Marie-Thérèse will admit to the jealousy. Nicole resembles their mother, whose ancestral past has bled into the present.

A people who remember the expulsions, Le Grand Dérangement, arranged quite handily by Charles Lawrence's and the Nova Scotia Council's attempts to kick their kin's collective ass out and over to Prince Edward Island or past the U.S. border. And if that didn't work, deportation to France. Once, Marie-Thérèse heard a writer speak of the building of culture on an expulsion that happened hundreds of years ago, wondering out loud what new narrative might define the Acadians, if there was even need of one … and what about those who were half Acadian or a quarter? More than two-hundred years of history; identity is strange that way. Whenever she's camping or meeting up with fellow activists down in the States, Marie-Thérèse enjoys a great solo jubilee when she hears her mother's maiden name. Barely makes up for everything they've had to deal with since being kids (not so much now), the "Goddamned Frenchie" shit. Nicole, more confrontational, answered with threats and fists, until the assholes knew to shut their mouths.

Easy enough to draw up a legion of Davids facing Goliaths, when you're staring through the gun barrels of history. Whether or not it's folly to feel closer to their dad's side, Marie-Thérèse feels somehow more invested in their Scottish roots, the girls' paternal grandparents from a small settlement below the Salisbury Crags. The Scots certainly had their share of ostracising. "Fanny Wright would've been my hero," she told Nicole. "Nicknamed Frances," a Dundee-born abolitionist, feminist and free-thinker, friends with Lafayette, who moistened his chops on revolution.

"Crazy Tigre." Releasing the brush, Marie-Thérèse embraces his snowy mane. Then, from nowhere, it arrives: a flaming river of grief. Tigre tries to free himself, as Marie-Thérèse clamps her lids shut, holds on. Flames leap up, consumed by flood tides. Coughing, she releases her friend, as she gives into the rising inside.

Along the bay, heavy fog has collected; it curls and snakes around all earthly objects like small, mischievous spirits. Early August, and the girls are spending the season with their uncle's family, in the sweet Annapolis Valley. Today, they're to go out to help trap lobsters. Wheeled up on a pulley, one trap swings above, drops to deck. Later, the unlucky prisoners will be transferred to wooden crates. Nicole, leaning over the boat, wind in her hair, is enjoying the view. Marie-Thérèse walks up behind. Nicole screams.

"Whadd'ya doing, Marie?"

"I'm pulling you back. You're going to fall in."

"Stupid, no one's falling."

"Not today!" Their cousin laughs, as he reels in the thickly braided rope. "This is a pretty good catch today. You girls are lucky; must've brought a pretty piece of that luck out with you today!"

Marie-Thérèse turns from her sibling. "Boil them alive?"

"Well, yes. That's what you have to do. Another amazing lobster dinner."

"Thought you were going to sell them."

His hand circles his belly. "Marie-Thérèse, my good-luck cuz, we get some to ourselves — on account of your being here. You're a good luck charm."

Marie-Thérèse kneels by the crates, a hand on the wooden siding. She pulls away for a split-second, worried about those darn splinters. Then, suddenly, she's not worried anymore but caught in those dark bead eyes, turning, then settling, the pinkish-orange pincers pincing. It's this moment, and in this moment, it's the ocean, the boat, her cousin, her uncle, her sister tailing the salt-wind in her hair. And one orange-pink lobster, rolling on top of the others, ribbed pincers slicing the air.

"CAREFUL!"

She just stuck her hand in.

But no, not this one with the blackest eyes.

Through the slats, what does this creature see? And what does Marie-Thérèse look like, from the lobster's perspective? Hand on her own face, her nose.

Lobsters live 'til 70, her cousin told her. "You can tell the older ones because their shells are different; they're not moulting anymore."

What if … do lobsters have birthdays? The lobster stares with coal-bead eyes.

'I'm sorry,' she wants to say. 'This is the way things are.' And then, there's nothing: just the lobster's moving eyes and crazy antennae … until, the creature freezes. She freezes.

Closer now, "What're you saying?" she asks.

Combing Tigre's fur, pinching out stray burrs. Marie-Thérèse wonders what is so compelling about the capital–D Dog? Sure, her own species has never been a match for the Dog. Out-of-control breeding and territorial-hunting make for a dangerous mix. But by now, the years have equitably distributed her passion. Almost twenty years ago, she began contemplating revolutionary acts, long before the 'dis' was tacked onto the magical 'illusion.'

Slowly, methodically, she moves, her boots sinking into manure. Inside her mind, her body, there's a growing terrible silence, but this is an essential ingredient. Another is slow breathing. Lifeless is what they all have to be – simple, meditative, with only the smallest spark within. Unfortunately, Marie-Thérèse's brain won't switch off. Slopping through dirt, thinking of a university lecture on philosophy and the will, Marie-Thérèse contemplates hers: free and strong, unlike her sister's; Nicole, who goes along with everyone, who name-calls. 'Tree hugger,' she calls her, insisting that the larger the heart, the more easily it punctures.

Despite their dark suiting and ski masks, beneath the open night sky, the fifteen activists are exposed. Marie-Thérèse feels a pang. The threat of breaking out in language, in sound, in any sound is burning up inside her.

The sharp ammonia in her nostrils tickles, burns, and she's worried about sneezing. As the barn comes into view, her pulse picks up speed. The place needs a paint job, the broken shutters desperately need repairing. This pig farmer has left on a dim but constant light, the kind of technology her father never had: a red intensity for night vision, generally what chicken farmers use. Industry standards maintain that a steady stream of light increase nursing and eating, fattens them up. Odd habit: scalding animals into obeisance. The whole world's orbit around the sun is one odd habit. And here she is, trying to break through. Don't look back. Walk. 'Towards the spectacle of light, in birth, in death, our lives and theirs, bookended by light,' their priest once said.

Now, in the doorframe of the house there's a sliver of light. Is that – Holy Shit! Someone's standing there! She blinks. A child?

She stops to signal the others, turns back to the farmhouse, sees no one. A fellow activist notices her hesitation. "I could swear," she whispers through cotton. "I saw someone."

To this day, she asks herself. Was it a vision? Who was that child, framed in the doorway? Maybe, with her pulse quickening, her heart racing, she'd seen right on through to the other side.

After liberating a few – only a few babies, no mothers – the numbers of activists dwindled. One guy, a little too curious, too disruptive instead of cautionary, left way too quickly, his whereabouts unknown. Soon after, some activists received knocks on their doors. Who to believe? 'Caution' was flashing.

Their fourth and fifth liberation would be of chickens; the sixth, of cows.

*In the dying moonlight, with its bright exterior, the barn shines like
a docked alien ship. Closer; beyond the stained windows, they see the
dairy heifers. Corralled in tie-stalls, the cows flick their plumed tails.
The activists use their cellphone flashlights. "Our 'torches of solidarity,
Olympic bound,' " one guy jokes.*

In winter, sound travels as if through tulle, between cotton
silences. It was January when their mother died. Recently,
Nicole gained access to the priest's eulogy, archived along with
other church documents. Marie-Thérèse and Nicole read about
'hoarfrost' along bare branches and 'dressed' spruce. "Mushy"
was the brutal agreement. Toddlers at the time, they weren't
taken to the funeral. After reading through the eulogy, Marie-
Thérèse saw winter's 'hoarfrost' everywhere. Not butterflies but
hoarfrost.

There, on the table, sits her birthday present from Nicole.
Along the wrapping paper are picket fences covered in puffy
snow: hoarfrost. Sparrows tuck their beaks into small bodies.
Silliness, of course. Aren't those birds south for the winter?

"Whadd'ya think?"

The tear in the wrapping paper reveals a book. *The Sisters from
Hardscrabble Bay*, by Nicole Jensen. Nicole! Same name! On the
front cover, a photograph: circa 1920s, two sisters, leaning against
a car out of *Great Gatsby*.

After thanking her sister, Marie-Thérèse pointed. "So, which
one is you?"

"The one holding onto her wide-brim hat. You know, the
book was published posthumously by … take a guess who."

"Can't. Won't guess. Tell me."

"Stephen King! How crazy is that?"

"Crazy."

"It's a story about two sisters who live with their father. Their mother's dead."

"Their mother's dead," Marie-Thérèse repeats, softly. "And you're this one? Holding her hat?"

"Maybe, but –" Nicole tilts her head. "Isn't there something here for me? A gift, perhaps?"

"I'm dog sitting for you. You'll get another gift when you get back."

"So secretive."

Marie-Thérèse's present to her sister is a photograph. How odd, another twin thing: The photograph matches the book cover photo. It's a relic, found almost a year ago, while the two were rummaging through their father's belongings, before everything came down … the house, the barn. It's a photo of the sisters. But strangest of all, she's never showed it to Nicole. Marie-Thérèse breathes in suddenly. No reason to remember what happened, what she did to the barn back over a year ago. She takes another look at the photograph. Yesterday, after Tigre had been dropped off, Marie-Thérèse exchanged this relic of the two sisters with a painting she had in the entranceway. Then she stood back. Behind Nicole's joyful eyes was something unconquerable. Back then, her sister was building. Mortar in hand, she was standing on a scaffold, creating the greatest wall ever.

They were having dinner, both sisters having moved to Moncton. "You know the story about twins and a mother cow?" Marie-Thérèse was helping out in the kitchen.

"I don't want to hear it. You know that."

"Even after the farmer took the mother's calf away, she returned from the fields, dry. No milk."

"Like I said, I don't want to –"

"The farmer found another baby out in the woods. Twins."

Her sister looked away.

"Twins."

"I heard you."

"The mother was hiding her other baby. She'd given birth in the woods, knew to give birth there, to escape the farmer's knife. Despite everyone's pleas to show mercy, what do you think the farmer did?"

"You know I know."

"Sent her baby off to slaughter. True story. Funny you should shy away from the truth."

"Just a moment ... gotcha!"

There! With special tweezers, Marie-Thérèse pinches the tick, burying in Tigre's skin. Maybe the smallest of the three – human, dog, tick – is sensing the inevitable end.

She pries it free. Amazingly, the insect is wriggling. Racing to the bathroom; she shoots it in, lowers the lid. Damn, she hates killing. Yes, crazy ... maybe.

Funny thing, her sister has only now begun sharing. Imagine the worst. Or don't. Marie-Thérèse has always wanted to tell her sister that a lie repeated becomes the truth. Still, how in blessed hell could Nicole ever talk about what happened? She's not her sister; her sister isn't her. Not Marie-Thérèse, begging the world to show itself in plain sight. In plain sight, she's wanted to tell Nicole, there must be something those animals feel, sunk in despair, something even bordering on hope. Even in their darkest moments, they must feel joy. It's obvious in the actions of the ones who've been saved, kicking their heels, stored up and away, as is the case with any incarcerated human. And while they're waiting their turn on the kill-floor, do they carry that same possibility, as they fight for life and, as she's heard, fight for the others out there on the floor with them? Do they struggle every day for that lightness of being?

Light figures prominently in farming. This was a lesson learned in church.

Along country roads, steeples look like harboured ships' masts gaining on Heaven. One promise to their mother that their father kept was raising the girls Catholic, although he was a non-practicing former Presbyterian. Still, he'd made a promise, and promises are for keeping.

It's Easter, the chill "packing its bags, singing its farewell song," their mother's words, remembered only because they've been repeated. Light = rebirth. Singing = love.

Morning enters through the church windows, consumes the parishioners. At the front, the balding priest, 'Father,' in his para-chuting white surplice, calls upon this hungry light to heal.

Sunken in the pews, that delicious perfume ... she's heard churches carry the odour of pine boughs. What about places of worship where there are no pines? Marie-Thérèse turns her father's expression around in her head: 'That's something to hang my coat on'. Around and around.

Light streams in through the stained-glass enactment of Christ's calling and Mary's open arms. Alongside, their father sits, stoic. Behind him, the Fourth Station of the Cross. They're in the very back pew. Marie-Thérèse stares ahead, at all those people from the great long past, wondering ... how did they all wind up here? Nicole brushes a hand against the chair. Too loud. Their father throws the girls a remonstrative stare.

When they dress up in their Sunday frills, sans père, it's their aunt who brings them to church, their aunt who wouldn't go otherwise, as she was never as devout as her sister. When they enter, old women pat the empty spaces alongside, gesturing for them to take a seat along-side. Nicole, fidgeting, always fidgeting, tries to listen. Sometimes, Marie-Thérèse has a book, which she somehow manages to hide inside the Lord's prayer book.

Of course, her aunt knew.

This time, Marie-Thérèse's book contains a story about a burning barn. It's a book her teacher has lent just her, saying that she can try reading them ... or not ... and come back to the teacher with whatever she thinks they mean: short stories by Faulkner. Rhymes with chalk'ner. When Marie-Thérèse gets to the part on the burning barn, she inhales so deeply, Nicole slaps her knee.

"Shhh," shushes their aunt.

On the pulpit, the priest's sermon changes to flowers and songs. "Odes to Christ." Spring, the lengthening days, growth and nursing time (for animals). And now he's tallying up instances of light in "harvesting the land." The pig and chicken farmers, like her father, the cattle ranchers ... everything circumscribed by houses of light.

It's like they say: This life has chosen her. Not, as Nicole insists, has it ever, ever been a lifestyle choice.

Along with the pigs, their farm has a few chickens; one crazy, howling rooster; three hens. She's raised them, named them all, brought them into the nest of her arms. Her father tells her that "finally" she'll be able to "take the axe" for the rare family get-together, cousins, uncles and aunts. Two chickens. One for her to kill. One for Nicole to slaughter. But Marie-Thérèse can't. She won't!

"Damn, child! Now, or ... damn, you're getting fuzzy in the head. You'd better, or else ..."

How was it that the 'or else' was so terrible she'd do anything? How?

Below her hands, against the chopping log, the chicken cries. This cry she knows. This chicken she knows.

"Close down on its throat!" That's her father. She shuts her eyes, keeps them shut and finishes the deed, wishing she could shut her ears as well.

"Almost chopped your damned hand off," her father admonishes.

Far worse than that – with her eyes still shut, she feels the warm blood slide over her fingers. Behind, Nicole is laughing herself silly. "Ya' almost did! Ya' almost chopped your goddamned hand off!"

Marie-Thérèse hears a SMACK! A scream. Through the darkness of her closed lids, her sister's scream reverberates through the darkness. Then her father: "I NEVER wanna hear those words from your mouth! Now, step up, Nicole. We need another chicken for that delicious feast with your cousins tomorrow. Marie-Thérèse, open your eyes, for God's sakes. Both of you should be happy! Damn. My daughters, you're farmer's daughters. Remember that!"

After flushing the tick into the toilet, she stares at the faucet, the running water, sliding up to her reflection in the bathroom mirror. Deep eye pockets, irises bursting with gelatinous fibrous tunic (the exact make-up given by a woman she dated who was studying optics). Deep inside, she knows she'll never let things rest with the practical and observable. Just last year, Marie-Thérèse reaffirmed the eye and all that it witnesses in the flames of a promise.

Alongside the collection of elderberry bushes, her spying revealed something she could never … ever speak about.

In the full-moon night, Marie-Thérèse wakes. Rubbing her eyes. Probably a hooting owl that had woken her. She draws the drapes just a little. Across the room, no Nicole in bed, only crumpled sheets and a crease in the white pillowcase: Oh no. Rising burn in her throat. Phlegm clogs her nose, and she reaches for a Kleenex. Nicole's out, night-walking most probably. On the rare occasion her sister makes it outside, she never gets far. Marie-Thérèse sighs, breathes. The fence will keep Nicole in and any predators out. Besides, sleep-walkers are kind of awake, not in danger, like in that TV movie, where the older sister watches her little sister sleepwalk right into a lake and drown.

This time, though, Marie-Thérèse will do some detective work. Maybe her sister's out with a boyfriend – about the only secret she'll share with Marie-Thérèse: Two guys are after her – yep, that's Nicole for you.

The front door's unlocked.

The substance of promises, that's what eyes are made of.

Beneath the splash of moon, Marie-Thérèse is fearless. She's focused more on the year ahead than anything else. A new year in mid-dle school. As usual, Nicole will be hanging out with the popular crowd. So strong and beautiful, so frickin' sure of herself. And there was that: their father's renovation of the guest room, a new bedroom for Nicole. He's let the girls decide. Marie-Thérèse's decided to keep their room, its first coat of yellow paint, chosen by their mother and still on the wall surrounding the beds – that's what their father has told them they could keep, even when the paint's chipping off. "Your mother will be with you like this," he'd said, probably unaware of the undying power of those words or how Marie-Thérèse would think of them as her mother's words. There was a window overlook-ing the pine woods, cut with a few of the deciduous variety. And, finally, the one thing every sibling craves: Privacy!

The grass is deliciously wet beneath her bare feet. The gate's shut. It's all a bit scary. Like getting ready to pour maple syrup on pan-cakes and by accident you choose a poison-laced potion. But no poi-son. No awful stepmother administrating the poison. Their father had never remarried.

In the autumn crispness, Marie-Thérèse breathes in the rot of dying leaves, a peculiarly aromatic odour: about the only kind of dying that's aromatic. Beneath the overbearing stink of manure, there's the exciting change of season.

She passes the pig barn, warm and protected. Her quiet place, where she'll often nod off alongside the animals. They, unlike people, never judged. She could talk to them about anything … she could go in right now, but evening's mystery is far too fragrant.

Thing is, this new year of middle school isn't a huge a deal for Nicole, who's solid. Truth be told, Marie-Thérèse has no frickin' idea who that person is who's no longer going to share her room. Her sister's speeding into a separate orbit. Like the moon up there. Canyons on its face. No, not a face. Clearly, those are canyons. She stops. Surely, her sister is out partying with one of the two boys. Probably she's left the front door unlocked, so she won't have to sneak in through the dormer window. Nicole loves taking chances.

It's been a few years since their father planted anything in this area, which rises above the rest of the field. Last year, the neighbours were speaking wistfully about his quixotic attempts. Wistfully, since it was a particularly cold year. This summer, though, the cluster of elderberry bushes are bursting. She'd pull just one, holding out for that bit of tartness that cuts through the astringent nothingness, a bitterness that oddly sweetened the journey. Then she'll return, maybe lock the front door (a cruel trick on Nicole but well-deserved. And there's always the ladder in the barn).

Moonlight streams through the trees, the deep purple berries almost luminescent. Their father named the berries and the wine after their mother – used their mother's name: Abdélina. The full name, Abdélina Blais, is what Marie-Thérèse whispers now, as she savours the berries' bursting bitterness. Naming, she carries her mother's voice.

When she bought this house on Indian Road, one of the first remodelling activities was repainting the bathroom dark violet.

Later, she found out that what she was really doing was 'flooding,' a psychological term for flushing out (pun intended) the fear – the secrets. Give in to the nightmares until they vanish. At the local hardware store, she found tiles decorated with vines and grapes. No, no elderberries, but grapes would do.

The cluster explodes against her tongue. Smiling, Marie-Thérèse turns. Someone's murmuring – her sister! Closer, and ... two crazies, the night sky illuminating their bodies. She steals a look. Just one. Damn! Their father's gonna be pissed to hell. No way she'll breathe a word, though. Not like Nicole, who'd for sure tell on Marie-Thérèse, if that were her in the grass with a boyfriend. Closer. There's Nicole's long, long hair. But who's that? Who, with the thickness of belly? Not a boyfriend. Not by any stretch of the imagination.

At the sink, Marie-Thérèse runs a hand through her hair. Like Tigre's, it's all tangles. From the living room, there's a distinct scratching: Tigre, ruining the floor. There's a moan, followed by a gruff bark: *Walk! Let's go!* Watching her lips in the mirror, she yells: "But we've just gotten back!"

The softened afternoon light enters the bathroom window, settling on an old towel, folded along its length, the dye worn from years of unfolding along sandy shores. All those beaches! Along the red to rose-pink fabric is a ghostly sailboat, its one billowy sail puffed out in the wind.

Absence of light, or rather too high a frequency, is used to blind and disorient chickens. In such a light, it's easier to string up the birds, slit their throats. The victims, dizzy and blinded, struggle less. In the agricultural business, it's called 'calming.' Agri-business profiteers claim it's 'more humane.'

Marie-Thérèse pulls at the towel. The ghost sailboat remains. Sand beneath her feet; Nicole, their aunt, their father, all of them laughing. Sandcastles, moats and … what's that, edging through? A fortress of discarded shells. Now, how did she salvage that? At least hers, theirs, is a summertime birthday: Summer, a wholly different length of being. Hours before the sun sets; skies full of clouds, tipped with eternal blue, magnificent against the paler tones of blue. Being a sister is like that: paler against a greater blue sky.

Thing is, sisters never listen.

Two years ago, Marie-Thérèse was invited for dinner at Nicole's friend's, where she was politely served a vegan meal. Veal was the main course, pork pie an addition and politeness the problem. Coincidentally, Marie-Thérèse had just shared a little fact with her sister: In neighbouring Québec, white veal calves, pulled from their wailing mothers, spend the whole of their short lives in darkness. Objective: less muscle, so their flesh becomes bright red. At dinner, Marie-Thérèse excused herself one-third of the way through, said she had to leave "in all good conscience."

Nicole called her the next day only to hurl reproaches. "What an idiotic thing to do! You're insane, you know? That's how you come across."

By the end of the year during which that thing happened, the event Marie-Thérèse has labelled 'the elderberry incident', she'd seen everything. All joking aside. She'd seen it all. The elderberry incident was her first baptism. The second occurred under the sun's broad strokes.

A day before winter charges in, the chickens strut around the barn, clucking. Marie-Thérèse strokes the soft feathers of one of their four hens. Standing, she breathes in, opens the barnyard door, the rusted hinges protesting.

As her pupils adjust to the barn's dimmer light, her brain pairs sight to the strangest sound, like the crinkling unwrapping of a Crush candy, Marie-Thérèse moves forward. Not far from the runt her father let her "manage," there they are: the two of them, skein of skin.

Did she catch sight of clothing, knotted in a pile? Father? Sister? Backsides, arms, legs? Years of mostly useless therapy has had her admitting to the most screwed-up question of all. Why had he chosen Nicole and not her? Pulling the shit apart, examining every sick crevice has only brought confusion. And probably Marie-Thérèse has lost her sanity along the way.

When her father walks into the thick-slatted housing for the animals, white paint along the Dutch weathered doors, she feels hot acid rise in her throat. The fresh coat of paint along the doors is her own proud job.

She's outside, as her father pulls the barnyard doors shut. Unlike some of their neighbours, her father kills them himself, is proud of this.

Surrounded by the red-hot sun, she focuses on next week, when school begins – fifth grade. After Labour Day. Hey! Why another day of labour? From inside the barn, grunt-screams. Hands over ears. She shouldn't have wandered over here, shouldn't have stayed. She shouldn't have named them. She'd been warned.

In the hallway, Marie-Thérèse pauses before the photo of the sisters. What will Nicole think? The photograph was snapped with a Nelson Rolleiflex; their father proudly looking down into the lens, creating a resilient image, leagues-removed in beauty from a Polaroid's. The sisters are all smiles and scuffed knees. Nicole's arm crosses the canvas, covering part of her face. There, the barest hint of joy. Yes. There was joy. Seems like a century ago, which of course it was: the last heedless one. But it has occurred to Marie-Thérèse that the *who* she yearns for is a brother. Phantom-limb kind of thing. While sisters have their differing opinions, maybe it would've been different with a brother.

Below, Tigre is grinning, lips sticking to gums, fangs bared not to terrorize but in a shining crescent-smile. This no trick of her imagination. It's a genuine smile, his tail thumping against the floor.

From inside the barn, the pigs' wailing is like an entreaty to heaven. Only, what kind of heaven? The ensuing silence, engulfing. Hand covering her mouth, she focuses on the circles her toe has just drawn in the soil. This small patch of earth is hers. Once a substitute teacher said that they should lay claim to the ground beneath, stay strong with that claim, a claim to the patch upon which they stood. This little square is perfect.

There's a sick, familiar metallic smell and … is that burning? Can't be. Flesh doesn't burn. This flesh has been sliced.

Catching the sky, as she turns — too late. Mucous pools gather beneath the barn doors, miniature streams running into mottled soil. Flexing bare toes, drilling into spongy earth.

Really? Is this what she remembers? Blood travelling from the barn and pooling around her ankles? Maybe she imagined the whole thing. Maybe she looked away to the clouds. Maybe she did feel the liquid, warm, around her ankles. Maybe the pigs cried and the chickens clucked furiously. Maybe she heard them, and maybe all their voices sounded like crying.

Memories, like words, mean nothing, the act of nothing. It's an act of being aware, then going to take down your notes and coming up empty.

At this moment, WALK is the Word, carried down from the Mount, through the desert of stasis, passed down through stories like Tigre's. WALK has meaning. WALK is absolute. So, what's her word, god or equivalent? It has to be Relativism. If you look into their eyes, match their gelatinous mass with your own, what god could distinguish but Relativism, slinking away toward Bethlehem. Yeah, the ancient story of the Sphinx. Sphinxes – beast and human creation, forged from the stone of awe … from the non-human animal and the human. A bridge. She likes the mutt-idea of them.

In fires, human flesh smells like a pig's. Last summer, at a barbeque, a volunteer firefighter revealed this tidbit of information, before announcing "Seconds!" of the "cow's bum steak," smiling at his cleverness, hands over stomach, leaning back on the two legs of his patio chair.

For Tigre, 'walk' equals 'Truth,' and 'Truth,' action. Recently, Marie-Thérèse heard a radio interview with a graphic novelist who makes a living as a journalist; she'd converted to Islam. When the author was young and naïve about the religious views on covering one's body with permanent ink, she'd tattooed one of the over-ninety-nine words for God along her back. Al-Haqq. Ultimate reality; ultimate truth. Nothing is permanent, as the author/journalist well knows.

Summer's come quickly this year, their sixteenth birthday! "Truth or dare?"

"Dare." Marie-Thérèse shoulder-punches her sister.

"Dare what?"

"Dunno."

"How about truth, then?"

Tongue pushing against teeth, pocket-pooling her saliva. Marie-Thérèse spits. Dares are about climbing trees. Last year, she fell; bruised her arm; shushed Nicole, who went and told their father anyways. Marie-Thérèse was grounded for a week. This is a biggie, though. Marie-Thérèse is gonna finally ask.

Annoyed, Nicole scrunches up her face. "Truth. That's what you want?"

"Yep." Impossible question. "I want to know —"

"What? Whadd'ya want to know? What the hell d'ya want to know?"

"I … about you, Dad." There. The cat is out of the bag, but this feline's all prickly and awful. No way she'll be able to return it to its secret box.

Nicole's dark eyes are jumping out of their sockets. Slowly, she sets down her blade of grass and stands. "That's it then."

And … she's off. There's not a soul around Nicole can't outrun.

Marie-Thérèse carries no thoughts. Big fat BLANK. Straightening out her bare legs, she pulls on the long-bladed grass, until one glides willingly from the ground. Broadening the blade between thumbs and forefingers, she whispers in the wind … out comes a tremendous bugle chord.

Tigre's leash feels strange in her hands. He's pulling, his harness bulking. "Okay, Tigre. One more walk."

They'll be going further into the country tomorrow. "You and me?" There's a mink farm she has to scout out. Probably a bad idea bringing him along. Tigre plants his wide paws before the door. She stops, thinking about the mink farm, planning. In a sense, her work will be the fulfillment of a promise.

Recently, while biking along country roads, in Restigouche, she stopped at an over-one-hundred-year-old vegetable farm. At the edge of the fields, rolling hills span the fir-backed New Brunswick land. A roadside vegetable stand blends into the landscape. Inside, simply, is a till. No one is 'manning' the till. Instructions for payment are written on a chalkboard above the bins. Fragrant carrots, peppers and fresh greens are there for the taking. She was picking out some fat peppers, when a couple from Ontario pulled up. "Nice how you do things out here."

Nope, she wouldn't disabuse them of their stories, not this one. "Sure," she answered. "In this province, we believe in people's honesty." Operative word – 'believe.' Lately, she's heard that all over the country, farm stands are standing, empty of vendors, with everything left up to the purchaser's honesty.

Closing in on the barn, she sees the windows are splashed with shit. Her flashlight illuminates rows of gestation crates. There's movement inside. Emerging from the darkness, and now she can see blue lines along pinkish backs … bruises and open wounds. With a nod, her friend flips the switch on the portable generator, brought along to mute the pigs' crying.

After what seems like a harrowing, sweat-drenched full twenty-four hours – but half an hour at most – they remove many of the babies and, somehow this time, two sows. The other sows have to be left behind.

The two mother pigs can barely move, but there are twenty-one humans, with (for the first time, and they're proud of this) four large wheelbarrows. They've also wheeled the generator over. Long ago, she learned that success is the art of thinking of everything. The pigs' cries might alert the family, snug under their plucked-feather duvets. And their blueprints for this revolutionary act must contain structural integrity. They'd even run a dress rehearsal, to assess the quality and efficacy of the generator's rich humming vibrato.

Consensus: Once the animals are in the trucks, they'll get the hell out. Only Marie-Thérèse will remain. Takes someone with that kind of muscle, gripping the proverbial cloth between clenched jaw. Slice of moon pools in the narrow rivulets of rain. Tasting shit in her mouth, breathing in sulphur. Paces away, the house is staring from its two-storey windows. With its wide roof, charming porch, it's all nothing short of epic. The white slats, luminescent. Behind the house, the long barn's prison doors are closed.

Marie-Thérèse clips a leash to Tigre's harness. With uncharacteristic strength, she pushes against the door. Since April, the wood's been bulking. Time to repair or replace. That's what happens, doors lasting only so long before they prevent a person from getting out.

After the pigs are liberated, she stays on, crying, wiping away her tears. No, no room, no time. Outside, through one of the upstairs windows, a light comes on. Stepping backwards, wiping out her tracks. Methodical, though, and that ole heart of hers is pounding.

Concentrate. Breathe. Step. Smell that fear. With a start, she realizes the fear isn't just hers. Here, in the mud lie years of captivity and confining. Surrounding her, brushing against the leaves, undeterred is the rustling of rust-iron ghosts. One more step, and … the light remains. She's close to the road now. Quietly, she opens the car door. If she looks back, like Orpheus, who, with a catch of breath, realizes what he's lost … damn! What's the use? Those sows who remain will have to meet their fate. And the farmer will fill up the stalls with so many more victims.

Maybe it was after her father suffered his first stroke. His second came two years later. That's when she realized patience is worth far more than an old house and barn. She'd leave nothing. Absolutely nothing. No residue. She waited until that ole will came their way.

Evening's moon-crescent lights up the country darkness. It's been roughly a year since he died. Odd how quickly an idea can spring into action. Next year, there'll be a lunar eclipse: appropriately enough, a rather lucky year. But there's no time to waste. This season, winter's cold dampness serves as cover for the fire. The flame won't catch any unintended victim.

Under night's veil, she brings the car to a rolling stop. Dungeon of dreaming. The farm, however, is as real as the weeds growing solid and strong: les mauvaises herbes. What will Nicole say? Fuck that. Here is Marie-Thérèse; and there, back home, asleep beneath warm sheets, is her sister. Marie-Thérèse turns off the motor. Weariness floods her bones. Keeping the headlights on, she opens the door, unlocks the trunk, takes out the kerosene jug and lugs it to the barn.

She senses a weird surge of energy through her muscles. This patch of earth is hers. At her feet, the kerosene, still firmly capped, releases its potent fumes. Here, where her father made her butcher each and every one.

He insisted. She persisted, kept on naming them, refusing to help him, even when he asked, then commanded her, knowing she'd get the belt.

One day, she relented.

It'll be the smallest runt, someone she's raised. Evenings, driving the nightmares away, she would make a bed in the hay, alongside the littlest one.

No exaggeration to call her property destroyer. The point isn't avoiding pain. Billions are hurting. Billions have been hurting. It's about lighting a match. Primary rule – confront your own demons. A few months ago, her latest therapist grabbed a book from a shelf and practically threw it into her lap. The title was German: *Ein Psycholog.* "This." The therapist pointed.

"I don't read German."

"You know Nietzsche. 'He who has a *Why* to live for can bear almost any *How*.'"

"*We-ell,* Nietzsche's idea of will is interesting, but –"

"Finding happiness, searching, isn't the goal." The therapist folded her hands. "The search for happiness defeats its pursuit. You need something more. The real fear, claims this author, is the possibility of experiencing suffering without meaning." She stopped, breathed, collapsed her hands in her lap. "You need meaning in suffering."

"That sounds stupid. And …" Marie-Thérèse turned over the book, skimmed the blurbs. "So, you're saying I need meaning in my suffering? What about –" She wanted to say "the animals" but refrained. No use. Not even with this therapist, who at least seemed to get that elemental thing that compelled Marie-Thérèse to go out, into night's swollen mercy.

Therapist-wise words: "This is Vicktor Frenkl's understanding of Nietzsche. Frenkl dictated this in NINE days, after surviving a concentration camp. When they made the selections, he scraped his cheeks red with bits of glass to look healthy. It's not enough, to find meaning. This is the first step, the realization that it's there. The second is to create from this something more."

The therapist paused, looking pleased with herself. "Marie-Thérèse, what you have to realize is you've done this already."

Suckling pig, her father's called him. Her secret name for him is more truthful – Little Burning Fire.

A little guy with a huge personality, pulling comical gestures, sharing his world with a thousand different vocalizations. Marie-Thérèse understands every word. Like the others, he has special sound-words for humour, for laughter, for grief. For love. His words, like those of the other pigs, are nuanced, particular to him. And he's saved her.

Her father is angry.

"What're waiting for? I'm speaking to you! Good God, it's for you. I'm doing this for you. Go on."

Not a whip, not a gun. He's holding nothing to her head.

Only now she wonders how she could have felt the cold metal barrel against her scalp.

Two more young pigs cower in the corner – they're being fattened up. Pigs will eat themselves into obesity. History has archived their ancestors as composters, garbage dispensers. But those people who know pigs know they're far cleaner and wiser than most any animal, including humans.

"I'm sorry," she cries, closing her eyes against her friend's pleading.

After their father's death, Marie-Thérèse stood in front of the sisters' inheritance: the barn. There was a gasoline container at her feet.

Standing before the barn now, kerosene below, "I made you a promise," she says out loud, her voice resonating in night's silence, her breath's steam dissipating. No bats out tonight. No hooting winter owls.

To her left, there's a dumpster. Parts of their house. Here, on the fresh snow are splinters and broken planks, the work of a crew the sisters hired.

Just a few weeks ago, she and Nicole were scrounging around for anything left in the house. Nicole's scream shook the house. Their mother's violin! It had been buried beneath the floorboards of their father's bedroom. He'd shut the instrument in its case and inserted it beneath the floorboards: a little ole coffin. "It's a miracle," the luthier informed them. The wood wasn't so damaged that the instrument couldn't be refurbished. Marie-Thérèse hasn't told Nicole about the photo of the two sisters, which she'd found almost as soon as Nicole had left.

Marie-Thérèse glances to the right. In the fallow field lie tools of a lost era: a thresher and tractor. Deserted landscape of forgetfulness.

The snow will be more forgiving.

"You're next," she says, staring at the barn. Startled by the strength of her voice, Marie-Thérèse kicks the container, mesmerized by the viscous stream of gasoline, clearing the bottom of the rotting doors. She breathes in the candied fumes of poison.

As for any mice who might be left, she's tried flushing them. Generally, these rodents are remarkable escape artists, but, yes, there may be some left. Hopefully, the smoke will scare them off. The fire will be isolated from the woods, a landscape of snow between.

The lit match draws a perfect arc in the clear, windless night. Celebrations and rituals, death and life – they all leave residue.

She flings another. Cinders rise; embers sparking, like miniature silver birds. With a flash, the barn becomes a raging inferno, crackling, consuming the familiar lumbar beams. The weirdest pain ever crushes her, bringing her down, fittingly perhaps, to her knees. Orange, red, vectors of blue transform the serenity. There's an audible rushing, like the fast flood tides of the Bay of Fundy. One Titan orange flame springs, its great tongue licking the charcoal air. Marie-Thérèse's coughing but smiling, then laughing. She rises as the flames stretch up, up to salvation.

The front door creaks on its hinges. Her laugh comes unexpectedly, like a welcomed sneeze. Tigre bounds out the door and off the porch, into the present-day. The first step must seem like heaven to him.

Love Along the 63rd – A Symphony

EARLIER, NADINE, her sister Virginie and her niece Joy had been deposited by the bus driver in the middle of nowhere and everywhere, the tires coughing up silt as the driver started up again, halting further down the gravel road for playful ground squirrels. Touring Denali Park, Nadine felt queasy, as her uncertainty read the unknown. And now, "Look!" Joy shouts, mapping the gravel road with dogged steps: steps like ink to the story – the story being this: Nadine's trip to snow-capped Denali.

Movement I. Adagio

Denali National Park, lying six million acres north of Anchorage. Big Mountain, Tall One, named by the many First people of the region, in the language of Koyukon of the Athabasca Nation, Tanana, Deg Xinag, and Holikachuk, Kuskokwim, Ahtna and Dena'ina. Over 6,100 metres to sky. Beneath its summit, clouds convene, in competing languages of mist. Nadine and Virginie were *en route*, from Anchorage, Virginie's home, with Joy, "ma cocotte," Nadine called her. Only Joy isn't so little anymore. On their way to the park, Virginie shrieked, freaked out Nadine, who caught her sister's hands flying off the wheel. "Drive! You're driving."

"Look! Denali's peak is visible! Nous sommes tellement chanceuses! Superbe. Mon Dieu."

Nadine's attention was captured by the stillness of the ghost mountain, sliced by clouds.

In the early afternoon, the sweet aroma of pine invaded all senses. The sisters set down two neat bundles. Her sister tried persuading la cocotte to help them stake in the tents.

Now, at a beaming seven years old, Joy eerily resembles their dad, who died years ago.

The child has offered to help, but offers are no match for the caprice and exuberance of childhood. "Mommy, *you* promised we'd go hiking!"

Virginie sighed.

"But you promised!"

"A promise is a promise," claimed the mother. "Now, come over and help us, ma cocotte."

Movement I. Allegro molto (development of theme)

It was February. "Come out this July," Virginie tunnelled into the phone. Nadine, who kept their childhood home, Montréal, had lamented that she did need a change. This first visit to Virginie's place in Anchorage would be welcome. Virginie had been living in BC and following her divorce had jumped at the opportunity for a job as a botanist in Alaska. "Why not move there?" she asked rhetorically, mentioning the sisters' dual citizenship through their mother.

And perhaps Nadine should be happy for her sister, who's found love in her field and peace with her ex, Joy's father, who's taken his earnings on pipelines and gone to build "experimental" wells in Southwest BC, along the Flathead River that flows into Montana. The custody agreement has given him most of summer with Joy. But this year he'd decided to take his dream journey to Thailand, so Joy would spend the months with her mother.

"If I can afford the fare, I'll come." A journey to Alaska! Then, lucrative heavens above! Nadine's audition had successfully landed her second violinist for Montréal's symphonic orchestra.

Movement I. Allegro molto, E minor

Jumping off the bus in Denali, Nadine felt assailed by berries. They were everywhere, among brambled vegetation. Kneeling down, plying them from clusters, she felt like she was on that final crawl before a child's first step. Tundra brush and ochre peaks. Nature's inference, a composition in motion; her musician's ear tuned to rolling tundra, scrubbed close, like a child alongside its mother's yellow skirts. Dream clouds. In their wake, ominous shadows, shape shifting along mountainsides. She felt pushed, anxious, not unlike that time, during practice, when their conductor forced more bow from the strings than the composer Bartok, himself, would've advised.

If Nadine were to play this scene? Probably, Dvořák's *New World Symphony*, No. 9. Perfect number nine. But ... and here's a very *looong* 'but', the 'new world' view would have to be modified. New to her, oui, but not to those living here, to those who have lived here for millennia.

Sure, it's possible, she thinks. *We could be anything out here.* Thoughts of childhood, hiking with their father; then, skiing. Cross-country laces through snow had brought her sister close to Olympic tryouts. Botany turned out to be her mainstay, poetry her hobby. Virginie's been clearing up the misnomer ever since. "Hobby? It's in my blood. Is blood fed by a hobby?"

Virginie's dreams steered her north, to study the paths of plants without borders: the sedge along Alaskan rivers. "Incredible similarities between the sedge down south and their tundra brethren."

Brethren? Botany becomes poetry. Another quirk in her sister's DNA: poetry. As for this botanist's recent poem? *The way a needle means everything, the thick-spun conifer rising to meet the wind, though throttled and thrown by its anger, never releasing its robe. The way a seed disturbs those who live on fruit, seeking shelter beneath.* Nadine had emailed a trite "Interesting verse," hoping her sister wouldn't ask for more.

Movement II. Largo, E major

Nadine too needs editing, only with relationships. Six-and-a-half years gone in one *poof!* On that fateful evening, her girlfriend, Suzanne, claimed she didn't know how to say this, but (oh, the perdition of love, especially as it's being taken away) …

"Say what?!"

"C'est la fin, Nadine," Suzanne's wild hair, framed by the window, Nadine's perspective placing Mont Royal's cross directly on top of her now ex-lover's head. Suzanne's explanation was lifted from jazz lyrics: "I love you but can't reach you."

Nadine was hyperventilating.

"Are you okay?"

"Course not! Jeezus!" So, who else was around when …

1. Nadine had spent many months consoling Suzanne over her bankruptcy declaration.

2. Nadine had offered compassion after Suzanne's failed course in "The ONE program that matched [her] talents."

3. Nadine had listened to Suzanne's broken record lament about her HUGE compromise in taking decent work at the bakery but with a "MASSIVE" salary hit.

4. Throughout it all, Nadine had been more than present. Moments are remembered in minutia: broken tiles along the counter, sifting flour, rolling out sourdough, taking the fermenting dough, "a pet," with them, to visit Nadine's mother. That's what Suzanne loved – making bread. And Nadine's mother, with her delusions: "She was always talking about herself, how she helped you. A LOT of self-praise coming from this woman."

"What the fuck?"

"Don't swear. It's just what I … I'm … forget it."

"Course I won't forget it. And if Suzanne were a guy, you'd be fine."

"Absolutely not!"

Nadine almost added: 'When it came to Virginie's ex-husband, you said nothing.' Instead: "What *things* did you see Suzanne getting away with?"

Endless, circular avoidance: this was the geometric shape to her mother's fear.

The fear of loneliness, Nadine's certain, is what drove Virginie into her ex's arms, before, of course, he became (thank God) her ex. Excitement, along the border of fear, had given Virginie a home in Anchorage, not far, Nadine was happy to learn, from the stunning Chugach mountains.

Nadine's fear? Is her job secure? Is any violinist's *or* musician's *or* anyone's job secure? Her job? "Call it 'profession'," her sister has advised, seeing as it is a way of being. Nadine is second violin, bowing her way through assonant and dissonant tonal curves, carrying the harmonics, "the embroidered cushions," joked her stand-partner, whose house is full of embroidery brought over from her home in Bengaluru. This has been Nadine's life so far: Playing strings in the land of snow, crystalized along sidewalks, bringing down the unassuming pedestrian to *crack!* Happened one winter. Instead of giving in, Nadine took up running. Perhaps that's why, heart beating, she raced along one Denali Park hillside to pull up monkshood. Virginie's brutal "Careful!" rang in her ears. Years ago, a young actor, hiking in Newfoundland, had pulled up the flower, labelled arsenic by the Roman naturalist, Pliny the Elder. In the actor's case, the flower had left deadly residue on his hand. People should respect plants, her sister pointed out. Not fear them but respect them. But Pliny, Virginie told her, was allergic to women, an allergy that manifested in a treatise on how to treat them when their menstrual blood was flowing.

And mountains: Respect them as well, claimed Virginie. A forestry intern in the park had fallen to her death down a deceivingly slippery slope. "It's not the bears," Virginie said. "It's what you least imagine: poisonous plants and mountains."

"And sometimes the blood from a woman's womb," Nadine said, smirking.

Movement II. Largo (harmonic progression)

For Nadine, another vocation (as critical to her well-being as music) is cycling. Treaded rubber along packed snow or in summer, as she and Suzanne would bike, observing Montréal's porch loungers, passing staircases winding into iron lattices and the 'Fashionables,' Suzanne called them, as the two biked along. "Hey, that's Farhat-Frames," strolling with "Crystal Blue Persuasion."

When Nadine biked through Montréal's parc La Fontaine on her drum-brake antique with wood pedals, retirees playing pétanque turned around to call: "C'est une belle bicyclette, là! – est vieille, eh?"

Passing snarled traffic, darting into alleyways, coming upon secret gardens. Earlier this summer, Nadine invested in a good multi-speed titanium. She was off to Vermont's Northeast Kingdom, with a stopover in Stanstead, at the home of the Birdman, who carves miniature birds out of wood scavenged from the forest floor. Nadine was choosing a gift, when his boyfriend walked in, leading a New Guinea dog: an astonishing creature with short-cropped fur. "Listen to this." The boyfriend lifted his hands, conducting the dog – to sing! More like the sound of a seal becoming a wolf. Nadine surprised herself, punctuating the recital with unusual plaudit.

"New Guineas are rare," he said, visibly glowing with pride. "Different pitches."

"I'm a musician," she professed. "Yes, the dog does have talent."

Returning to her bicycle, she paused at a miniature windmill alongside a miniature pond. "Luna moths die in there," the Birdman said, coming up behind. "Tricked by the reflection of moonlight."

Jumping, Nadine smiled. When she looked back at the miniature candy-cane coloured mill with its mouse-sized pond, she remembered Suzanne's Sholem Aleichem story of the wise, aka fools, of Chelm capturing the moon in a barrel of rainwater. But these moths weren't fools, only dying to reach the light.

"A bike! That's a long way. And maybe a bit crazy. Wait. I have a gift." The Birdman ran in, returned with a palm-sized carving of a goose, fanned feathers. Now, how did he do that? So skilful. "Here's something Canadian." He smiled. Nadine bit her tongue.

Along the route, she was assailed by bitter fuel, the perfume of fresh fields. What orchestration!

Out on the tundra, collecting berries and beneath mountains' shadows, Nadine tried to "delete her brain store." Soon she'd be returning to the pedestrian from this Elysian landscape – to the steel-spiked Mount Royal cross, whose residence Jacques Cartier initiated for King François I, shaking hands with the Iroquois to seal the deal. Mount Royal and Mount McKinley, both extinct volcanoes. 'McKinley,' named after the assassinated president, by settlers, or white ghost Ohio legislators, who wouldn't let go. But Nadine's let go. Hasn't she?

Crowberries have a sum-zero taste – like forgetting or never having been born.

"Yuck!" Joy screamed into the silence, spitting out the mushed berry.

They're rare, crowberries. It's been a summer of rare sightings – eagles, one shy lynx – and not so rare Dall sheep, in white kernels along sesame-brown ridges; a moose; four caribou.

Green-patch mountains, shrouded by oblong clouds. In the distance, slate-grey ridges, land chiselled from glaciers. Beneath Denali's ghostly presence, Nadine has accepted love as tasting like rivers. Picking berries and glancing towards the rises, she felt shame or lust, the aching that Thoreau described in watching a groundhog move along the grass.

"Not rare, these berries." Joy kept spitting. "Just yuck."

Crowberries, part of the heather family. *Love at first sight. Simplicity, as taste vanishes.*

In the spread of mountainside, Nadine realized taste is two-tiered. While the story, like a some berries' tartness, arrives in the second chapter (a symphonic musical score, orchestrated for brass), the crowberry's is given in the opening chord ... but not before the connection's made, when there's more to lose.

"Hey!" Joy, framed in arc of sky; oval eyes, buzzing brown hair. Spitting image of their father, the same incorrigible wonder.

"How do they get it so beautiful out here," she asked her niece.

Joy held up her hands. "It just comes that way." Bubbly child laughter.

Movement II. Largo, D♭ major

Seeding. To seed. Suzanne wanted children, and Nadine would carry, since she was the one with "the better DNA."

Out in Vermont, while listening to the singing dog, Nadine wondered if such a companion could've saved their relationship. Singing dogs, Vermont mountains; a story that perhaps had started with Nadine's father, who passed away ten years after leaving their mother. As a doctor of broken hearts, he'd overlooked his own.

Love, Nadine has realized is best read by those who know how to bank seeds. Never for those who die of broken hearts or drown, trying to reach the moon.

Lunch on the mountain was freshly picked berries, hummus sandwiches and apples with peanut butter. That's when Nadine learned about Johnny Appleseed, gifting seeds to settlers moving across the prairies. "The Puritans fermented the apples into spirits," Virginie told her.

"Cider?"

"Not exactly, but what's interesting is the grafting that led to all those varieties of apples."

Nadine yanked up a blade of grass. "Apple wine for the settlers."

"You need fat grass!" Joy pressed thumbs and forefingers into her blade, producing a painful re bemol, then sol dièse.

Nadine repositioned her niece's thumbs, thinking about their conversation on the ride over, on how the Aleut state – later, Alaska – went to the Americans. America's deal with Russia sealed Canada's Confederation with the Brits and swept up land from the Coastal and Inland Nations in what is now BC. Alaska was sold for pennies.

Virginie was munching. "Farming for spirits."

"What's spirits?" That was Joy.

Childhood, with legs for trees, tongues for questioning. Nadine dipped into the bread, broke off a doughy wheel. "Spirits, for adults."

"Like ghosts?"

The sisters burst out laughing. Joy stomped about.

"Yes, sweetheart," Virginie consoled.

Nadine was considering. "Hmm, ghosts, distilling cider."

Finally, Joy had it: the grass-blade song!

"Well done," Nadine congratulated. She sat back against the dry grass, eyes closed, blinked once. "So, that's who they learn about here in the U S of A."

"Who?" Virginie sounded as naïve as her daughter.

"Johnathan Appleseed." Nadine sensed that her own voice was being spoken not by her, through her own vocal chords, but sung by someone else: the ghosts of this mountain. She laughed, turned to her sister, who said: "Nadine, you're crazy, vraiment. But you're right. Those are the people we learn about here, sing about. The so-called 'pioneers'."

Above her body, her spine against the solidness of the mountain, Nadine flexed her fingers in air quotes. "Not about Louis Riel, we don't learn about him either: his battle for his people, the Métis, to save their land from MacDonald's push to build the railroad. Not about Sitting Bull and Wovoka."

"No," Virginie said. "We don't hear about them."

The sisters had learned of Wovoka on a childhood trip to Nevada, much later saw the name resurface, as they combed the internet for 70s music and found the group *Redbone*, inspired by the Paiute-born Wovoka, who, it is said, gifted the Lakota of Wounded Knee with the Ghost Dance.

"We're not *taught* about them, so our ears aren't given the chance to *hear!*" Nadine stood so quickly, blood rushed to her head. She widened her jaw, put a hand to her head, focused on the remains of their picnic. The crumbs: Would they be eaten by bears, ground squirrels or birds? Not as many birds as she'd expected. In fact, the skies weren't teeming with birds *or* insects. Odd, wasn't it? She asked Virginie, who didn't seem to have answers to this one. But no bears either. Would they see even one? Caribou, Dall sheep, ground squirrels, but no bears.

Virginie murmured, "Joy gets nothing at school."

"What?!" Joy sashayed over.

"Nothing, ma cocotte. Well, actually, yes, something, Pumpkin. We're just talking about how you don't learn *anything* about the people who lived here first." She drew an arc in the air. "Here, everywhere. Whose land was stolen."

"Who stole it?"

"Good question. Short answer: our ancestors. Long answer: forthcoming. Tonight, we'll catch up with that story at the campsite."

"They're starting to add more to the curriculum by us," Nadine said.

"Hmm," Virginie answered, standing. She carefully folded one unused napkin – dexterity spiced with nerve-wracking meticulousness. Nadine scanned the horizon. How to articulate this beauty?

On the bike to Vermont, she'd brought along a cheap violin. Not as difficult to carry such an instrument, not as difficult as had been prophesized by Suzanne. Nothing was as difficult anymore. Playing at night, solo campsite, Nadine had regained her sanity.

So, the tune for these mountains? What resounds is the kind she plays for a living, classical. Sonata in A minor. A few flats: la bémol or une mineure harmonique, bringing sol bémol to natural.

From every point in the park, Denali's peak is visible. Below, glacially cut fissures make up the finger lakes. After lunch, they'd hiked down. From tundra to glacial sediment, ice has sculpted these valleys, trailing wet sediment, like snail's slime. To Nadine, it has become more, not less, inconceivable that glaciers move over dry land. Perhaps a more appropriate interpretation for this magnificence: solo violin piece, veering into empty.

Down in the valley, Joy wrote her name in the silt. To no one in particular, Virginie murmured: "In geological terms, these mountains are young." How unfathomable, Time, hidden by being too large to comprehend.

Movement III. Scherzo: Molto vivace – Poco sostenuto

Joy trills her "Lo-o-o-ok!"

In the creek-bed nearby, the water runs percussive, polishing rocks. Nadine's intention: to meet those waters, then cut a perpendicular path to the two above. In view of thunderous, snow-clad Mount Denali, she might continue forever deep in thought, until Joy's trilling call and Virginie's "Nadine!"

In the distance … a bear! This beast is actually not so close; over a crest, along another hillside, but all warnings convene: "Grizzlies reach thirty-five miles an hour." Holding her breath, Nadine ventures another look. The grizzly is sniffing the air.

"WALK," Virginie yells. Nadine begins the ascent, glancing once only, catching her breath. The bear is running now, thick swatches of skin dancing over musculature. *Focus!* On the snaking striations of colour, the soil and parched grass of the tundra. Fear is odourless.

Her eyes, sharpened, forge a pathway to the two above. Resounding thuds echo inside her own tremulous gasps.

Bear. Human. Imprinting soil with sound, touch, odour.

Joy, above her, along the gravel road, sprints forward. Nadine hears her sister's reprimanding. Sudden movements tantalize curious predators. With strong knees, Nadine takes the incline, firmly planting each foot on a rock, observing all there is to take in, regarding that rock. No, she won't look up. Not yet! She remembers a Tlingit legend of a heroine who takes off her clothes. The bear, ashamed, turns away.

"You're close!" Virginie's voice, a spear through her heart.

Movement III. Scherzo: Molto vivace, Trio in C major

Bear. Insurgent warrior. Lone traveller. Mothers protecting children from dads who may consume them. Virginie's offered some biologists' theory that cubs are raised near humans to thwart infanticide. Which means they risk the bullet, Nadine had thought.

Caribou. Quiet, strong eyes. Bird's eye, different perspective. Can animals reinvent themselves? *I hope this serves to lure you back one day,* Virginie's friend has written on the inside cover of her book on Alaska. With one deep inhalation, Nadine joins the duo. Sweat in her pits, pressure in her chest.

"Look." Virginie pulls Nadine close. The bear has stopped and … what's that? Up now on two hind legs, s/he lifts a snout into the air. Sniffing again.

Nadine's vision tunnels into beaded eyes, until it's no longer about proximity. Here is Nadine, and, here, the bear … now, dropping to all fours. Clear movement through broad shoulders. The bear's shrugging! And, now, the formidable creature turns away.

Movement IV. Finale: Allegro con fuoco, E minor

"Creature," Virginie sings in the evening breeze. "'From 'creation'; assumes a creator."

This is how the story ends: Along E minor, with love and memory, perhaps a residue of fear, held in the uncanny nature of any piece with sharps (as Nadine has always found) and ending with Denali's snow peak; only imagined, as now unseen.

Every animal has a name for love.

Near the 63rd, the summer-night sky is chalk-navy. When Joy and Virginie visited Québec, Virginie recounted for Nadine the story of her friend's toddler, born in upper Alaska, in autumn, and, therefore, unfamiliar with the sun. Below the 60th, the sun was fearsome. "Imagine that," Nadine murmured. "Imaginez d'avoir peur du soleil."

Campfire flames thread through dust veils. The mountains' outline is pen-stroked into darker blue; midnight's sunlight, dim at this witching hour of 22h, moulding fantastical shapes.

Virginie yawns. "It's late."

Nadine squeezes Joy's shoulders.

"Hey!" Joy's voice rides the sparkling embers. "Aunt Nadine?" Palms on the ground, yoga style: body slanted forward. "What do you think?"

"About your downward dog pose?"

"Not dogs. About bears."

Must be something in those flames. Nadine's thoughts are on horrors, deeper to the mystery of life, how a bear's skeleton resembles a human's. *The brutal, unforgiving tempo of relationships.*

Movement IV. Finale: Allegro con fuoco, E major

"Aunt Nadine!"

Virginie throws in a twig. "Don't scream, Pumpkin."

"But I'm asking something."

"Go ahead." Nadine moves closer to her niece and the popping embers – a little, burning village inside the disintegrating logs.

"Will bears hurt us?"

"Not here," Virginie's voice rises above the pastiche of campers' voices. "And only those protecting their babies will even *think* about hurting us … but not to hurt us."

Nadine falls back into the cushioned soil. "Good point."

Virginie's in teacher mode. "Mama bears, of course, but I'd do the same. Still, they've never attacked here, in this park, not to my knowledge."

Nadine sits up. "I think that grizzly was curious. We're strangers to her land."

"Her?" Joy stands straight up.

"Franchement, I think she just wanted to check us out."

"Check *you* out," Joy says, tailing with laughter.

"Probably curious," Virginie says.

The flames lick the subarctic *crepuscule* – dusk. There's a wizardly crackling, the incense of wood, a potpourri that Nadine configures as love or as a love letter to Love, signed: 'With deepest gratitude, Time.' The fragrance is grounding, onion-y, a playful onion-y fugue. If only they could stay here. If only … Nadine turns to her sister. "It's beautiful out here."

Virginie stands, brushes off her behind, evidently pleased with the freedom to do so. "C'est l'heure de faire dodo, Joy. Time for bed. Way past that time, in fact. Here, along the 63rd, we'll be sung to sleep by love," she sings, echoing Nadine's thoughts. "Love … like … well, you should know this, Nadine. It's like a symphony."

"Con fuoco, and with one, lone sharp," Nadine says, smiling at her niece.

Raw Sugar

Have you heard these blues
That I'm going to sing to you
When you hear them, they will thrill you
Through and through
They're the sweetest blues you ever heard
Now listen and don't say a word
Sugar blues, everybody singing sugar blues
—*Sugar Blues,* Lucy Fletcher

SHE'S WAITING to be seated, as her boyfriend converses with strangers in the queue. Social ease, his middle name. *Entropy* is what she's thinking: The restaurant's glasses, intact, their factory seams outlining technological innovation; the water somewhere beneath Montréal streets, in pipes cut from polyvinyl chloride or steel.

Only a half hour later, when the glass shatters and the water spills, when the beast descends, will she realize that it's her fault, that she has been and will forever be on the shit side of the equation.

Right now, they're still in line at this café in Montréal's Mile End. Couches and mismatched chairs butler jean-clad bottoms and yoga pants – which probably fuel the premonition, a fiery speculative inferno. Coffee blues or nausea from odours that weren't *this* powerful yesterday. Surely not. And why not? Why not?! No, can't be!

In the now of this moment, there's a hot gush of recycled air, almost tempting, along her thighs. Generally, she likes this place, but weirdly right now the generally inviting aroma of roasting coffee (though she doesn't drink coffee) is pulling the acidic remains of yesterday's combustion from her stomach.

"Let's go somewhere else."

"Don't be silly." Perfect teeth. She knows there's more in the thin foam of saliva along his lips, more in the insipid cajoling: an acknowledgement, perhaps.

"Being here is what we need. Good sandwiches, great coffee –"

"I don't drink coffee."

"Great company," he says, smiling but moving no closer.

"Combien? Deux?"

The hostess must've spent a good year cultivating that look. Trustworthy brown eyes, lips slightly open, arms in a perfect L, shoulder to wrist, tasty line from crotch to knee, tight yoga-stretch jeans. Holding two menus like a fan, she chaperones the two to their seats, each lovely half-circle of her bottom moving in syncopation. Ends with her dance alongside a table that's sandwiched between two occupied tables: One of mirth and one of sorrow.

Table of Two, Table of Mirth: Two women, laughing over heaping sandwiches; closer, their lips almost touching.

Table of One, Table of Sorrow: One man; straight chin; sucked-in chest; firm, black jean-jacketed shoulders. Drinking … is that tea?

"Merci." She smiles at the hostess, then gestures to the man's saucer.

"Thé de menthe … tea, s'il vous plaît."

Her boyfriend orders coffee. The hostess nods politely and tells them that someone will be coming by to take the rest of their orders. Yes, of course, and probably the owner, who likes to take on all the tasks of her employees.

Saturday interlude. Pause before Sunday. Time to relax. But that isn't going to happen, especially considering what she needs to tell him, to tell her boyfriend, who now is tilting his chair forward, ready to offer something intriguing, something erudite: a curiosity. Caramelized, his words, sweet-coated. There's a well-known play she's re-reading, by Shakespeare. Hamlet, with his Ophelia. Nope, not *his* Ophelia, not Hamlet's. If anything, Ophelia is her own woman. Anyways, the more suitable theatrical ensemble for this situation would be *Othello*. Only in this particular case at this particular café, Iago isn't lying.

That's what she has to say to this man: 'Iago isn't lying.' But her attention is diverted to the table. If she were the proprietor, she'd place photographs of women between transparent glass and wood. On the walls, she'd hang portraits of women, chested in lace. Dark midnight curls – Ouf! She clutches her stomach, rides a hand down. It's not her stomach, no. Shit!

He's still talking. *Focus.* Forget the midnight curls … focus on this strange sense of nausea, with no bile, just pain. Concentrate on the abstract circle paintings decorating the wall behind his head, a few with a red dot on the bottom-right frame, marking their recent sale. On their table, twin watermarks, one from his glass, one from hers. And near his saucer: a raw sugar packet, ripped open. The jagged top resembles Lilliputian mountains, salted sea. So like her home, on the other side of this continent, where the earth reaches to the obliqueness of clouds.

He runs a thumb along this jagged edge. How effortless everything is for him; how easily things enter, make their way through, come to him rather than he to them.

"That's it," she says.

"What is?"

"Just realized."

"Oui?" But she doesn't answer right away. Lifting her water glass, the ice crackling. *This is the thing,* she thinks. *The thing that unites us.* Out loud: "I just realized that we're alike, you and I, from the land of mountains."

He laughs. Fine, let him. Her belief system is flawless. They're both from ruptured land. Hers is made up of pointed glacial peaks. His, tapered summits brushed of youth.

Stirring his cup o' coffee, pool of caffeine absorbing the sugar, his metal spoon pulling in any stray crystals. *Rain* is her thought. *Always raining where I'm from.* Her tea bag listlessly rounds out the saucer. And the nausea – from the tea? From. The. Tea??? No, she's been feeling this way since before she woke up … this she knows because of her dreams. Been feeling this way since – NO! Do NOT go there.

His face – what can you call that face? *Chiselled* is a good word, the 'consensus among friends. Today, though, his pallor is unusually pale, almost granite, like all the faces here. Silently, she sings: *Oh, wintry face, I may not love you anymore.* One exception being the tanned snowbird retirees, in Florida now, who occasionally return for a medical visit or just for a visit. None here now. Come late June, the olive in his complexion will take its rightful place. *Or …* she practically shivers at the thought. This cold may well last forever, the frost a wintry Midas, exploiting a fundamental something-*ness* from everything it touches.

Out west, they've capitalized on the snow and mountains, fashioned an industry for skiers. Here, in the province of Québec, in Montréal, to be exact, the snow's a slice of the damp, bone-chilling sky she'd rather do without. Yes, he MUST feel it in his bones as well, this man from desert sun, from Algeria, where they the moon's craters are shadow tears. Wasn't that the name they used for Earth's shadows on the moon? Why has she forgotten? Anyhow, the image is much more lyrical than the tired man on the moon or the mouse-magnet, Swiss cheese.

But this man, who moments earlier tore open the sugar pack (and, ages ago, nearly her heart, back when they first met, claiming he wasn't sure it would work out), this boyfriend, from the land of poetry, is motioning with his spoon towards the walls, stating that he likes the artwork, although it's costly, he adds. She agrees, but her distaste for this city is an opinion he doesn't share. He loves Montréal as much as he does his home, Médéa.

Maybe it's not the cold or the coffee or the tea. Not the honey – maybe the honey and those poor bees. Maybe it's the lack of … how many days since her last period? He's been talking about current events, about politics, about the current regime and the very possible regime change in Algeria and about the protests in front of the Consulate in Montréal. Soon, he said. They'd go together to protest in solidarity with Algerians here and with everyone back in Algeria. But politics is not what's bothering her. If anything, the renewed optimism sweeping through his country is a cause to celebrate. Nope, a big fat ABSOLUMENT PAS! Not what's bothering her. It's something else.

But, true, she can't say it's not in way he's just grabbed that packet, as if he were still in the lab, not caring about the general picture, his head in the clouds, poring over minutia. Erudite *what-ifs* shoot out from tightened lines around his eyes. From these lines, pencil marks connecting the dots, she calculates a hypothesis: *How might this solid affect the liquid?* He points to the empty sugar packet and diverges from the discussion on hope and Algeria. "This stuff is as deadly as sucralose. They've just reported that the scientists in the 60s worked closely with the sugar industry."

"Of course." She knows that a person's one-third more likely to suffer from cardiovascular disease, with a diet 'rich' in sugar (take soft drinks, for instance), that the food industries pretended everything was fine by taking out the fat but then adding sugar.

"So, I also heard about those scientists working on sugar and fat. The report by the more obnoxious researcher –"

"Yes."

He tells her what she already knows, that the more 'dynamic' scientist claimed that fat was worse than sugar. He had received accolades, while the other, shyer researcher found sugar was the culprit. The sugar-is-the-culprit research was disregarded because … drum roll here … the researcher was shy.

She interrupts. "Maybe it's fake, that story, made up by an envious bystander, an envious colleague of the two. You know how it can be." Yes, he knows. Some of their colleagues in the lab can be a bit … 'restless' is a good word. Recalibrate. Back up. She's moving beyond sucrose, to fructose and strawberries, like the ones they picked when things were … when they were *together,* laughing, hanging out, actively *doing,* not sitting around waiting for Saturday brunch. And NOT just following formulae. Back when there was passion. It's a tricky business, feigning concern, especially when one of the pair is droning on about fatal sugar. She keeps her eyes wide, hoping he won't notice. "Sugar? You're kidding. Bad? Triglycerides, you mean?"

He laughs. There it is, his curve-ball smile. "Especially the processing. Horrible, and even this shit – terrible. Although people will tell you that raw sugar is healthy."

"What? It's sugar," she says. "And: I have no idea what you're talking about. Besides, it's not the worst thing. But there *are* terrible things we consume."

He lifts one eyebrow, steely dark and just incredibly sexy. "Nope. Merde, pure shit. Interacts with our blood cells. And the refined white contains pig."

"Pig?"

"Lard. Used in the processing. Helps with the functioning of those brutal machines. Et bien sûr, you know about amylase."

"Maybe, but what's that got to do with – ?"

"E-eleven-hundred, from the pancreas of a pig, or, as you know, from mushroom mould but generally from pigs."

"In sugar? E-eleven-hundred, amylase?"

"Of course not."

"Then why?"

"Relational analysis. Amylase – they're considering it for a diet supplement. You see? Diet, sugar –"

"Got it."

He lifts the packet, presses a thumb into the paper. "I'm speaking about the simple truth of sugar."

The simple truth of sugar: What will she do without his words?

"Thing is —"

She pulls the tea to her lips. *All we want to say is felt especially keenly in the silences.* A phrase that enters as a whisper. She's back in bed, sheets being pulled up to chins, two lovers, two suspects. She and ... he wasn't involved. Her lips close over a pinhole of air. Despite her attempts, they're meagre compared to imagination, which doesn't take well to fences. In through the bolted gate, the image enters: A woman, her new friend. Antidote for rain and snow. How to tell him about this recent invasion into her dreams? Into real life? Into their bed? Grabbing her stomach —

"Are you alright?"

He's noticed.

"I'm ... yes, some kind of virus ... or ... my period, maybe."

"The food should come soon."

"I'm fine, really."

The waitress plops down a basket of pita. He picks up one, drives it into his coffee. Corner comes up, soaked. "Very good," he says.

Around their table, conversations spool out. To her left, the two women are laughing. On her right, the Boroughs-like man is on his phone. Back to the women, leaning into the table, hands centre-pieced, fingers steepled. *And here are the people.*

Across this stage of tea, coffee, sugar and pita, he's oblivious. She wants to scream, pull down a shade over that too-brilliant February sun; over this damn winter, with its snowy circumference of forgetting. Who the hell wants to live in a freezer? Maybe the diehard snow lovers, trekking through precipitation, the ones who've figured out how to enjoy damp winters. Snow is precipitation; just another solid from a liquid, another formation. Easy deception, in the land of perpetual winter, especially for someone from the land of rain and mountains and ocean. Somewhere beneath the nausea, she feels disoriented. *Is destiny a combatant or a friend?* In the lab, destiny is an expected yield from a chemical reaction. So, yeah, pretty much, friend. As long as the landscape is absent of any grand explosions. That's all her lab partner was supposed to be, a friend. Not an explosion. And here it is again. Her lab partner. Her friend. No, not just a friend.

As he speaks of sugar, she can't help the picture: Lab partner to both of them, naked, darker areola to nipples, dense curls, a penchant for Shakespeare, even for misguided Hemingway, a fascination with Hildegard von Bingen and symbols in Ingeborg Bachmann's stories – stories in which small objects, like eyeglasses, stand in for larger concepts, like loneliness. How can she tell him? They all work together, but he's never listened, never heard the new lab partner talk about her conservation work, the capture and release program to save species or about her working visit to Mauritius, helping populations of sea turtles and other amphibians to bounce back … or at least trying; trying in Brazil to save the Orange Lion Tamarind; creating new marshland in Canada, for endangered frogs. "Creating," the woman said, the corners of her lips turned up. "We created habitat." What an amazing smile!

Now, over his shoulders, a good metre away, the proprietor is gliding a wet cloth over a countertop, singing, her voice reminiscent of the voice of the Iranian poet on the radio the other day. On the CBC, the woman spoke about the loyalty of memory, about being ripped from one's homeland and the terror of losing that land.

His lips on his coffee cup. "Tasty coffee but unfortunately tastier with sugar."

"Try maple syrup … or agave."

"You know I hate agave. What about honey?"

Hate? What kind of word is that for liquid sugar, and "Honey? No –" She almost tells him why, the bees, how the honey is not meant for humans, how it's meant to feed the hive and nourish the queen. She decides instead on silence. His tongue moves along his lips, as he sweeps in stray sugar crystals.

"Sugar's deceitful, its molecules circling a sun-like star." How will she live without his phrases? But more insanely, how is it possible he still doesn't know about her indiscretion? As he sips, she sees him turning over thoughts, like pages. He jogs ahead, speculating on why people have grown so used to the pairing of caffeine and other stimulants.

Still battling the odds to quell her nausea, she reaches for the mint tea, drinks greedily, puts down the cup and intercedes with speculation on bitter and sweet. He concedes with a nod. She thinks about the beauty of his country, of sun, mountains, fig trees and honey, of the bees and the land she's been hoping to visit since … well, frankly, since meeting him.

His mother has wanted to meet her, but when he last left for a visit a couple years back, he went alone. Sure, he'd invited her. It's just that her uncle had died, and she needed to be at the funeral.

"So," she asked recently, "what about this summer?"

"What about it?" He was planting cells. Before her pipette, she was vying with a recent explosion in her heart. An explosion that had ended events that had unfolded the previous evening, when he'd decided to stay home.

At the bar, lights were flashing, as the two women danced closer and … quite unexpectedly, the touch. Then, in the bathroom, that delicious kiss. Quick escalation, and they had found themselves in a stall; the toilet, thank God, lidded.

Now she was contending with … hell, really. Recently, the two women met at a nearby falafel place. "You know," said their new lab partner, slate greys fixed on heaping green and red platters.

"Know what?"

"You know what's happening here –"

Sucking in. "Yes." More quietly: "Yes."

"You also know that the ball, to be perfectly metaphoric, is in your court. But I … I can't be a part of whatever you're playing. Do you have any idea? It's impossible with him in your life. What I'm trying to say is you have me pinned. Whatever is going on with your boyfriend, I can't be a part."

"I know. You're right, but I don't … damn. Yeah, it's unfair." *It takes two to tango.* These were her thoughts, but she slowly nodded when her friend added: "Yeah, right, damn! But I like you. So …" Heavy sigh. "We're stuck, I guess."

That's why in the lab the other day, she had to tune it all out with Algeria, with a question whose answer she dreaded. "You're always talking about us visiting your mother again. You know I'd love to see where you grew up, to see your country. What about going?"

"My country?"

"Your other country."

"Not this summer." Maybe his initial invitations had meant nothing. Maybe he'd wanted her to stand there, mouth open like a transgenic fly's, right before the pin comes down. Maybe, just maybe, he knew.

Here, in the café, the beast enters with a vengeance. She remembers the movie, their first date. She recalls, along with the faint scent of popcorn, the South Korean film they watched, about a radioactive monster, lurking beneath the harbour, about a father whose mission is to rescue his daughter. Over drinks, they'd laughed about their lab findings, having their own monsters lurking in the lab. Back then, there had been possibility. She had to believe, she had – it was everything, finding him.

Right now, she's skating along the thin edge of his monologue, trying to not lose sight of the shore, as he discusses the
origins of sucrose and "our crazy love of all things artificial," how
one American guy who worked for the FDA alongside Don-
ald Rumsfeld – Rumsfeld, then CEO of GD Searle, producers
of aspartame – how "just one man," later indicted for embez-
zling, stopped the miracle berry from entering North America.
Except, briefly, when someone had managed to get the berries in
as frozen fruit popsicles. And now the possibility that they'll be
allowed in markets here.

"Great for diabetes."

This berry from the African continent, his continent, the fruit
that "transfigures comestibles" and "sweetens the palette," lasting
over half an hour, is a "real miracle," he says, enthusiastically, exag-
gerating that enthusiasm, as if this is how she's supposed to feel.
She wonders if anyone has timed this miracle. Maybe he'll tell her.
"If we took this sugar molecule, set it under a microscope –"

Sugar from afar, he tells her, is granular, not like under a
microscope, where its molecular structure is ... wait, he's thinking ... is horse-like. He laughs. His lips too close to the caffeinated surface. Coffee spray. She wipes a cheek. *Who gives a
shit? Not about the raw, refined or artificial.* His voice blends
into the din. There's a roar of laughter nearby – one middle-age
guy, garrulous, sitting next to a thinner, younger man, whose
earlobe is punctured with discs, on the left side of his head,
hair shaved. Next to that dude is a woman who's holding up a
shrimp, puckering as she consumes the shell-stripped creature.
"Hmm, tasty!" Even from here, the sickly-pink coloured pin-
wheel of shrimp is visible in all its shrivelled detail. Shrimp,
trawled from the sea or fished out of stagnant beds. *Bed of
shrimp, bed of lettuce; bedded, wedded.* Her boyfriend interrupts.
"Are you listening?"

"Yes." But is she? Has this philosopher of 'terrible sugar,' so observant to evidence, made the link between caffeine and heart palpitations? Across the table, he's discussing how molecular structures are repeated in the greater world.

Her turn! She tells him what she's reading – does he care? What would palpitations be in the larger universe? Magnetic rings? There's her cue – he's on the sugar-train again. She barges into his monologue with her concern about cane planta-tions, the cultivation by Haitian and Dominican workers, the manipulation of the colonized and the way people gravitate towards the deplorable, basing their economy on trafficking: the wealthier nations leaning heavily on the industry, while the victims harvest the material that's used to fashion the weapons that kill them.

"How terrible is that?"

"Ironic maybe."

"Sure, ironic."

He lifts a brow. What's he thinking? This one completely rel-evant, most important answer isn't found in the molecular world. With her finger, she circles the water ring below, murmuring: "And we complain about human trafficking but use sugar from those plantations in our …"

She glances up. "In *your* coffee. No sugar in my tea."

Did she catch some eye-rolling? He's nodding; then: *"Ye-es?"*

Mocking her. She inhales. *Ouf! Not again.* That pain! Could be her uterus, the seed: the seed of pain. But they'd been using condoms! As she lifts her cup, stray drops pool in the saucer. In the lab, these drops could be significant. In the lab, they could contain whole cities of particles. *A drip, a drop* could carry the planned or accidental. Beneath fresh sheets she had moved into her new friend's scent: A woman's is so different from a man's. And … what if this need to vomit – CAN'T BE!

Sunlight elbows its way into their community of chatterers and rabble-rousers, huddled before doses of caffeinated and non-caffeinated pleasures. The bitterness of coffee assails her. There's a phrase she's learned from his friend: *Khalas*. The word contains many meanings, but 'stop overthinking' is her favourite. She's nearing a black hole, a magnetic field, remembering the evening when she first heard the phrase. They were out with another couple, when perhaps … no, she's certain, when she loved him. She reaches for the little brown packet. *Bam!* His hand comes down on hers. "Nah, this one's mine."

Laughing to himself. She chooses another from the ceramic container. She needs to tear it open, to watch the pale crystals running into the dish.

He's talking about his work on ions. In the lab … and she has something to say, right now. But how to tell this man, with his long face and words from another country, words so familiar? How to hand him the news, with the sun shining in? Holding her cup, thinking there's nothing like fresh mint to help with nausea.

"Our body is at war with itself." It's the book he's reading, a more philosophic than scientific study of altruism and altruistic systems.

How odd, life's coincidences. Just the other day, she was having a conversation with her new friend about the Russian nineteenth-century anarchist, Peter Kropotkin, who lived in a world where questioning altruism was the rage: Altruism or competition?

Was it ever that simple?

"Kropotkin disputed Darwin's theory of competition," her new friend said. "Yet, Kropotkin's critics claimed he'd misunderstood Darwin, hadn't read him carefully." The woman's voice, hands … hands and lips, speculation that most of what is known is misguided, that it's really the lens that decides. The lens of history or science? The lens through which the object is seen. Take relativity in a bee's world, the world through the bumblebee's lens. "The yellow-banded bumblebee hasn't been seen in most parts of their U.S. range since 1999." Cool voice, hand against naked thigh. "But the government hasn't placed it on the endangered list until now. The common backyard bee, gone."

While they lay, naked, they discussed disappearance, the flaws of interpretation, the essence of extinction and evolution, hours later ending with some aphorism on the need to know everything. And now, she's hearing a story about Darwin from this man across the table, a microbiologist chemist. *Focus.*

"So, the author's winking at Darwin?" she asks.

"He's giving Darwin a nudge, arguing that bodies are in constant war with themselves; the *self,* just a unit of cells waging war, like groups of people, like cultures. While these cell groups are warring, individual cells can be collaborating."

He pauses, enough time for her ... "Collaboration? But how, if cells are vying for – if they're trying to survive?"

"Survival depends on cooperation. The body ... I mean, what's très intéressant is that when cells start dying, they become selfish. Each one out for himself."

"*She.*"

"What's that?"

"*She.*"

"Oui, of course. *She* for *herself.* It's about the body breaking down – individual cells leaving the group."

"Maybe *your* body's breaking down."

He stiffens. She breathes in hard. What about ... could it be? Is there a creature inside of her, inside her belly?

"I've got to tell you."

"It's more about cooperation, more than natural selection. In mitosis, on the cellular level, it's not really birth. What? What do you have to tell me?"

He looks startled, like he's been walking in the desert and has come upon a bed, with her and ... no, not with him in the bed.

"We screwed up, in the lab, and ..."

"What?"

"I mean, we screwed up, this week."

"What are you talking about?"

"I ... I mean, we didn't do a good job in the lab; we didn't mix the right amount –"

He's suddenly Mr. Hyde, irascible. Nose twitching, lips pursed. Arguing. Everything's *all right with the world, except* ... except for her indecisiveness, her cavalier set-up in the lab, and sometimes, no, too often, her procedure, conventions and lack of due respect to their work. Conclusion: When it comes to the lab, she could do better.

She steadies herself. *Time to Disengage.* Hypothesis: *Will it work here?* It's a trick she learned after her parents divorced and her stepfather was ranting on about her "insubordinate-ness." She took off to find her real father, whom she found living on the streets. That's when she chose to leave the land of rain. She blinks. Still here, in Montréal – seven years after having graduated in chemistry, three-going-on-four in this relationship. The buttery aroma of croissants spills into the stories around them by poets and drama queens. Add two chemists. She feels hemmed-in, suffocated. Borders are impassable, odours for the first time stomach-churning. *Shit.*

"As I was saying."

"You were?"

She searches his hands for a sign. There's another phrase from his friend, an Arabic expression for 'slow down,' but she can't remember it. What a shame her vocabulary isn't richer, her Arabic more fluent, her English more eloquent. If it were, she could – in the conditional sense of the verb – string together word displays.

In that conditional sense of things, they would be somewhere else, not here, maybe standing before a display of engagement rings. In this, the only known universe, she's having trouble with the simple present. She lifts the sugar packet from his palm; his skin soft. He relinquishes the treasure. She brings the packet closer. Larger than life, than him. A brown packet = *au naturel* in the sugar industry. Sucrose. Crystalline. $CnH2On$. Carbon, hydrogen, oxygen. Groupings of altruistic individuals. How she craves the last one now: $O2$. An apology is what's needed. "Sorry," she says.

He's quiet, clear-eyed, crème de menthe lips ... why is that? Every pair of lips, a different taste, always temporary: the taste, the lips. Like after you've had a bite. Never as tasty when *you* make the dish. For this, she admits, there is no recipe. Those crème-de-menthe lips are the last of their kind. "It's about us."

"Us?"

His eyebrows arch. Lovely brows, lovely eyes. She exhales. "In the lab."

"What does –"

"In the lab, yesterday."

"I have no idea, no idea what you're talking about." He tips his chair back, closes his eyes. Two legs, she thinks. Will he fall?

"We screwed up. We could've done things differently –"

Bang! His chair lands on all fours. She sucks in. "I have no idea what you're talking about!" He punctures every consonant with a stare. Fixating on her. On her eyes or a on point right above, on her forehead? She brushes back some hair, directs her hand to her stomach ... so, really, what is going on in there ... in her uterus? Panning out to the wood counter behind him. The décor is nice enough; the food, tasty. Huge change from last year, when the owner's ex-husband went bankrupt and left the marriage. The new proprietor, a cause celebre, bided her time, trimming, hammering, throwing open the doors. From Formica and constipating-dinner beige, light-grain is the outcome. When business is slow, she loves to talk about the surface and marrow of relationships, the "turquoise oxidized kind," when "la beauté plus foncée" is still visible, after five years or so, when there's a settling-in but when possibility still exists.

Once, if memory serves, the owner's ex-husband was ranting on about lattés. Arguing with her for no reason that this type of foaming drink was no more or less than coffee latticed with steamed milk. And if a person wanted steamed milk, she'd do best to ask "dans une langage précisée!" That's the point of steamed milk, the coffee just the base.

But! she wanted to cry, before he was pulled aside. *I'm asking for soymilk. Plus, I'm a chemist. Of course, I know about bases!*

Behind the counter, the new owner is angling a steaming-milk tin beneath the espresso machine, all shiny silver; the steam, doing its thing. *Waaaalllllsssssssshhhh,* while here she, a chemist in vocation and in soul, is attempting equilibrium between what is and what, *que sera,* will simply be. Among the tables; chairs and couches, every movement seems forced, sclerotic, the newcomers searching for seats as if combing the sand for signs of gold.

Waaaalllllsssssssshhhh. What's he saying? "If you're trying to equate the stuff in the lab to our relationship, I'm changing the subject."

Along her jaw, her skin tightens. He leans over. "Here's the new subject or … challenge. Digestion."

"You're kidding."

His elbows skate around his coffee mug. She wonders if he's about to take her hands, but no.

"It's a pun. Digestion. Sugar. Na2."

Despite her anger, this randomness teases out a smile. Sugar and potassium nitrate – a story she's shared with him about university.

Boom! Atoms breaking apart, falling together. One crazy professor almost blew up the lab. Sure, she gets it: breaking apart, coming together. They've done this before ... and now, wide and mocking, his eyes reflecting what he sees of this absurdity, of this inconsequentiality. Dream catchers, those brows. Her breath arrives in short bursts. He pushes her water glass forward, a small gesture in which she sees shadows and stunning sunsets, years stinking up persimmon sheets. She'd joked about wanting to be lavished in thread counts. His commitment? A gift of 400 threads (*and* he'd considered her request for a unionized labour tag). Years, months, and he has her. Her knees jerks forward, touches his. There's an imperceptible movement, and she realizes he's moving his away.

"I have to –" She's coughing.

"Drink," he says.

She sips, saving the rest, as if water has become scarce. Tipping her glass. As the cool water flows down her throat, an ice cube jabs into her lips. Their new lab partner, her – *lover?* – had almost choked to death on ice. Imagine that. Asphyxiation on a solid that could transform to a liquid, but not soon enough. She considers these past few months. All they've been is suffocating, inside a circumference of rigid indifference.

From above, the proprietor's voice simmers. "Can I get you two anything, while you wait?"

"No, merci," he says.

"Merci," she says.

The proprietor nods, steps away.

"I'll finish."

"Yes. Please. Thought you had." He reaches for his water.

"I mean, you –"

"Go on." He returns his glass to the water ring.

"I think you contaminated the last mixture we were working on in the lab."

"With what?"

Placing a hand like a visor over her eyes: "With the additive solution."

"Which additive solution?"

"Hydrogen sulphite." She leans into the table, the hard surface against her chest comforting. "Didn't you notice?"

"I took every precaution, as I always do."

Her glass is far too close to the edge, her elbow too close to the glass, but she does nothing about either. Against the light, he's turned into a silhouette, face smoothed by the sun, shock of blackberry hair, crème-de-menthe lips. "Nice light, this time of winter. Nice light, and ..." He smiles. "You must have been dreaming, as you do when we're working with hydrogen. I'm always cautious."

Obstinacy is distilled water, a poor conductor of electricity, unless impurities are present. Cryogenic tanks of oxygen, hydrogen gas. She contemplates the sugar explosion in university, the equation for digestion he's just referenced. Gripping her stomach, her mind retracing a childhood event. Climbing up the geologically young ranges to clouds, the warmth of her mother's hand, wondering if there'd be something up there, something other than a view.

His eyes are saying, *Fully here, fully me; can't change that.* His lips form around recalcitrant vowels; eyes jog. She imagines herself caught along the back of his retinas, her concave-spoon face. Scaling the interior of her thoughts to the counter, behind which the proprietor is running boiling liquid over macerated beans. Remembering is like a pin through skin. In a lab where they sliced through mice, the bite of a rat who was trying to break free. She won't work for those companies anymore. In the new lab, she'd met him, the man who, like her, no longer would experiment on animals. Maybe she can tell him.

"I'm pre –"

"Here you are. Yours is the hummus on bagel?" The proprietor is parachuting down a plate with an open-faced, sesame-seed bagel, swigged with lettuce and rosemary twigs – *olive branches*. For him, a bouquet of romaine, reds and yellows, with a sandwich of tofu scramble.

"Looks good." How refreshing to say something positive. He's staring.

"Pregnant? You're pregnant?"

He's breathing heavily. It was the bees, the woman told her, the woman with the heart of honey. Insects? No, not insects. Apoidean (meaning lineage). "The root of the soul is in there, a complete being in that small body. Scientists have found bees experience happiness, depression. Emotions are related to the hive. Not being able to produce honey brings on grief."

Is she depressed? No. Just – "Pregnant, yes."

A stray breath sends her napkin sailing onto the floor. Kneeling over, she knows before lifting her head, before smashing against the bubble-gummed bottom what is going to happen. It's like that movie, "Arrival," like Chiang's "Story of Your Life." She's learned from the aliens how to read time. *Crash!* A diminutive stream soaks the napkin, slipping through glass shards that glint like diamonds.

"Are you okay?!" Voices whir, fret, crash like calamitous waves. Consonance and condolence. She lifts her head, which is throbbing. And now there are changes to the still-life before her, to the composition of the room. Change is good, except of course for this ringing in her ears.

The owner's presence is felt more than seen, as a bright-red broom handle, then dustpan come into focus. Grey mop sponges up the mess. The woman's lips are steel, her silver tempo voice surrounding like a sea. "How are *you?*"

"I'm fine. Should I –"

"No, no worries."

Across the table, his eyes hold a strange blend of incredulity and humour, a wonderful layered complexity. Over the speakers … can't be. Ella Fitzgerald's deep vocals, *Sugar Blues!* This is their song. That's what he's told her. Ella Fitzgerald and Fats Waller, performing Clarence Williams' and Lucy Fletcher's lyrics. *Have you heard these blues / that I'm gonna sing to you / when you hear them, they will thrill you / through and* this is the song her real father played for her mother, the house reeking of booze and sugar blues. This is how he met her mother, in a world full of sugar.

The proprietor moves closer. "No worries. Mops take care of everything. It's you I'm worried about. Looks like you've done a number on your head."

She pats down several unwashed strands. Across the table, he's staring, as she massages her temple. As for this … embryo? Zygote? Is there ever cooperation in the world of human interaction? Should she keep it?

Through spasms of pain, she sees the sun-drenched room is ablaze, people laughing, *rhump-rhumping* on a number of subjects. Peculiar shadows climb the walls, alongside those acrylic paintings. She has the sense they're in someone's living room, a cottage or cave; the place, round and woodsy. Could be a bistro near Hemingway's valleys of Ebro (without, of course, the snow), sunlight streaming in the audience's laughter. A bluesy melody, with, maybe, this soon-to-be stranger across the table. To her left, Gertrude Stein and her Alice are singing. To her right, the far too-sober Boroughs is staring at her. She places a hand on her head, the other arm across her uterus. Difficult to determine where the physical strangeness ends and where the more existential kind begins, but the centre is intuited or known in the way an infant knows the smell of its mother.

She reaches across the table, to him; his face, frozen; her sigh carrying far too much weight for life's grand design. His sweet breath washes over her face, as the crazy beast surrounds. A beast, she realizes, on an unstoppable course and now leaning back in its glass-bottom boat, ever so merrily disappearing into the brackish wasteland of some comedian's sun-water dreams.

The Bard of Dorchester Square

As YOU MAKE your way through the park, you take in the early dawn. A time that's intangible, circumspect. The trees' dusty branches nodding off to some transient lullaby. This is your favourite thing to do, to walk through Dominion Square so early, you can avoid everyone and anyone. You pass park benches, brushstroked in darkest navy. The scene reminds you of one in Chekhov's *Seagull,* a decent rendition you caught last week at Théâtre Nouveau Monde, with Chekhov's ode to gulls, crowding urban centres, feasting on sparrows they've chased into office windows. Mostly, however, it was Chekhov's desperate cry for lost youth that resonated.

Very soon, it'll be time to plunge into the markets. Far easier now, with no one at the office – unless someone's decided to spend the night.

It's almost too quiet now, like being inside the eye of a hurricane, here, in Montréal's downtown oasis. This land was acquisitioned in the late 19th century: The northern section of this square aptly named Dominion, changed to Dorchester, some say to appease the federalists. Across the wide asphalt thruway is Place du Canada, the country inserting its big toe in the middle of the city. This boulevard belt running through the south and the north section of the square has been christened René-Lévesque. Lévesque, a man of the people, who would do what was needed to carve a country out of a province. To your right, Sir Wilfred Laurier, stands statesmanlike holding … a feathered pen? *Sign here* is what that assured pose says. The soles of his polished spats roof his celebrated words: 'harmoniser les différents éléments, se compose notre pays,' a useful credo to this day, one you use for dealing with egos at the office. Along the snow-swept squares, you tread carefully, their engraved crosses slippery with residual ice. There was a cemetery here, probably cholera victims, whose skeletons may still lie below ... you've never checked, needing to hold this one mystery close, like a pirate's cutlass buried beneath a salt-worn suit.

It's freezing, each breath slicing through like a knife. April; yes, it's April, for Chrissakes! This morning, you opted for a change of wardrobe. No way in hell were you going to suffer one more day buried beneath that heavy winter parka. In this latest prize from the London Fog collection, easy to act the role: big guy, the can-handle-anything type they've gilded into 'Vice Prez' on the door, expecting the substance beneath to comply. A cold dose of winter falls on a shoulder – just one shoulder. Winter's mark falls heavy and bleak. Closing your eyes, and ... there! Songbirds! For one brief moment, it's May; you're out in the country. Opening your eyes to the city. The silence of those songbirds, you realize, is an inevitable reality.

So are the layoffs, buyouts, mergers inside these steel and win-ter-proof glass behemoths, following you around daily, like your shadow.

But that's the joy. It was your choice, business school, after that stale degree in literature. Still, Shakespeare at least did serve this student well. Before you, Robbie Burns stands, cast in bronze. There's a voice, faint, a woman's ... and she's humming, her tune growing more distinct. Really? Leonard Cohen's *Secret Life?* You whip around. But no one's there; not a soul. Wiping your brow. It's too damn early, the strangest time of the 24-hour (and then some) clock. Down here, where the flesh isn't so solid, narratives and their ghosts are everywhere.

Clutching your briefcase, you catch a whiff of diesel's sweet poison. At home, when you uncovered yourself from dreaming, you'd resigned yourself to a day of low clarity. Still feels like you're dreaming, so you don't notice him right away – the man, to the right of the path, near the bench, shot up like a reed in the crosswinds. His half-mitted hand is draped over a shopping cart. His eyes are closed, but ... that face looks so familiar, minus the puffy eye-pouches and scruffy chin. Whose face could it possibly be? Underneath his *Canadiens* tuque, scraggly hair falls over scavenged skin. One arm's folded against his chest, all of him draped in a coat, his figure wavering, like a mirage. Behind, the Boer War Memorial Horse rears on muscular legs.

It's probably the way the wind brushes your skin, but you stop. Travellers to this park always cull some piece of you. While you might offer pocket change, you're generally uncomfortable. He unfolds his arm; a faint line ripples across his cheekbones. One palpable beat. His eyelids lift. Wide pupils fix on yours. "Bonjour! Hi. Je m'appelle MB. Short for 'mon bébé'."

Your legs won't move. "MB?" He looks so damned familiar.

"MB, named by my maman. Almost died day I was born, but she wouldn't let go of me. So, they rushed both of us both to the hospital, the whole time trying to yank me free. All night, toute la soirée, she kept on yellin': 'Mon bébé!' À l'hôpital, the nurses, les infirmières, lui ont donné des sédatives. But no one, y'know, can believe what she did. Outwitted them AND the pills, exited those grey hospital doors and got me home somehow. My 'ole man, a red cad, he named me."

"She ran out of the hospital?"

"What's that?"

"She left ... with you?"

He's silent; then smiles, wheezes, pushes aside his cart. "Viens icitte." He gestures towards the bench. "Room enough pour deux."

Your head, heavy; the rest, freezing. "Désolé." You catch yourself. Generally, you're one step ahead, and now you're losing that step. "Je n'ai pas de change."

He shrugs, then softly shimmers, as he deflates onto the bench. "Don't need no change. Seems you need this bench, though."

Nope. Not on your life, but you just shake your head. He's reaching towards his cart and a book on top of a moth-eaten blanket – a book, you swear, that has magically appeared.

"William Gibson, my man! Met him in Vancouver."

Walk! Now! Your brain, on fire.

He opens the cover, points to a squirrely signature, barely visible in this blue dawn. "Gibson signed it. Man, oh, man." MB's smiling. Even in this duskiness, you can see a few of his teeth are missing.

Words rise in your throat, meeting your percussive "Shit!" Such a strange morning interlocutor, possibly full-blown lunatic, reminding you of – who is it? He's got one arm draped over the bench, smiling like the Cheshire Cat, his tongue swooshing over cracked teeth. "Good stuff," he murmurs.

It's morbid curiosity, compelling you to remain where you are. But along the outer range of being, there's a twinge of fear. He's strangely mesmerizing, more ghost than substance, as the blue-black moves through him. Who does he remind you of? *Gotta go. Disappear.* But your legs, your feet, not one part complies.

Laugh-groaning, he searches the sky. "Long time ago, my parents dragged me to Trois-Rivières." He pulls on his nose. "Dragged me by this, my ole man. By my very nose."

Inside, something catches. You were dragged around until, like Gregor Samsa, you became a giant insect. Your dad couldn't get you to budge.

The ghosts swarm … speak as one … Each has left something undone – who penned that? Her name whispers along your neck: Rae Armantrout. You smile, touch your head. Good thing. Memory's still intact. What about your poems? So long ago. Wasn't there that line? *Stop chasing the dead.* Once, verse was your anchor.

There's the swish of a taxi, the spluttering of an anguished city bus motor. Back to MB, murmuring, smiling, cupping his palms. He blows into the mitted channel.

"I have places –" you begin to say.

"All of us do, my man. We all got to be somewhere, somewhere other than where we are. Et j'ai les yeux dans l'même trou. Me? Tellement fatigué of being somewhere else." His weary eyes open, it seems, to collect what little light there is. What appears to be a sneer draws out to laughter, echoing against the still barely visible sky. Above, the office windows reflect this almost-sky, pierced by thrones of interlocking steel girders. Beyond one of those windows is a desk. On that desk, a blank screen that needs to light up soon, with clients and numbers, questions that need responding to.

You lift your chin, rub your hands together, turn to leave. The strange fella's pulling down his tuque, whistling a tune you can't place, a strangely bitter melody. There's a pinch of cold. Sourness wells up from your stomach, so you open your lips for some air. Crazy nonsense he's spouting, something about the "wild park" of Gibson's imagination.

"Gotta go," you say.

One lone songbird's trill filters through. Should you give him time instead of loonies? No. Leave it be. As you walk away, something unseen, almost imperceptible, brushes against your coat. You turn. He's rubbing a bristled half-mitt down his own threadbare coat, brushing off errant dust. Most has probably set up residency. Your throat burns; the brusque air carrying the dead. How many stories does this apparition have?

He smiles, calls out: "So, like I told you, my mama …"

Sighing, you walk slowly back to the bench. There's a uric whiff; you bring a gloved hand to your nose. Close on the tails of that stink is … roasting coffee? What barista would be up this early?

Resting your briefcase against your knees, you're uneasy, unsure, un-everything.

"Ah, ma maman. Proud woman. Acadian. Met my ole man after the war, in that Land of Acadia, where she was born. A bread-maker's daughter. Folks used to buy unbaked dough from grandpapa, finish the baking chez eux." He crosses one stained denim-jean leg across the other. "Now, it's all the rage, the unbaked stuff, in the freezer section."

The pungency, thankfully, is gone, the roasting coffee left. Olfactory heaven. Just the other day, a colleague took up your precious time, talking about Dionne Brand's book on smell. While this idiot extolled on the dependency humans have on this sense (who knew?), you wanted to scream, *The absurd upon the turd of the absurd!* Just standing there was painful, reminding you of your dad's endless discussions on chemistry, particularly the chemistry of sleep. He was always heating, incubating. Damn! He would've flipped over the latest discovery linking human genes to circadian rhythm. The one thing he did well was tell a story, feeding your dreams with angry chemists sparring with pipetted concoctions. As for that colleague, the absurdity of crunching numbers to manage … well, shit, really, wasn't lost on you.

With MB below, you scan the sky. Morning's breaking through. Beneath what's left of this cloud face, the saints' legacies are preserved in stone. What were their real lives like, those men? Across the street, along the baroque Basilique Cathédrale Marie-Reine-du-Monde, they stand, heralding God's existence, offering absolutions. One guy is holding Baby Jesus. Below them, the cathedral's ostentatious columns. Columns everywhere here, now in celebration to the almighty dollar more than Baby Jesus. But it wasn't so long ago that this was the avenue of the gentry class. After last Thursday, the Church has given her campaign a rest: those columns previously cloaked in long drapeaux, which announced in French and in English that Jesus was the greatest rocker who ever lived.

There's a phrase that comes to you: *The dead more alive than the living.*

Is MB part of the dead? Along his trench coat, a patchwork of holes, stray threads along his mitts. Oddly, the rancidness is gone.

"Aren't you cold?"

He sucks in his cheeks.

"Nah. Pas si pire. My skin's thick."

A lone pedestrian floats past, hands in pockets. You turn once again with every intent to leave. Hightail it out of here, go get what the markets, the world, your life all are calling on you to do.

MB's pressing a fist into his side. "Me, my whole life's been about movin'. Got up to Labrador. Then James Bay. But that trip to New Brunswick –" He shakes his head. "Went looking for my grandpa's bakery. Ugly goddamned mall now. But I can say for certain it's not so bad here in April."

There's a café near here, where a neon-orange poster proclaims: "April! Poetry Month!" The lunch crowd finds this particularly funny. "So, what's May? Month of turgid prose?" Just the other day, you were reading about a Google AI that spits out random pits of poetry: *He was silent for a long moment … silent for a moment … it was quiet for a moment … dark and cold.* Like Apple's Newton, bottling chaos in verse … although nothing's entirely random.

MB grabs his cart, an entire home without lock or key. He wheezes, catches his breath, closes his eyes and speaks, like he's breaking through a fog of recollection, painting a portrait of the woman he left behind in James Bay, when he was working on the LG dam. Her dad, an overseer, wasn't impressed with his daughter's choice. "Tried to kill me! Fed me poisoned soup! Luckily, I didn't clean my bowl. Was sick for DAYS! She swore it was the flu. Course it wasn't."

Your briefcase feels heavy, your legs too ... no. You won't sit down. A siren wails. Wasn't it here? Same spot, years ago, you were crossing to the Queen E. Hotel, to catch the airport shuttle. Off to New York City's Corporate Headquarters. Finding your seat, putrid though it was, you sank into its first-class finery (they *were* more luxurious back then) with an aged scotch, taking the plane's turbulence as a sign of better times to come. Back then, you were so optimistic.

Twenty-five years almost to the day, and now everyone's expecting you to bring in the glory. At home, dust reigns over Shakespeare's kingdoms, over Prince Hal and Falstaff and their doomed relationship.

But you're dust-free in your office, tallying up productivity, rattling on about corporate projections. *Life ... is strangely boring,* some poet wrote. Strange lies of nature. Should've been Wilde, with his *Thinking ... most unhealthy ... people die of it just as they die of any other disease.* Too crazy, here, where dawn threatens to pull you under.

MB's talking. "That woman, her ole man –" He scratches his jaw. Shadow of a beard. You notice how deeply life's been etched along his face.

"He poisoned you?" you say.

"Yah. Sure. But her and me, we *had* something. But ..." He's shaking his head. "Y'know, shit happens. I ... I had to leave." There's a faint sigh from somewhere. Abruptly, you turn. Against the Boer War statue, a young couple's embracing. You place your briefcase down.

"Mon cœur n'était jamais aussi seul, but no heart of mine's ever going back." MB hammers the final consonant, his tuque riding up. Resting a hand along its ribbing, he sings to the misty air. "Got your reasons for leaving ... I'll give you that, just let me keep pretending one day you comin' back."

Shifting your weight, you're conscious of interminability in the momentary, of the immutability of time.

"Y'ever heard that tune?"

"I —"

"Montréal's very own. Michael Jerome Brown. Why don't you sit?"

No, no. Something's bothering you.

"Had to leave you said?"

"What?"

"You said, you *had* to leave."

Deeply, methodically. "Yep, couldn't fucking stay."

He's just hurled a bolt of lightning. Sears through, reminding you of that night ... one night ... two nights ... many nights. But one night in particular, with your mom's late-night shot of nightmare: "Tell him! Tell your son that you're taking off with that bitch whore!"

Dad wasn't blameless. Still, at that moment, it was her you hated. Confronted with this filial cul-de-sac, you flew out the door. And now self-accusation rings like a five-tone bell. For god's sakes, who hasn't dealt with a divorce? It wasn't a catastrophe, was it? Not like when you finally told your dad the 'news' that nearly killed him.

Pulling in your shoulders, you pick up your briefcase, resting it against your crotch like a fig leaf. Inside those buildings, all it's about is being ever vigilant at cave's entrance. Long ago, they called you professorial, yanking on the strings of your poetry kite. And that boyfriend you followed into the Communist cell, the Trotskyist. *Il faut être de son temps,* wrote Daumier.

You should go / from place to place / recovering the poems / that have been written for you – Leonard Cohen, whose lead you almost took and headed for India. It was your uncle, rated top CEO by Forbes, who delivered the ass-kick you needed. Money's the thing, he insisted, the stench of bitters on his breath. (He always was a good drinking partner.)

Taking no notice of your absence, MB's like the captain of a ship. More like lorry driver, chauffeuring you through *la belle province.*

Pain shoots through. Kicking out a cramp, you stare at the cart's woeful blanket. Gibson's pages flutter … it's as if the wind's skimming the book before considering purchase. A cyclist flies by.

While someone else is eating or opening a window or just walking dully along / About suffering they were never wrong / The old Masters: how well they understood. Auden.

"What about this?" MB's voice scythes through. "It's all the poets. Whosever's words get in your head – that's who calls the shots. Take the folks that bronzed that statue there, in Lake George. Battlefield Park."

Lake George?

"Got it in my head, y'know. Was buzzin' through, not long ago."

Your whole family used to visit the town, back when you all were still together: You and your sister dipping into frigid waters, sand-painting your toes. Lake George: Tourist trap for Montréalers, second to Plattsburgh, Shopping Mecca.

MB's going on about its beleaguered history, the first inhabitants, "the Nations and their battles."

So, you wonder. How the hell does he know all this?

"Reeks of blood," he murmurs. "Y'can smell it."

In your head, *winds change things … the wind from the sea steady and high … some breakthroughs of sun … released from forms.* Trust A.R. Ammons to understand.

"Yeah," the man beneath you spits. Thank god in the opposite direction. Something inside, acidic and grisly, rises inside your throat.

"Oh," he's saying. "That ole Champlain, pissed to hell he couldn't slaughter more. Stealin' for his king, for the glory."

"For the glory?" Despite your rising nausea, you have to let out the rest: "Maybe it was just land he was after. Not the glory."

MB meets your smile. "Yeah, sure. Next century, y' got King George's troops pullin' in the Iroquois. Williams is leading, fighting the Algonquin, who're fighting with the French, the Algonquin set up to battle the Iroquois and English. All of 'em cannon fodder for the thieves that stole their land."

He throws himself against the bench. "Guns in their hands ... God at their side."

Dylan's name is on your tongue, but MB's strangely iridescent, folding into the haze. Exhaustion swoops in. MB's motioning with a cordial wave, not unlike the usher's, the other day, at the theatre. Clearing his throat, MB furiously shakes his head like he's trying to rid it of snakes. And you're suddenly aware of the traffic. More pedestrians now heading up Peel.

What are you doing ... who the hell knows?

"That Gibson book –" you begin, then shut your mouth. Gibson avoided the draft, unlike your dad, who eventually left the treachery of his country for Canada, where he went into chemistry – appropriate occupation for someone who sprayed fields with poisons.

How old is this MB? His face – that weirdly familiar face – is a map of eddies and streams. "Done some fighting?" you ask.

"Me?" Wide, bony grin. He coughs, splutters into his knitted half-mitts; you promise yourself: NO handshaking.

Along the bench, inside the magical world of some glistening ice, there's a flash of sun, which is still so low in the sky, it's almost like the reflection is all there is. Dad did have some interesting things to say, informing you that the setting sun isn't actually *the* celestial body, only a refraction of the Earth's atmosphere. Could it be the same at sunrise?

"Match to flame," MB's saying. "There's always someone messin' with things. Yah, I fought. Vietnam ... or as worn-out characters call it, 'Nam."

Clearing your throat, you stretch your neck to sky. Your ole man finally shared stories about the deaths, the smell of the jungle. "We washed in that stench," he told you. "Inside the jungle ... well, it made us clean, so we could go back out into that crazy fucking world."

MB laughs. "Weird, huh? Me, Canadian, enlisting in the war the Americans wanted. They stationed us in Ho Chi Minh –" Grabbing the bench, he sways. "Every one of us. I mean, *all of us* pulled the trigger. Blew away whole families." He waves his hands around. "Yah, my regiment, just like all the others. Best thing was getting killed early on, before you could do the damage ... or get so damaged up. Swatting insects – bugs everywhere. Big critters in the jungle."

He sinks into the bench, like he's falling into a small, strange universe.

"That's why I gotta move all the time," he says suddenly. Sounds like he's been moving throughout his life. "Followed the Mississippi south. Got by pumping gas, workin' lunch counters, profiting from the hunger that drives people to seek more than stomach stuffin'. Zombies, with vacancy signs hanging from their necks. Folks needing someone to hear their stories. For me, y'know, they pulled up their sweaty T's. Big, fat welts on their backs. Crazy field managers, whacking the guys with aluminum poles. Irrigation wasn't going fast enough. Oh yeah, those were foremen with tempers to light whole cities on fire."

His midnight eyes are trained on Robbie Burns, who is watching the westerly-bound traffic. All the other statues here of are soldiers and politicians, masquerading as poets and dreamers. MB swallows. "Plenty of room for the wicked; no room for best-laid plans. Y'know, in Mississippi, I learned all anyone ever needs to know from a guy who was stationed in Indonesia."

Indonesia?!

Temptation tells you to turn your wrist. But checking the time would be like breaking the glass between this world and some other place you dare not enter right now. *Poetry slips into dreams / like a driver in a lake.* The author's name, somewhere near the surface, like a stone polished by running water – oh, right. Bolaño, Gómez Roberto.

"Guy who'd gone to one of those Indonesian islands: He was the one. Told me about this thing we don't feel here, don't have … ah, but I've come to the conclusion that we do. Liget. That's the name for it, the emotion."

"Liget?"

"Somethin' you get when you're about to, y'know, fall off the edge. Folks he met on one of those islands in Indonesia felt it. *Damn* powerful stuff. Made 'em wanna take a head!"

Vertigo enters; you catch yourself from falling backwards.

MB's silently laughing, his shoulders shaking.

His smile … so reminiscent … whose is it?

"Liget's a drug. When nothing is left, but you gotta deal … or die."

Filling in the blanks, you silently add, *when you can't fight anymore.*

MB's voice is a surge of electricity. "Yeah, when it's gonna kill you if you don't take a head. I felt it up in Alaska."

You've taken a step back but still can't seem to budge more than that.

"In Alaska," he says, pausing. "Under Denali. Ghost Mountain. Camped under its arching madness. Keeping an eye out for bears. They're not the ones to watch out for, y'know. It's falling down those mountains that'll kill you. Happened to a kid from

North Dakota when I was out camping. She was working for the parks. Moi, j'ai fait de camping, out in the tundra. Jumped off the park bus, pitched a tent. I was lucky. Nobody caught me. Slept beside those drunken trees, 'drunken', because they lean to one side, like they've been waiting there forever to hear what the mountains have to say. But those mountains never talk."

He smiles.

"Trees, losin' their footing. Permafrost loss kinda thing. Y'know, it's the papa bears that the bears gotta be worried about. They eat their own. That's why the babes, the cubs, can climb."

And just now it seems to you like this guy is a part of another world, or maybe a part of his very own piece of everything, stuffed with the bread of poets. Not the *would-be* but the *already-is,* wound tight.

"Gotta write it down some day." He sniffs. Stretching a hand down into a pocket, you land on your Blackberry: a relic. So is the pad of tissues that your fingers find in the dark. Tissues you carry around just in case you meet up with any papa bears. "Here," you say, as he sniffles some more.

"Thanks, but it's best to work these things out."

Alright then. As you stuff it back in your pocket, you wonder: What were you working out, sauntering around the city, carrying your books of poetry? *Henry's mind grew blacker the more he thought ... looked onto the world like the act of ... Delmore, Delmore. / He flung to pieces and they hit the floor.* And here comes Eliot, entering stage left, whenever the world's collapsing into the maddening state of the poet. This time, the vertigo is stronger; the world slides to one side. Breathe, slow. Slow. Your knees buckle. Steady.

"Back when I was workin' in James Bay, learned some Cree, bit of Atikamekw." MB shakes his head. "And let me tell you, I was no prince; more like pauper of the iambic, though trochaic's what I love."

What? How the hell ... trochaic? Paupers?

"But I couldn't make it work. No one needed my shredded meter. Much better stickin' to the free. Free verse. Vivre la liberté! Up north, met some real poets. Ever heard someone speaking Cree?"

"Nope." Is he a poet? Is that a poet's face?

He releases some phrases into the cold.

"Sounds like –" but you can't say and, so, refrain.

"In Cree, everything's crawling with meaning, electrifyin', limbed – the *who* inside the *what*."

"Aren't all languages like that?" You're thinking of a credo for people who work in your field: In convincing shareholders, persuasion comes when the *what*, the drive, takes over the *who*. Of course that's not enough, if you want to make a killing.

"Maybe, but Cree's solid. Seein' the world through the word. Being in the here and now. Now, that's solid." He falls against the bench. "Rememberin' forward. Not chasing our tails. Brothers, Sisters, their language's about the 'where' too. Riding the turtle's back. That's poetry." He lifts his hand, dances his half-naked fingers in the air. Who the hell does he remind ... holy shit! Once upon a time, you were racing home, to watch the Canadiens beat the Buffalo Sabres in the semi-finals. You were supposed to watch with your dad, but of course *that* never happened. Final score: Sabres 3, Canadiens, 0. When your ole man finally got in, Mom's voice rang out like a siren in the dark. And all he ever had was criticism on *your* wasted life.

Soon after, he left all of you – your mom, you, your sister. And soon after that, a woman from his office was his next victim, her son older and without the bags under the eyes that MB has ... or maybe with them – that's who MB looks like. Those eyes, haunting.

You breathe in the cold air. Deep down, you know it's ridiculous, but this particular manifestation of that other son your dad had for awhile is like a mirror image. Must be a mirage. Come to think of it, so is this guy on the bench. He knows things he couldn't possibly know.

You catch him pointing at Burns' statue. "Wish I had the proper hat; would've taken it off to that guy. Mows right over a mouse's nest, and what's he do? Composes a poem. To a rodent! That's me. A rodent. Always trying to outwit the nightmares. Got rid of some of them in Alaska and then in Dawson City."

"You mean 'outrun the nightmares'," you say, falling into fits of coughing.

"You alright?"

You nod reassuringly, but inside something's rising. Despite your anger, despite the salmon sky, despite your desk and the papers upon it. "Did you say you left your wife?"

"Terrible stuff. Me and the girls' mom didn't get along."

"Kids?"

"Two. Must be married, with kids of their own." He stares down at his fingers. "No, it wasn't good, leaving."

"Well," you say, wondering still why you can't leave, wondering why MB doesn't smell anymore.

Sun's breaking through, or maybe its hot bubbly refracted image. The birds sing in striated chords. MB murmurs: "The rain."

It's only rained twice since March, odd for Montréal. You're shivering. There's this bot that intentionally pricks the finger's fleshy pad. The inventor wanted to see how far humans would go in accepting their mechanized kin.

As for MB, it's like there's this doubling-thing going on: One guy is lifting himself up from the bench, the other casually calling you back with "days of rain out west." The clouds never bothered him, he says. "Weather, poetry, same."

On the wisps of a whisper: "Like Baudelaire's flâneur,"

Wiping your eyes. "Baudelaire?"

Amusedly, MB stares.

There's that strange voice again, riding out the wind: "Like a flâneur, leaving signs."

MB's lips haven't moved! Turning, you look for the source. Pedestrians aplenty out on the sidewalk. No one nearby. Baudelaire was your favourite once.

Here, in the city, you've seen the signs: *Flânage interdit,* iron spikes to ward off the ones who want to stay in one place too long. Flânage: the word a cipher from university days, when you were taking classes that got you "Nowhere!" your dad screamed. "Spending our money on poetry and French philosophers."

"Baudelaire's a poet," you shot back. Pathetic.

"I don't give a damn who he is!" In your dad's wisdom, pursuing the sciences (he'd been alright with business too) was the only path forward. "Literature's for sissies. Are you girl?"

Your answer came on wings, the weight lifting: "If you're asking if I like guys, I do." Bam! Years of silence. Best thing he'd ever done was leave. And what a relief when he was again out of your life. Wasn't it … a relief?

MB's wringing his hands, his smile, a flash in what's left of the dark; the sun, demanding its place in the sky. "Nah. J'te niaise." A fog comes up, sweeping into your thoughts. *Flâneur – it's a kind of book browser. Enterprisin' witness of the modern metropolis.*

MB exhales a miniature cloud. Nodding in the direction of Burns' statue and without taking a breath and in the Scots tongue, he begins to recite. *But Mousie, thou art no thy-lane, / In proving foresight may be vain: / The best-laid schemes o' mice an' men Gang aft agley.*

Now, how the hell does he know the words? But you want to ask, does he fear the future, have regrets?

Traffic rolls up the hill. Once, your uncle told you engineers were going to add a humming sound, more like noise, to electric cars, so everyone would know to get out of the way. That's how things are in this world. Everyone having to get out of the way.

Along the wind, it seems, MB speaks, more to himself than to you. "Y'know, at night, there's little light on Burns over there but a whole lot of glare on that soldier and stallion, celebratin' war. And there, those words Burns had, bout a day when fightin's done, men get along, 'brithers and brithers.'"

Really? You've passed that statue a million times, never noticed a thing on 'brithers.'

In the light of dawn, the cries of seagulls split through the air. At this time of year? There's no glimmer of wing. Just cloud and more than a hint of belligerent sun. Everything's out of focus; like you and MB are seaside, both of you pirates. More cries, from some elusive pathway of sky. Citrus rays hit the bench, and it's like you and MB are posed at the imminent break between now and possibility, the smooth oil diptych of your separate worlds inaugurating a tableau of impressions. MB scratches a cheek. "How do poets get by?" Pointing to himself. "Forget it for this old fart."

This time it's your ethereal voice: "Keats found poetry to be like death. Slow and painful. Wanted to commit suicide, to end the pain."

"Of writing?"

"Of TB. Course, they never figured out what got him in the end."

MB pulls in the cart. Orchestra of the city, bows across steel strings. He leans in. "Y'know those words by Godin, up on that wall, at the métro over there, at Mount Royal?"

So odd he's mentioned the poem. Of course, you know the words along the wall – words engraved on golden plates, pounded into brick. *Tango de Montréal.* Godin's *le vieux coeur de la ville, le vieux coeur usé.* Immigrants waking up god-awful early (like you, but you're no immigrant), the city's beating heart: these, the people with *all the reason in the world* to give up.

MB shifts, murmurs: "Thanks to the early birds."

You feel you've been lifted, placed down, told to walk along a dotted line towards the future.

"So, y'know, I thought this one up on my own. Call it 'Asphalt Songs.' Slam-dunk free verse." Sucking in his chest, MB begins.

Telling lies, we compromise
Singing high, low
Sailors set out, as
Cargo slides, sweep of tide
   Asphalt highway
Packed in jagged stones
On city sidewalks, ghosts of Doctor Mesmer walk
   Neon and stiletto bliss, newlyweds
Sway past vendors of Old Jerusalem.
Box-store windows, jutting jaws
Holding chalk corpses
Misfits of a lost age
Play shopping limbo, slip-sliding
   Strolling by, wearing their lives like sideshows, fake jewels
The whole fuckin' time, in our bones, there's the hunger
And the drive
'Seize the day', they say
But loose change tumbles
From torn pockets
Every newborn, baptized
The one child, 'Hoped-For,' never arrives.

The city moves along that red-hot wire
No sleep for slung-on walkways, for the rough and tumble
No middle ground, no real common.

Silence, not from the waking city. From you. You feel a palpable brush with the inevitable.

Someone is speaking. "There's something Shelley said about poets –" With a start, you realize it's your voice.

MB's pulling at his tuque.

"Percy Shelley, married to Frankenstein's monster creator, Mary Shelley. Her husband said, 'poets know the world.'"

Actually, that's a pinch of a lie. Shelley called poets the most unacknowledged legislators of the world.

"That's it." MB's eyes wide: carved-out orbs reflecting your world. This world. Warbling pigeons settle on the blue-grey squares. Slowly, he leans over, calling: "Where've you been?" He sits up again. "Y'know, once these skies were filled with passenger pigeons. All of them shot dead." He mimics a trigger-pull.

Near your feet, the pigeons strut, with their iridescent collars and starched blue-black suits. Parlour dilettantes. *In the room where the women come and go.* Of course. Eliot again.

MB reaches inside a half-shorn pocket, pulls out a bun. Not a gun. For a second, you were worried.

"Usually the gulls are here first," he says, fanning out breadcrumbs like wildflower seeds. "Today, these soldiers beat them to it. One thing about those pesky gulls is the droplets on their back wings."

From above, despite winter's damp, the screeching gulls have magically appeared. Maybe they've overheard MB's disparaging comment and have come to wield their mighty beaks. One pierces the air. *J'accuse!* Sure enough, there they are: miniature black dots along each and every wing.

"If you listen, my friend: that's language. Like that lil' ole mouse Burns destroyed, these birds plan everything. That's the cleverest part. And no regrets."

"As far as we know."

"Oh, we know," he says.

It was a year ago. Dad's funeral. Surprising, the number of people who showed up. And that minister, droning on, when all you desperately wanted was to smash through the stained-glass wall.

Darling Death shouted in his ear, his ear made to record the least, the most finespun of worm-cries and dragonfly-jubilations – Denise Levertov, a favourite poet of yours. Died the day your dad decided to phone, welcoming you back into his fold of one.

Two weeks before his final days, your sister flew in from Vancouver. As you both stood over his bed, you found yourself staring at a stranger, perversely enough, alongside other strangers: his other family you hadn't seen in years. Saline solution flowing in, other liquids flowing out. At some point, it was just you and your sister, and she advised you to go home. That was the night he died. Over the phone, she broke into sobs. "When he was in that death fog, he was going on … going on about death masks, all being alike, all like his in the end."

"Masks?" Nothing made sense; the wretched miasma coming through the fog in your brain spoke: *You've never forgiven him, never told him that.* So what? Who cares about neglectful dads, about statesmen or poets or even about those buried below? Certainly not about MB, feeding breadcrumbs to these maligned city dwellers.

A few metres away, Sir W. Laurier berates you, with his magisterial robe and oh-so-familiar pleated trousers. *We are left alone with our day, and the time is short, and / History to the defeated / May say Alas but cannot help or pardon.* Auden.

Driving through stained glass …

"Liget," you mumble. "The emotion that hits you profoundly when you get an opportunity to feel again."

"What's that?"

"Nothing."

"Well then, my friend."

Briefcase in one hand, you offer the other, no longer worrying about what he's spluttered into his half-mitts. He hands you Gibson's book, and you notice pustules along his boney knuckles. "The street," he says.

You wait, then, nodding, finish Gibson's line: "It 'finds its own uses for things.' Thanks, but you keep the book."

He smiles. "Okay then. Bonne voyage and all."

Along the path, you glance back. Almost translucent, MB's waving, But ... what's this?! It's like he's disappearing. Later, you realize you were dreaming. The elusive bard's nowhere to be found, not in Dorchester Square, not on any street corner. No ghosts spouting non-sequiturs in free verse or regaling you with stories. No one who notices the droplets along the back wings of those pesky gulls.

Then They Went on Their Way

There is my country / wrapped in calm of night / steeped in steel-cold ice ...
—Gerry Kristyn

HERE, IN REYKJAVIK'S Harpa Convention Centre, the voices from the main corridor are indistinct. Outside this little alcove, people are grabbing a coffee or just hanging out, probably for the simple pleasure of being inside an enormous crystal. While leisure is their pleasure, waiting is your cross to bear. Fear – a good, healthy dose – rides through. Imagination serves as a welcome distraction. Should you let L know you've caught an earlier flight? He has no idea you've changed the itinerary. Hard to believe that only a few hours ago you'd left Montréal, soaring through the heavens, on a journey through Lost. As the pilots circled Iceland, you noticed threads of the familiar, the unfamiliar running roughshod over the uneven. Tricot medley, chromatic shades, dull greens and tan, to snow-capped peaks, masked in fog. 'Urður,' 'fate,' cognate of 'weird,' suited your disorientation.

From Keflavik, the bus through Landslagið headed into that furious blue ... through open windows, you swore you caught the incense of caves, volcanoes and lava fields. Beyond where you were sitting, the sea convened in lead-blue lifts, where, as you've seen in photos, barren rock faces stand as choirs. Inside your nostrils, along your tongue, slipped the fish-salt knowledge that these were Norwegian waters, the meeting of the Arctic and Atlantic. L has shared his people's legends, like the one about Mysing, who killed King *Fróð,* brought the king's slave women on a boat and ordered them to grind salt. When the boat sank ... so the salt sea.

So, yes, he has no idea you're waiting and worrying about how he's going to take this change of plans, the fact that you booked an earlier flight. Here's a thought: Can two men show affection in Reykjavik or anywhere in Iceland? L was adamant. "Of course! It's Iceland! Not Ah-MER-i-ca."

L: quick witted, descendant of Egil (if his genealogical map is to be believed), fervent greens, lightly lidded. In heart-stopping Icelandic lilt, L's asking questions carved from answers he already knows.

Harpa's pyramid windows throw triangles of light onto your face and arms. For fun, you touch the bevelled glass. Everything here, it seems (although only in this space), is curvilinear, with some Euclidian geometry. There's a chunk of pyramid that's been thrusted into this room. A glacier. Seems as though the sea's driving in. Pythagorean *tour de force,* touch of Miesian and Buckminster Fuller's Brutalism. In an ideal world, universities like McGill would dispatch their architect hopefuls (e.g., you) here. Forget the seven wonders. You're inside a hub of shapes, unbidden impressions, odd angles, pillars and pinions, imaginative squalls whipped around, pulled apart, brought together again. From your two years studying with architectural wizards (and some not so wizardly), it's easy to see this as the virtual gone viral in real time, Iceland's porthole to another world.

And it's right here, inside the centre, that L's rehearsing with the orchestra! Your breath shortens, as you straighten, try to clutch at whatever calm you have left. Soon, you'll see him. Soon, you'll text. No harm in down-time. Slipping a hand in a pocket, you pull out your cell. Below, your suitcase rests against a Sunkist-yellow Scandinavian block-seat, on which the *Icelandic Review* is open to a critique of L's ensemble, a group he plays with, on the side. *Innovative,* wrote the critic. That's cheery. Like L himself. Music, his calling. Yours, architecture and sound laboratories.

Hljóð, sound. 'Gallalaus,' flawless. Both of you having travelled along similar paths. Music and architecture; both musing on the pauses and empty spaces between.

Back when you were beginning your MA at McGill, late October, on a whim, you decided to end the evening with a concert. For a fifteen-dollar student ticket to Redpath Hall, you'd be treated to an hour of oboes and clarinets. Arriving late, you threw the student attendant a wry smile, opened the closed doors, checking your concert bill. Things being as they are, serendipitous, especially with the harvest moon busting out of its straight jacket, there, on the bill was 'Iceland.' Not the composer or composition (you were disappointed) but the birthplace of one of the student oboists. Somehow you knew you'd be charting this country, the skies of your future shadowing your present.

Earlier that very day, in the library, you'd been reading about Nordic architecture. Alongside paintings of twelfth and thirteenth-century homes, the author discussed the influence of Icelandic sensibility on the architecture of residential dwellings in certain parts of the world: the lack of trees reflected in the thatched grass roofs of the beehive Scandinavian homes, down south to Ireland's stone clocháns. Despite their dark interiors, the corbelled and thatched roofs and layered stone spoke of the quest for photosynthesis. Light, you thought, stronger in its absence. Then, that evening, there, on the concert bill, an Icelandic oboist who gave you a hard-on.

For a good hour, students breathed magical interpretations through wood. The oboe's rich, wide notes cajoled like a trickster. Reeling in apprehension, you introduced yourself, praising the musician's interpretation of Telemann. Circled by fans, he smiled. Secretly, you swooned. Turns out he was studying at McGill's Faculty of Music and used to live in Reykjavik ("not born there, in the city, I mean," he said, winking, with his obvious accent, probably Icelandic). Throwing your concert bill over the tightness in your jeans, you shook his hand. Those eyes, lift of hair, head in the shape the ancients used to plan cities (a joke you never shared). And one amazing, melting-heart smile. Your type. A+.

He complimented your musical knowledge, adding: "I can't understand why they let you in so late. You destroyed ... no, worse, fucked up my concentration!"

"But you hadn't yet begun! And how is 'fucked up' worse than destroyed?"

Over his face, gleeful smirk, quick wink.

L, for his part, carefree as they come, always turning your effusiveness into an aside. That evening, he told you to stick with him: Like Telemann, he'd steer you wrong. Walking home, you googled Telemann, found the composer was self-taught and went into music against his family's wishes and, basically, experienced a terrible love life. Tapping your phone's contact icon, you entered L's info. After two days of painful anticipation, you texted. Later, beneath sweat-soaked sheets, he made it clear that in Iceland, the fog pulls in before the downpour. "Before, after, all the time, we have rain, in all its glory."

His idiosyncratic phrasing in English made your already racing heart quicken. Your surprise at his English was embarrassingly communicated. But English, he told you, is, after all, spoken in Iceland's coastal cities. "Breaking up our usage of our mother tongue: what happens when we allow in the American military, paving our roads, our main arteries," leaving you deliberating different meanings of the word 'artery': What would it mean to let somebody in?

Uncontrollable jitters. You return your cellphone to your pocket. Later, this evening, you'll be listening to L sharpen his trill along the oboe's deep assonance. Here, under his sky, beside his sea, where the world runs along the sixty-sixth parallel, a guy could find himself forever in one spot, while trying his damnedest to turn away – which is what L did, when he first left here for Montréal.

And now he's given you an assignment. You're to critique the acoustics of the orchestra's production in Eldborg, Harpa's main concert hall, to gauge how well the strings ring out during the Brahms, under the able bowing of one young Russian violinist. As well, you're to focus on the resonating tones from his section: the product of breath through conical bore and flared bell.

But now is now, and the sun, brilliant. Next month, Iceland will be illuminated by midnight's cast from this very same celestial joy. When that happens, you'll be back in Montréal. This year apart has been hellish. A prism rainbow catches your eye. L was right about everything to do with this place. As the bus entered Reykjavik, the driver told passengers that it was unusually clear. Passing beautiful houses, roofs in Crayola's reminding you of home: St. Johns, Newfoundland. Polychromic façades, electric indigo – divergent shapes, glinting fences. Yes, almost the same terrain as in St. Johns. Maybe the craggy is a bit less relentless. Those crazy Atlantic winds are similar. And maybe there are as many clients in therapists' offices, if L is to be believed ... though you have heard that the Nordic are some of the happiest people around. "But who knows? We aren't a talking ... a *talkative* people," L confided once. Another tidbit he shared was that per capita, Iceland boasts the greatest percentage of Coca-Cola drinkers.

The strangest confession (L seemed to think it was a confession) is that he "*loooves* sitting along that seawall," letting the wind *mess* him up, his phrasing, contagion, from some trope (satirical) in a Québec novel you read to one another, pillow-side, a ritual that made you realize you'd been born into the wrong century. Still, considering your relationship: Good effin' question how that would've gone down.

Reserves of sun bounce off rippled glass, fracturing in rectilinear and polygon 1960s coral-orange and yellow panels. Impeccable fenestration, a shattering of light. 'Charming Prism Egotism.' Hats-off to the enfilade and modular interior. Symmetry, amid chaos; folly, whimsy, the out-of-place exactly where it belongs. Like you. Out of place and exactly where you belong. On your left, unknown doors lead to hidden chambers. There's a staircase. Nothing so heavenly up there that can't be found down here. Hard to believe the whole building's bustling with convention-goers. Inside this alcove, it's quiet. Alcove, 'cagibi,' from Montréal French, although the word's Italian. This whole interior is like a *Dr. Caligari* set.

In Montréal, on winter weekends, with the radiators bucking, you and your *chum* ('boyfriend' in Québec) hunkered down. L claimed Iceland's "much warmer in February."

"But here our immune system's strong as steel."

While watching *The Cabinet of Dr. Caligari,* he knew exactly what you meant, when you spoke of the subconsciousness captured in the film sets, lifted from nightmare's stuffing. As winter entered the city, both of you became more reclusive, the film choices growing crazier, like Tarkovsky's noir *Stalker* or, just to appease L's craving for action, Tarkovsky's *Ivan's Childhood.* "Leave it to me," you said, simulating his turn of phrase.

And, sure, St. Johns (after Confederacy) and Reykjavik could be sister cities. L's descriptions are travel brochures. You made him promise to take you to the ancient rock, Alþingi, seat of Parliament. Rule not by sword but by law. Then, to Þingvellir, in Thingvellir, a park, alongside Lake Thingvallavatn. The word, þingi, assembly of things: Music to your architect's soul. Magic, which Icelanders must find proof of along rocky shores, carrying lava rocks like jewels in their pockets. In a book you've been zipping through (great title), *The Geography of Bliss*, the author quotes Freud, who believed that the geography of the human brain isn't geared toward attaining heavenly bliss, but … hold on … you're blissful and shit-worried. Everything you've built could be dashed against the rocks. Or …

The talk of whaling almost finished the deal, with L swearing that everyone wanted to take Icelanders down. Took hours … no, days for you to agree that *every* culture has made a fine mess of things. But that was almost it, almost it for nights, knees buckling, both of you tumbling onto the bed. Chests heaving, cocks riding against sweating thighs … all to say that if there were any epidemiological evidence for the links between love, culture and weather, well, there you have it – here actually, about forty-five minutes from Keflavik's International Airport.

When you'd hopped off the bus and walked towards the sea-wall, there it was! Harpa, in its post-industrial, windowed glory. Just as you wondered how you'd gone so long without the sea, you wondered how you'd gone on so long without ever seeing a building this amazing. Then, along the sea-walk, Árnason's shining-steel Viking ship, the Sun Voyager, the genus loci, 'protective spirit of the place.'

Now, inside, protected from bitterly cold waters, you imagine taking L in your arms, Titian locks framing jocular brows, sporting the cap you bought him in Edinburgh. Clasping his oboe like an earnest sentry. "This way, my love," he'll sing. Of course, you'll kiss. "The best tincture," you've told yourself. And now, come to think of it, you're not *that* far from the Lewis Islands, home to the legendary chess set, carved from walrus tusks, by Margaret the Adroit (or so it's been theorized), *'Clever Margaret.'* Like your dear friend Margaret, who was studying at MIT. Last year, far too soon and soon after receiving the chilling diagnosis of breast cancer, she was gone … how incredible if she could have joined you here, breathing in the wild birch salt air. "That fragrance! Enough of the stuck-in-the-mud 21st century! I'm inventing a camera that captures aroma."

"You mean an instrument that *records* smells."

Clever Margaret, smiling, would offer historical relevance to this place, to the ewes and rams, feasting on fragrant grass with their lambs.

"See that wedding cake?" This was a year ago, and she was pointing to the crème de la crème of wedding cakes, her multi-coloured scarf wrapped about her head, her eyebrows almost all gone. Around the table, friends were discussing weddings and how they weren't much the thing.

"Maybe it's ego speaking," she whispered. "I'm like that dessert."

"You? Dessert?" Trying to make headway through her puzzle, wondering too if the next wedding would be yours and L's.

Margaret pointed at the cake. "Temporary, I mean. Of course, *life* is, but edible works of art … they're …" She smiled. "Transitory. I'll be crumbs. And this time next year, I'll be –"

You stopped her from saying more.

The harbour enters through an intersection of glass, refracting light within sharp edges. Beyond, sails folded along their masts pin the air, alongside tethered fishing boats, unencumbered with any aesthetic duty to muse about their surroundings. A crystal palace is what this is – as a kid, you stretched out pockets with nature's architecture, scrunching up your face against a microscope lens to view intersecting lines and caverns. Patterns in those crystals repeated in the larger universe. One university professor gave a lecture about the smallest to largest item in the universe, how even immeasurable mass displaces space and how the universe can be re-imagined as a folding-in. On Halloween, the same prof offered: "Not implausible that future physicists will find ghosts hidden within the corners, tucked-away." The metaphor?

The Mobius strip!

L's tried convincing you there is definitely light during the dark winters, the sudden squalls and rain. Leaning to one side, placing his cheek into an invisible rivet – something he does when he's about to extemporize: "And at least in Iceland, we jailed the bankers." Then, one grand leap to imperialism. "Danes, Norwegians, even the U.K., recently, with the Cod Wars: all imperialists, who sought our demise, to colonize us and demand our beautiful island, its legends, its stories, as their own. Certainly," he added. "Who wouldn't? But I cannot advise anyone to worship or care about such thieves."

Annoyed, you countered: "You're an island in a raging sea," not an entirely literal pronouncement. But the bitterness in his words was familiar. With your parents, it's always been about Newfoundland's precarious standing among the Confederate provinces. L grew quarrelsome. "We've managed to put away some of the capitalist bankers, something no one else did."

And what can you offer, cocooned inside Canadian history, watching Montréal's long-standing Anglo-Franco divide, reading about the Quiet Revolution, the resentment still tangible? Even more egregious, what have you learned about stolen land? L's berated you for not knowing more. "It's your responsibility to learn," he said, after you pointed out your formal education contained NOTHING on residential schools. "We've been fighting the colonizers, have become pretty good at sniffing out treachery. Our own schools taught us … or certainly we took the time to find out."

You'd opened your mouth, closed on a thought. Relieved you'd kept silent.

L's called you a melancholy realist, the worst.

"And you're a reckless optimist."

"I *am* from reckless winter nights."

"Maybe, but Newfoundland's winters can be pretty reckless … and feckless."

That's when he promised you'd be his guide through "this Newfoundland." Only he's never visited, just thrown out promises like roses along an aisle.

Once, under a particularly dreary Montréal January, he suggested a guy in Iceland would have to *while* away the endless endlessness. Going back to the solid *Wow!* of his phrasing, you remember leaping up to embrace him.

"What's this?" He pulled you closer.

"I'm thinking, therefore, I am –"A horrible image came to mind, from Clever Margaret: Descartes, cutting open puppies, charting their cries of pain, as he tested his hypothesis that non-human animals were mechanized clocks. Their suffering, apparently, he didn't notice.

L kissed you. "You're … skörungskapr, thinking all the time."

Almost untranslatable. Later, you learned that the word isn't about thinking at all but more to do with 'generosity' or 'nobility,' with 'leadership.' Maybe mostly to do with 'moxie,' what the Valkyries and Queen Gunnhild had, the kind of courage that once earned you land.

So, how has he been, this past year? Shitty, he claims. Missing you, he says, as you both face one another over Skype or Facetime. Easy to be sentimental, he's told you, and you suddenly realize that he was saying it's easy to be poetic if you're from this land. Definitely easier inside this crystal palace, expressing the sun and sea through a geometry of windows. Memory forms along the colour refraction. Egil and Erik. The sagas. Once, just so you could hear lyrical Icelandic read out loud, L narrated the lesser known *Ref, the Sly*. "Ref's called a sissy." He translated a bit into English, which is when you corrected: "Called *out* for being a sissy."

L didn't flinch. "Yes, homosexual. Queer. Thorgil, the Chieftain, describes Ref's shepherding in Greenland, calls him sissywoman."

"Hmm." Nope, this characterization was not one you'd add to your repertoire. But you didn't say this, instead: "They need more characterization, more about the lesser ones."

"You have no idea. This is a saga. All they need is the hero. This is the framework. The writers were concerned with heroes, with describing the natural life."

"But there's … I don't know. There's nothing on the characters' intentions and nothing much on anyone beyond the main character."

"Does that matter? We don't need the rest. Thorgil's sons call Ref 'Ref the Effeminate,' 'Ref the Gay.' It's through them, we see Ref. His nature is the reason he was kicked out of Eylenda." (Eylenda: Lýðveldið, Ísland. Ref, from refur, meaning fox.) "Ref will prove them wrong, not a sissy at all."

"And there you go."

"There I go?"

You bolted up in bed. "Using homosexuality, queerness as synonymous with deadbeat. Who cares if it was years ago?"

"*Hundred*s of years in the past."

"And Ref is the Exiled Queer. More than four hundred years of shit about queerness, and NOTHING's changed!"

L was silent.

"Even now! Can we hold hands in public? Kiss, for Christ's sakes? And all this about how Ref will prove them wrong, not queer at all?" Ego said your logic was flawless.

L closed the cover, smacked down the book on the night table. Lights out.

In the morning, you apologized, adding: "It's about the fucking homophobia."

The next saga you read alone: the Laxdæla saga, which may have been penned by a woman. "It apparently has the female touch, archetypical story," you said.

L turned over in bed, facing you. "I read it."

"It's about fratricide. Cain and Abel."

L visibly cringed. This was over a woman, he insisted, Guðrún, and while the story has a fraternal battle, it's not because of any god accepting a lamb sacrifice over a harvest.

"More about fate, you mean."

L rolled over, smiling this time. "Sure, Elskan mín ('my dear'). Fate."

Your lover has promised to guide you through Viking settlements, but with an important correction: "*Norse* settlements, since Vikings aren't fat men in horned hats," and 'Going on a viking' is going on a journey. He'll even present portholes to the worlds of the Huldufólk, the hidden people, as long as you don't "do circus-making summarizations of my culture."

So, you've bundled up your teen-like enthusiasm and fit it into a quiet interest. Quiet interest on the Huldufólk, who guide the reckless to safe shores, a passing interest of fishwomen (similar to selkies, in Scotland), who steal men's hearts. In a week, at volcanic mountains, you'll hear stories of giants, also steering travellers off-course. Seems this is what Icelandic other-people do: steer people (like you) off course. You catch yourself. Are you relegating all this island's beliefs to folksy mythology? Is L right? Sighing, you sit down, glance again at the review on L's ensemble. He's your less naughty (pun intended) guide, a Virgil, guiding you through rugged, poetic terrain. "Origin of poetry, started with a peace-meeting. The gods, at war with the Vanir, agreed to a truce and to demonstrate their agreement, spit into a pot." L grabbed the knife you were using to cut the tomatoes, sliced through a juicy one. "Their spit was a truth token, became a guy named Kvasir, who travelled around, answering questions."

You backed towards the fridge. "So, Kvasir's a symbol of answers inside questions, of asking all the time?"

With his knife finally stilled, L cut in verbally; "Yes, of interruptions. When Kvasir –"

"So, this guy Kvasir was Vanir's son?"

"And, like all guys with the task of dealing with so many questions, he was killed, his blood … but he wasn't killed in vain, you say in English?"

"In vain, in our veins."

L ignored your stupid pun. "Kvasir's blood mixed with honey, became mead. Odin discovered this mead-blood. Poetry is 'Odin's Catch.' Whoever drinks it becomes a poet."

You circle danced around L, who continued slicing into a blood-red tomato. "You've definitely had a sip."

L relaxed his shoulders. "I'm a man of prose."

Taking the knife from him, resting it on the counter. "You? Prosaic?"

"Maybe poetic. Poetry answers that elusive question, Elskan."

Kissing him. "Which is?"

"Has to do with honey. If it's sweet enough for the throat, then it's good enough."

"That's not a question. It's not elusive either."

The thick foam steppes of tidal water braise the seawall; the sea, shored up by a concrete plaza, could be skateboard Mecca. You're reminded of some Montréal ice sculptures you saw a couple years ago, the angles reflecting the sun's errant light, pitching it into your linked hands. L was lecturing about his country's auteur célèbre, Halldór Laxness, how Laxness' wit and telling prose illustrate the pastoral struggle. As you applauded his outstanding English, he called you patronizing. A few weeks later, you spotted *Sjálfstætt folk, Independent People,* on an after-Christmas sales rack.

Laxness's writing was impressive, from the first to last line, 'Then they went on their way,' which you read (this thing you do), right there at the store. L had read the book long ago and asked: "Why read the last line before all the rest?"

"You know I do that. Sometimes. Taste the succulent ends before beginning the novel. But this habit's never ruined a story."

"'Went on their way.' That's what I hope to do." He wrapped an arm around your shoulders, like the roof of a shelter in a squall. Now, you wonder: What did he mean?

Dancing through packed snow, down a path lined by ice sculptures: "Ástvinur," he called you. *Love friend.* A group of ass-holes were staring. "Let's kiss." Abruptly, he swung you around. You wanted to tell the a-holes to go to hell.

"Idiots who should be living their lives, not envying ours," he said, smiling. Laughter from high-school bullies echoed in your head.

"Storytelling's our inheritance. Goes back to the ancestors, to tales of the dead."

"Zombies!" you cried.

"Not exactly."

"Vampires!"

Again, he was dubious.

Being in L's arms has been like coasting, arriving at an abode, skáld-like. Intrepid traveller, you've placed your body in his arms, running a palm over their muscled halves.

'Then they went on their way' *was* an interesting line, but you opted for another novel: *Under the Glacier,* Laxness' tribute to the Icelandic wit, populated with philosophic somersaults and (of course) magic. Its supercilious cover caught your attention, the cover reminding you of Lawren Harris' surreal glacier. Harris' "I'm trying to get up to the summit of my soul and work there – there where the universe sings" was a line you'll never forget, from one museum wall. A few years ago, you heard, Harris' paintings were, weirdly enough, auctioned off by Imperial Shell Oil: fossil-fuel execs, wanting nothing to do with glaciers, melting or otherwise. The subject of Laxness' story? Take your pick: the game of love or love's elusiveness. Surprisingly, L never read this one.

A theology student, Embi ("Umbi," L corrected, revealing that he did know of the story and that it was based on the Eyrbyggja saga) is sent by a bishop to a small town to investigate rumours of a glacier burial, a very un-Christian burial. When Umbi arrives, the church is boarded up, the irreverent pastor, a silversmith. What's more, it's rumoured, the silversmith/ex-pastor has fallen in love with the elusive Úa. Problem is, Úa is a magical fishwoman, and the villagers are convinced she's a trickster. Your theory: She's a ghost.

Inevitably, Embi or Umbi falls in love with her.

Embi (to himself): Is this love?

Úa (obviously a trickster, since she's read his thoughts): "Could be, if you imagine it to be."

And the novel's ending – this side of crazy.

"Nordic," L said. "But I'm not a fan of fishwomen."

"What about mermen?"

"Maybe." He laughed.

Towards the end, Embi and Úa drive into a raging downpour. Their car stalls in the fast-rising mud. "Follow me," she calls. Embi does her bidding, follows her through the rainstorm to her house. Inside, he immediately finds himself alone, and the building, dilapidated, a woman's laughter echoing against broken beams. Scared out of his mind, he charges out, into the rain and probably away forever from love.

"That's it!" you yelled. L jumped. "Úa evaporates."

"Porthole to another world?"

"Could be."

Now you're in L's world. He's promised to take you to where he was born, a valley shadowed by an active volcano, not far from Hekla, gateway to hell, entrance to the underworld.

You turn quickly, catching … was that motion or a prism's reflection? Maybe L *has* jumped through a porthole. There's something familiar and equally strange about him, about you with him. What's not strange is brick-by-prevailing-brick the bridge between both your worlds, your shared Montréal residency. L claimed that Montréal is where he "grew into himself, this thing you do in your twenties," he said, as if he were decades older. "There's always room to be someone different from what you were meant to become. Always room to become –"

"A merman!"

Each of you finding the other quirky, sometimes uninformed. Like during that one St. Jean Baptiste parade, in Parc Jean-Drapeau, among a deluge of partiers; Québec's fleur de lys flags like superhero capes, draped around shoulders. Around wrists, blue and white arm-bracelets, worn as amulets. Soldiering tank-top chests, bare shoulders or tattooed artistry – you commented on sovereignty, said it hasn't been going anywhere. If anything, it's plateaued; not, as L suggested, on an incline to "God knows what," he said. "In twenty years, you'll see," he countered. "Revision of sovereignty. History's a needle in our veins." He should know, he insisted. His interest in Québec goes way back. "The chasms in your country have *always* been my desire."

"Rifts. Schisms. Not chasms."

"Rifts?"

What you were trying to say is that it's impossible to negotiate people's allegiances, while, on giant insect wings, crossing the geopolitical map. Yeah, sure, negotiating national allegiances … like relationships. Forget it.

Ping! Your phone.

Rehearsing. Miss u. Can't wait 2 c u.

You text, *Luv u 2,* pause over *Send,* ride a hand along the phone. *Here. I'm here now.*

Again, you wonder: Is it *really* acceptable here to show queerness, in all its glory?

"Of course!" L has thrown his hands in the air. "We'll do whatever we wish – fuck, if you'd like."

He's been insisting for a long time that you visit. Like last year, in Montréal, when he was pointing to an ice-sculpture, a chess set, the sun bouncing off the rook: a Lawren Harris futuristic, horizontally-coned marvel with turrets. "We have Reykjavik's Harpa, which you'd love. It's … I don't know, maybe it's like Montréal's Grande Bibliothèque? Only wilder. Hexagon honeycomb for windows."

"I can see how anything in Iceland would be wilder."

But your voice was consumed by prevailing winds. For a second, you wondered if you'd spoken, if in fact it wasn't a dream.

L turned to you, top of his tuque shining in the sun. "Doubled-wall glass, for Reykjavik's Convention Centre. Built by a Danish-Icelander. Set of triangles for windows." Scoping a hand over an eye: "You have to pretend you're looking through this."

"A kaleidoscope? Telescope?"

"Magic pieces of glass."

"Seems it's about transposing perspective."

"Sure, Elskan mín, perspective."

But you were off, running. "Like the Neo-concrete movement: all about metaphysics. Started with a manifesto: Brazilian artists in the 1960s wrote about transformation, opening doors to previously unknown hidden rooms. Mostly this transformation was about experiencing continuum with the object."

Ping! Your phone. *Wtf? How are you here?*

You text, *Earlier flight. I'm here @ Harpa.*

Once, during a heated discussion on language, L was throwing out ideas. Most you didn't get, but you did understand this: "Besides, many Icelandic authors are writing in English and Norwegian. We keep Icelandic alive. And, of course, we have November 16th."

"What's that?"

"Jónas Hallgrímsson's birthday. We celebrate poets' birthdays."

You'd never said otherwise. Caught in some bizarre storm's eye, you'd tried reframing. All you'd meant was that Icelanders should claim their language, offer incentives and support their artists.

He was surging, angry eyes. "You don't realize. Our writers receive adequate funding. We are EXTREMELY literate people."

Maybe it was the way you voiced your thoughts, the words you chose to transform meaning. Maybe you were being didactic and/or probably obtuse.

Icelandic is a brew, L's told you. "We have Papal Latin, Shetland; Hebrides; Orkney …" He paused. "Pict. Norse, Danish." He was counting on his fingers. "Anglo, Germanic. Our heritage for storytelling comes from all over the Atlantic."

Ping! If ur here, I'm coming.

You lower yourself onto the block-seat.

Cum all you want.

Texting him a photo, *I'm here, by the hexagon honeycomb.* You conjure up his voice, the way he rolls his r's. There's that French expression: 'il te manque,' 'he of you misses,' like he's holding a chunk of you.

It's been exactly a year. Last April, in Montréal, both of you were out late night, poetry slamming, listening to musicians wrangle the hell out of steel strings. Montréal was just waking to spring, the lightning-bolt season but without the thunderous blooms. Broken pavement was lined with human circuses, crumbling asphalt and potholes – the kind of rainy, bare-branched spring during which L was nodding to passers-by.

"You're too friendly," you blurted, immediately regretting. He'd been pushing you to visit Iceland. "Then, maybe Newfoundland," you'd said, afraid of his response.

"Sure." Then, more forcibly: "Certainly!"

Who'd guess he'd get chosen right after graduation? Maybe he's too optimistic, but he *did* land this job in the country's premier orchestra. One more year of architecture; then, maybe you'll take your father's given name as a surname, add *son* and, like Bobbie Fischer (minus the chess and the paranoid vitriol), call this island home. Or maybe (doubtful) L will return to Montréal. Maybe you'll try Paris or Chicago – *the* architectural Arcadia and not so bad for an oboist. Fine thing, dreaming.

Ping. Almost there.

Reykjavik's palace of light opens to voices. Laughter slides through. A *frisson* rides up your neck. Nagging winds tail in: *Will he? Will you?* Background voices grow distinct. You're surrounded not by a sea (true enough) but a lava lamp: oil-pustules elongating, dividing.

"Hey!"

And there he is, familiar case slung over his shoulders. Brows lifted, soft curls and YES! Wearing the Edinburgh cap. He strides over, his smile breaking ground the closer he gets. And then who cares? His tongue sweet, his lips, sweeter. "Always outdone by your trickery. How convincing, Elskan mín. Thought you'd be here right before the concert."

Between short breaths: "And so I am, here before it begins!"

"Trickster." Amazing lips.

"Same."

"Same? Can't be."

You pull back. "Remember that Telemann concert?"

"Sure," he murmurs.

"I rushed in after the doors closed."

He laughs. "You wrecked my performance." He reaches for your suitcase. "Just this, my minimalist friend?" He smiles at the paper, open to the review.

You lick his sweet saliva (pheromone paradise), grab your suitcase from his ready hands. "I've got it. You already have your oboe."

"But I'm your host. Let's go eat. You must be starving!"

"Aren't you too nerve-wracked?"

"No, silly." Amazing shoulders. "I'm a pro."

One last view of the symmetry of angles: "You're right; this place –"

Deep-chested laughter. "My *kærasti,* there's more to come. Reykjavik's … why, the whole of Iceland is waiting. Let's be on our way."

Stop. Rewind.

There's a man, standing, staring. In broken English, a woman, asking you who you're speaking to, her eyes glinting wildly. How the –?

And … L? Djákninn á Myrká, the Deacon of Dark River. Disappearing around the corner. Rippling laughter, faintly alluring. What? Please. What? Is? Going? On? L? Is he … ? Hold on. You steady yourself. Breathe. You steal a peek out to the salted sea. The breakers, silent from this side of the divide, roll in on a whisper: *Let it be for now.*

Memory Becomes You

ON SILENT WINDS, you move. There's purpose in your step. No doors need opening, no bells need ringing, as you move on through, like an afterthought. In the foyer, the garish red framing of Vermeer's *Astronomer* is still here. Surprising how much is still here. No disintegration of house or home.

And … one of your paintings. Ringed Saturn and a mysterious planet you named *Memory Becomes You*. Maybe you ought to throw in a tidy ending. So, you do. Right here. Right now. Something that the ever-observant might locate in the dark swirls. One black hole meeting another, a rendezvous, a gift, in Vantablack. Will he notice this pulsing in the depths of black, your answer to his call?

"Vermeer," he mumbled one evening.

"What about him?" Your tongue was heavy, brain asleep.

"Invented flash-fashion, only it became more than a flash."

"I've never heard about the fashion aspect, but I like what he did with camera lucida."

"Invention is the soul of necessity."

You shared your thoughts on paints, painters and astronomers; on mathematicians, like him, spinning gold. On doctors like you, who in previous iterations might have been able to do more for mathematicians like him or for patients like you.

"That blue must have been heaven to work with – the crushed semi-precious stone."

"The soul of distraction," he said. "That's painting. That's math."

"Scientific *and* poetic." From your usual place on the sofa, you stretched out your aching legs, realized humans don't need anything but massages and curiosity: the kind of massages he offered and the kind of wonder you explored in your painting. Dancing is what painting was, as you let the sabre bristle's swish over the canvas; all senses piqued. You savoured the chemical sweetness of linseed oil, grew joyous as the colours were squeezed out of their tubes onto the palette. Ribald Titanium White and its unflinching opacity. Burnt Sienna, capricious. The vibrancy of colour. Into the Alizarin, the Ivory Black dances, while remaining magically undetectable. "Add Munch's mystical orange," an instructor once advised. With this, your landscape was elevated into purple.

The corridor empties into the living room. You pass a tentative hand over the furnishings. Yes, appearances are indeed deceiving: the soft accordance of the substantive with what's become of you. Mesmerized, you watch your hand waterfall through.

On your left, through the window, flagstone steps to Paradise. Along the grass, crimson and orange leaves scatter. From the arching ceiba you planted, to the oak, to the fruit-bearing plum tree he nurtured into towering maturity, and beyond, where sunlight catches the surface of the sea, luminescent bodies splinter into veils, showering upon the water's surface – like a hundred jewelled arachnids. Long ago, you brought him along for your second visit to this place, the real estate agent close behind. The door swung open to ceilings festooned with morning's welcome. "You'll have to see the study," you sang. "No distractions!"

"Oceans can serve as a distraction," he replied, smiling.

"Not on my watch!"

Quickly, the fantasy of ripping your lives from habit and moving here had graduated to a possibility. In the end, it was a mutual decision to settle along this British coastline, buffered by Ireland from prevailing winds, synchronizing temperaments to the mercurial Atlantic waters spilling over cliffs, crashing into rocks, somehow peacefully settling along silken sands. At this precise moment, you're on a quest for the familiar: the wall in muted copper, the rest in sunbath yellow, a swathe allocated to Frida Kahlo's self-portraiture. Kahlo's in lush jungle green, punch of life, her chest ornamented with a thorn necklace and hummingbird. Over one of her shoulders, a spider monkey pensively regards the hummingbird and necklace. Behind the other shoulder, a bone-thin black cat slinks about. The cat resembles a member of your own household. Kahlo's coal eyes carry a frigid air of insouciance. If it hadn't been for your honeymoon to Mexico, your solo tour of her house in Coyoacán, you'd never have understood that stare.

Here, near the study, fractured prisms of light illuminate soft pine beams. Beneath the study's window, there he is: the mathematician you met that fateful day your professor lectured on the Stendhal syndrome, on confusion and hallucinations when viewing art, particularly in Florence. In that lecture hall, this man who became your husband turned to you, whispered a story about his own experience with art, his visualization of numbers as points along an infinite line. What followed was the strangest few months, the both of you soaring on that ridiculous equation of two.

The window across the desk reflects dusk's sweet brush of setting sun. Outside, foam tides break against the sandy shore. He looks fine without you, although somewhat Dickensian, hunched over that writing desk of his, modest twin to the unvarnished chair. Hmm, and just as always, he's jotting in his notebook. Beneath the familiar Shetland sweater, the curve of back. Along his left shoulder, tension.

Memory is odd on this side of the divide. It enters as texture. Glass is the texture of Southern France, you realized, as you surreptitiously ran fingers along Chagall's stained treasures. His leaping faith expressed in painted riddles of dance and music. And that same year, when both of you flew to New York; in front of

Chagall's dancing couple painting, he surprised you, twirling you round. Then the trip after your wedding to Mexico, when you went by yourself to visit Kahlo's house, painted yellow, amaranth, crimson and rosewood, the richness of absence in creamy white. Along the exterior, brilliant cobalt stucco.

It was perhaps fitting that you and your husband, both newlyweds, met at the Fountain of the Drinking Coyotes. Your voice rose, as you related Frida's life with Diego and everything you'd learned about their marriage, joking that your own very new marriage might end, if things ever teetered a fraction of an inch overboard.

"Ah, you have our marriage in its grave already." He was looking over his shoulder at the two sculptured coyotes. Children chased each other around the fountain, shouting. You were just out of med school, taking in the desert sun, with a mathematician, who was running imaginary numbers through eyes of needles.

You related the horror: Diego's visits to the morgue.

Eyebrows arched: "Morgue?"

"Yes! Rivera dined on corpses! 'Women's legs,' he wrote in his journal. They 'were the tastiest', he wrote."

His laughter met your unbounded anger.

Angrily, you added: "It's insane. What a misogynist monster."

"Sounds like he was being sardonic."

"Misogynist. And Diego was probably a bloody cannibal! I think this was after Frida died, though I'm not sure." Sitting, you straightened out your legs, clenched sandaled toes. Unclenched. "It'll require further investigation."

He slid an arm around your shoulders.

On this, the last day of your adventure in Mexico, it was all about history flipping into present-day. If only Diego hadn't met Frida and her monkeys, cats and birds. If only Frida, hadn't met Trotsky. What if you hadn't met this mathematician?

"You're being patronizing," you told him. "I don't see what's so damned funny."

"Curse of my kin. Our dragons are humour breathing fiends."

While you were ensconced in Frida's world, he'd paid a visit to a former mentor and related to you their discussion on math. But you were trying to dissect Diego's life, the 1930s rally he attended with other Communists and a speech given by Hitler. What would this mathematician you married make of Diego's friend's unexpected approbation concerning Adolf Hitler, whom some of the Communists found to be a terrifyingly effective speaker? "I could shoot him right now," whispered Diego's friend, pistol at his side. The friend, Jewish, was later killed.

Light glinted off the greys of your husband's irises, as he heard the story. "Hmm. We're creatures destined to be entrenched in past horrors, theorizing about changing one event in our ruinous past. Changing the present in consequential ways … well, it could of course be for the better when it comes to most of the twentieth century. And I can only speak to this century. You know, my love, common sense tells us there is no past, no future. Or perhaps yes, there is, but only as points along a graph. Nonexistent, except in the realm of numbers."

"Memory," you interjected. "This provides *some* hope horrible things don't happen again."

"Maybe," he said, dubiously. "But the terrible irony of that story about Hitler and the Communists, and Diego's friend's lack of courage in not pulling the trigger, is there's nothing left but speculation. 'For next time,' we'll say. There's a word: Maktub, Arabic. Loosely translated, 'It is written.' Not that I agree about a pre-written order to the world, but accepting this idea … I'm not speaking of inaction, not at all, and not of acceptance, no. I'm speaking of the sense the present makes of the past, that puzzling through these events inevitably leaves us despondent, craving retribution, more and more needy for the thought experiment, the counterfactual *what if*. You know, Dante banished fortune-tellers to one of the circles of Hell, their heads screwed on backwards."

"Why put them in Hell?"

He didn't answer right away. You waited. "As Diego's friend should've taken out his pistol, shot the bastard, it's also certain he wasn't going to. Interesting, the Communists were worried but opted for impassivity over mutiny; so strange how effective Hitler was in sleuthing about until he could ride through that open door and into everyone's consciousness."

"The fabric of unacknowledged hate," you said, shivering. "Why is it always a choice of fear and inaction rather than revolution?"

"Oh, there's always revolution."

Frida, Diego and the tragicomedy about love witnessed, passion in abundance. Maybe you were attracted to the idea that this act, Frida's and certainly Diego's, would never be yours. That night you realized relationships are like crime plays, like the one about Héloïse and Abélard.

The both of you were luxuriating in bedsheets at the hacienda. "Love? Forget it. Results in Abélard being castrated. He's banished. So is Héloïse."

Dozing in the lazy morning, your partner in crime brought up Stieglitz and O'Keeffe, de Beauvoir and Sartre: "Real criminals there."

"Hope not," you murmured.

He brushed a hand against your skin.

"You know, Sartre slept around," you said.

"Ah, then forget it." His breath, hot along your breasts.

Now, as you move past Kahlo's self-portrait, you notice that beneath the harmony and brash celebration there's an indiscriminate darkness. Surely, the hummingbird and thorn necklace have everything to do with what you'd been trying to tell him. You move forward, ready to kiss him entry into this world. It's been years since you left. As far as you know, he's been present … but only just. Passing the Bauhaus sofa, the *pièce de résistance,* in 'Irish green,' you once called the brash tone: Snot-green, Stephen Dedalus' "snot-green sea." Dedalus, who also called history "the nightmare from which" he was "trying to awaken," prophetic for what was to become of you; only, when you'd purchased this sofa, your nightmare was years off.

All those trips together, driving over borders, when the world was new and mystifying, listening to audio books, the whimsical reading of *Ulysses,* the narrator's tonal flourishes drawing distinct personalities out of endless, unbroken internal monologues, out of the frescos of dialogue and inner voice, demonstrating that Joyce's work was meant to be read aloud.

Out there, the setting sun is mesmerizing, even inside what is rapidly becoming cloud-cast sky. There's a clap of thunder. You smile at the call of time's passing. The mathematician adjusts his John Lennons: this man who once was your husband. You reach out, think better of moving closer. His hair, tousled brown, sliding into grey – surprising, since you've been away. And there's a bit of balding, tucked beneath a carefully brushed wave. There, against the left side of his neck, the birthmark whose map you once smoothed with a finger. Along his right cheek, a familiar scar, made in Italy, during his tumble down a hill in Cinque-Terre. Your cries tore through you, painfully, in a rush, as he smashed against the rocks. Scene of tragedy, the peppery fragrance of fresh olives accompanying your leaps down the hill.

After one frenzied lope through the grove, one blood-soaked face and surprised farmer and many stitches later, both of you were languid-wine laughing, speaking of the urgency to add Latinate-gone-Italian to your medical lexicon, wondering if it had been Athena who'd taught the mortals how to cultivate (meaning, how to pickle) olives. On a terrace overlooking ancient hills, you toasted your love for one another, feral cats mewing plaintively around your ankles.

Times like those, both of you kindred to one another's pain. And that Christmas Eve, when the on-duty cardiologist at the hospital where you worked diagnosed a very young woman with aggressive Non-Hodgkin lymphoma. Memory brings you along, as the patient asked whether she'd be allowed to spend Christmas with her family along the coast. Weeks later, when on one channel, there was a documentary on Van Gogh's *The Starry Night,* and the next day when you and the mathematician walked along the quay, the walk became prayer. Then, a year later, when the young woman hadn't pulled through, remembering how he held you, as you cried yourself to sleep.

It's a bit lighter, slower on this, your side, the calibration different. In his dimension of secret sorrows and wonder, things are heavier but also quicker. The sun's winking out, dissolution of light. Enter the shadows. There's a pang, the soft perfume of rain, a sudden and unexpected drizzle (no telling when it'll become a downpour). Thunder again. Closer now, and how odd, considering you haven't thought about things in this fashion in so very long. So, how can such a feeling possibly be moving inside you now? Thoughts of a writer who said that one should write, if only a little, every day. Feeds the soul, the halcyon infinite. For you, that infinite is being here with him.

Outside, the land recedes. The rain intensifies. Desire is a current …

You remember being beside him, jesting, contemplating 'what ifs,' playing chess and leaping out of your chair. "Checkmate!" Your queen and remaining bishop had his king. A blood bath!

"Can't be!" He was mortified.

"Have a look. Next time pay attention to the board, darling. Not on endless binomials."

"My God. How did you manage that?"

Along the sofa, you notice a faint contusion – here you used to sit, sipping from each other's stories, listening as he eulogized typewriters. Here too, where Gísla, the cat, napped beside Snorsi, a Bengal cat, who left life far too soon. To your left is the fawn-coloured settee and old mirror, more of cheap antique than kitsch prank. Through its silver-plated glass, a looking-glass window into a parallel room, every indiscretion captured, except when it comes to you. You daren't look. Probability tells you that you won't be there, reflected.

Hesitating – slavish adherence to the liminal space surrounding, then deciding to stay the course. His half-smile calls you from the shadows. Moving into empty: his world without yours. Shimmering sky, wrinkle in time.

Back when you'd decided to re-upholster the sofa, set it upside-down, you'd found a book with an intriguing footnote on green and blue, the lack of distinction between those two colours in ancient Asian cultures. His response was a quick signature along the line of your wondering. "Modernity was responsible for that need, I suppose."

"Need of what?"

"Need for distinction, maybe." He wasn't sure. "Modernity brought in a need for distinguishing one of those colours from the other … maybe."

"Well, *that* hadn't crossed my mind. Trade was responsible, more like it. Finding a common language."

You stop, consider. Where you're from, they say it can't be done. Not completely. Maybe in episodic blips and only when they truly call. Well, yes, he's called.

Another reason you're here: to see how he's changed, since constancy has become like the bow of a ship, viewed from the shore, through the haze of being. Outside, salty waters slosh against land. Autumn evening carries rain's sorrows; paint peels along the sill. Peculiar how the lamplight he's just turned on captures subtle changes to his face, reflects along his glasses, sifts through his frown like a hand through sand. Forehead wrinkling, eyebrows furled. Familiar tremor along his lips. You reach out, but there's no touching. He furiously dances his pencil along the page, tip to tempo, over numbers revealing ... creation, in a way. Sex, you think, smiling. Shapes, supernal circles, polygons within other polygons, atomic structures, points along an elliptical. Wait ... surely, this isn't what you want to see. Shouldn't he be somewhere else ... indeed, with someone else?

Frowning, you move closer.

There's melody to his scratchings. If you were engaged in frivolous amusement, you'd name one side of the opened page *Dark Matter*. The other, *Sonata of the Fibonacci Golden Key*. Wishing you could tell him. Wishing he could hear. Only he can't. He turns the page. At the bottom, his graphite lines shimmer in an almost phosphorescent glow; the lines, attempted answers to what light does through atmosphere, addition, subtraction, expansion, contraction. Calculus really. Equations, with their tabled certainty. Others, spilling into margins too small to contain them (Judge Fermat's phrasing of the solution to his theorem). Straightening, your eyes now level with the window, you stare into the night. There's an almost imperceptible shift in the increasing darkness, as if someone is walking through, leaving no prints in the cool sand.

Years ago, when young was everything, you travelled twice to Iceland, once in April, over lava, black-sand beaches, wind whipping about soft snowflakes – April's three seasons in a day, winter squalls arriving without warning. Beneath the clear-glass night, you pressed your backs into mossy damp, took in the tango of the Aurora Borealis: the sun's radioactive dance in night sky, over unending land. Above, funnels of incandescence lengthened. Pale, iridescent green became violet, pulsed across the stars. There it was: lapis lazuli, the bluest braid. You commented on this shade and Iceland's glacial, ultramarine blue. "In painting, you add white to achieve glacial unearthliness."

He suggested a watering down.

"No watering down with oils, silly. So, what do you think is really up there?"

"Collisions between electrically-charged particles from the sun." Under the spectacle of light, he seemed invaded by doubt.

Indulging him: "Maybe. Or maybe night coats worn by the gods." Adding: "There has to be a Somewhere Else beyond this world of objects and sharp corners."

Lasting is to stay as moment is to light.

A guide you'd had in Iceland had told you both that the up-there reflected the down-here: the souls of all animals, the first explorers believed. Your guide hadn't used the word 'Viking' but 'explorers.' You wondered who was first: who of the humans, who of other animals?

Pause. Rewind. Only you can't. It's raining steadily now, and you're standing over him, his notebook with the yellow cover on his lap, its pages filled with jewelled shapes. Fibonacci's and Fermat's Theorem. For his birthday, the last one you spent together, you gift-wrapped this notebook in newsprint from the *Sunday Times*. He carefully pulled it apart, lifting the corners of a Peter Brookes' cartoon. "Luminous," he said, trying unsuccessfully for a joke, but in a sense, he meant it: luminous.

Weak from all the chemo, you laboriously lifted a finger to point out the notebook's metal spirals. "You can purchase recycled paper, keep the book forever." It was imperative that he understand that he could use the gift long after ... well, long after.

He brought a hand to your shoulder, drew you near.

It comes to you now: Blue is thirst; green, turtle-neck sweaters, smelling of his sweat. Memories, playful, duck out of sight. Only here, where gravity's association with mass and space carries permanence in modest chairs, in desks and the papers upon them, are you surprised by the mechanism of gravity, of permanence, of life.

Back then, after the chemo and radiation, surprises were no longer interesting. You swore you felt the errant cells expanding. "Too large," you'd joked to her husband (citing Fermat's theorem) for your body to contain them. Cradled against his chest, listening to his voice – when your tongue, your lips, even your palms felt parched; when cold had become warm, warm, cold and the stench of vomit was everywhere – that's when you realized no one's plans were working (yours, his, nurses', the doctors'). Best thing: focus on trivia, playing the name game. With your insides exploding, tripping over phrases became a worthwhile avocation.

Countless musings spray into your present now. Memories of his attempts to divert your attention. Latin gone Nordic.

"Aurora Borealis, Daga."

His grey eyes flashed; lips curled in amusement. "Daga is a verb, silly."

"Elding then."

"You'll need Boreal, for north."

"I gave it to you already! Alright, Norðr." Rolling the o before the r-trill.

Along his tongue, Icelandic keened, as if skating on ice. Languages were a forte. He teased: "Fine thing, your Norse."

"It's not Norse."

"Of course not, dear. The language you're speaking is from no human tongue." He was laughing, as you wrestled him down.

During the ordeal of cancer and the 'cures,' you realized you'd have given anything for one hour of 'Before.' Before this pain. Before the diagnosis. Even after the diagnosis, time and promises were your allies, fashioned from lab-coats, statistics, pills and other gods; possibility dictated there had to be *something* out there that would work. And here, the most shocking revelation of all: All those years treating patients, and you'd never given a second's thought to the cost-cutting measures taken with the hospital gowns.

And you, "thin as a rake," commented your brother, during a family dinner. Mocking, when he fancied he was being helpful. "Have to add juice to those bones." At first, you'd spared everyone, but catching sight of yourself in the mirror, you decided. In this very living room, you shared your concerns with your husband. "I'll have to tell everyone. I mean, family, friends."

The man you loved slowly put his students' papers down. "You will."

"And I'll have to leave the hospital. More than sick leave."

"Yes."

"And the youth program I'm running for the ER patients."

"They'll manage. Don't forget what you've done for them."

"Just imagine, will you? Conquered by open-toothed irony."

"Why open-toothed?" His lips registered a brief smile. "And there's nothing ironic. You're not conquered. It's not the end. Don't say that."

You didn't answer, wanting to scream: 'Of course it's ironic, and isn't irony the rechargeable battery of life?!'

Five years back, give or take, in spring – now it's autumn – the fog was curling in at the shore. Before stepping out to take in sunset, you'd snuggled into his sweater, admitting you detested scarves, not admitting to watching scarf-clad mothers along the shore, with their children.

"You're in constant struggle with Vermeer," you said, gesturing toward Vermeer's heavily clothed astronomer out in the hallway. "I like that painting."

"I like yours. We should put up yours."

Inside your head: 'The pain is excruciating!' Instead: "I don't paint astronomers, only what astronomers expect is there."

You're behind his chair now. You call to him, but no sound penetrates. Happily, there's smell in all its glory. "Aurora Borealis," you whisper, breathing him in. "Proton dances. Dark matter. Only more colours here. Ultraviolet, as well."

He hesitates, trains his eyes on the window, adjusts his glasses. You reach out, your hands never meeting the chair. He remains focused on the rain. "Wishful thinking," he says, his voice deeper than you remember. More bass than tenor.

"I'm here," you murmur, following the compass of his gaze to the shore.

Once, when this world was a part of you – the rains, tides, the sand – everything had a name. Categories, sobriquet, monikers, appellations, English or Latin, Arabic numbers.

It comes to you now, like a needle puncturing skin. After the rain, in the dissolution of fog – that's when you realized it was you, not he, holding the key.

"Dark matter," he once said. "I'm reading an interesting article with a speculative theory on the dinosaurs' demise and particle discs through space. Extinction. Neutron star collisions – gold, thorium and plutonium, heavy elements falling to Earth. Still, I'm not crazy about the author's distinction between darkness and light. It's one explanation, I suppose. The darkness can be the light."

Shaking your head. "Always searching. When I'm gone, you'll know about dark matter, whether the darkness is really the light."

He put his book down, methodically unhooked his wire frames.

"And how will that be?"

"I'll come tell you."

He reached over to the iron poker, turned the logs. The embers ricocheted. Heat along your thighs, evening's warm breath against naked scalp.

"I wish you wouldn't talk that way," he said quietly.

He knew. The so-called professionals and modern-day alchemists were certain. Still, this was your body. Not an alembic, not a theory. Alchemy. Al – Arabic for God. Chemi – 'system.' Through the window comes autumn's sweet cider. Like spring, you realize. Renewal. Along the roof, the raindrops scamper. Anticipation.

On the evening of your decision, one live star dipped. Through the fog, bands of light seemed heaven-sent. You placed no significance on the how or when, only promised yourself that things would end differently. Leave the Fates to their weaving; you were thirsty for water, and salted would do. Unlike that Bloomsbury darling, you'd carry no stones in your stockings. You'd go barefoot, weighed down by the sweet pulp of not knowing. As you walked along the sand, a cool breeze swept in. Solid passed into fluctuation, the laissez-faire of water. The tide was breaking, seaweed's silken aggression against your ankles. Transition into the new, crescendo into spring.

He grabs the back of his chair, turns.

"If you're here, you know, yes?"

I love you, he says, without speaking. The ending returns to you now: as ready as the first droplets of rain along the coolest whispered secrets of the wind.

That evening you left, above the Atlantic tide, the world melted away. Inside the water, against the rocks, you felt the vibration of a door slamming, the low, quick thuds of someone running. His voice, apprehensive, calling your name. *But we've just determined names aren't solid,* you remember thinking, before falling, falling into ending.

Acknowledgements

A FIRST THANK-YOU to Montréal, my home of many years. To those who live and have lived on this beautiful continent, whose lives have inspired these stories. The Quebec Writers Federation and its great team of administrators and writers have been an anchor for me and for the community at large. My thanks as well to my writing group, to Su J. Sokol, who has kept the virtual and actual fires burning, to Cora Siré, who has critiqued many of these fictions with the eyes and ears of a poet, to Sivan Slapak, B.A. Markus, Deanna Radford, Dyane Forde and Ariela Freedman, who have assisted in the perilous journey known as the editing process. These stories have grown through workshops and conversations with writers at the Iceland Writers Retreat, at Toronto's Humber College Summer Workshop, with the late Richard B. Wright, and at UMass Amherst's Juniper Summer Writing Institute, with Noy Holland and the late Grace Paley.

I am deeply grateful to the editors at Guernica Editions for giving these stories a home, to Connie Guzzo-McParland and to Michael Mirolla for his superb editing that includes his uncanny ability to catch unintended puns.

For the warmth, food and expertise, a deep thank-you to those in other writing groups: to Janet Singleton, who has lent historical detail to many of the stories here, to Maria Worton, Sylvia Goldfarb, Simon McAslan, Louise Dessertine, Martha Tremblay-Vilao and Sebastian Piquette for their shared love of storytelling. To Nassim Noroozi for opening my eyes to wonder as a subject of research, and to Anita Kranjc for opening my heart to the Earthlings we often refuse to see. To Tiphaney Mark, Patricia Bittar, Shane Joseph, Michelle Wildgen and David Smith for their generous input and helping me chip through the paint to reveal the characters beneath. To my dear friend Jerry Weinstein for his unwavering support.

My family has been the earth, wind and sky: to John Detre, my Virgil, and to Annie and Louis, the spine of my creativity. My mother Evelyn has given endless support, not the least of which has been going through virtually every word in this book. My discussions and journeys with the Lax clan, with Brian and Stuart, Andromeda and Mildred, nourished much of the material here. Finally, to my father Louis, to his memory. Of the many stories he experienced, he never tired of telling me, "You have to write this, Sharon!" I'd like to think he's still lighting the flame.

About the Author

CURRENTLY, SHARON LAX calls Deux-Montagnes, near Montréal, her home. She's had several, all of which have given texture to these stories: L.A., Waukegan, Boston, Toronto, Vancouver and, of course, Montréal. A writer, teacher, activist and editor, her favourite pastime, besides writing and walking along forested mountain paths, is working for and with animals and educating the public on their behalf. Sharon Lax has published in the Quebec Writers' Federation's online journal *carte blanche*, in *The Dalhousie Review*, in *The Rover* and in *Montréal Serai*. Like all inhabitants of this planet, Sharon aspires to reach that one fine place, also a moment in time, that resounds like a perfect note, what Lawren S. Harris called the "summit of my soul … there where the universe sings."

Printed in March 2020
by Gauvin Press,
Gatineau, Québec